I0846941

THE Ultimate GOAL
BROOKLYN BLADES 1
FELICE STEVENS

BROOKLYN
BLADES

Published by Good Man Press

Edited by Keren Reed
Copyediting by Flat Earth Editing
Proofreading by Virginia Tesi Carey
Additional Proofreading by Lyrical Lines

Cover Art by Reese Dante
Cover Photography by: RafaCatalana

ISBN Digital: 979-8-88949-093-7
ISBN Print: 979-8-88949-094-4
ISBN Alternate Print: 979-8-88949-095-1

Published in the United States of America

DEDICATION

To the NY Rangers...maybe this year...or next...or not.

ACKNOWLEDGMENTS

Thanks as always to my editor, Keren Reed. To Hope and Jess from Flat Earth Editing, you are the best. To Dianne, from Lyrical Lines, I couldn't do it without you. To Reese, thank you for everything and more.
And to the readers, you are the reason and make it all worthwhile.

CHAPTER ONE

Rip

My blood ran warm, but I lived for the ice.

That crisp sound of my skates digging into the smooth, unvarnished surface of the rink was the music that filled my soul.

The second half of our season began tonight, and I couldn't wait. This was our time. Our year to win. My goal was the Stanley Cup. Nothing else mattered.

"Are you ready?" Seb asked. "We'll close the deal this year, am I right?"

I slipped my Blades jersey over my padding, pushed the hair out of my eyes, then answered Sebastian Crowe, All-Star right winger and my best friend on the team. "Yeah.

But we say that every year, and something always comes to bite us in the ass."

His dark eyes dancing, he nudged my shoulder. "I thought you liked that."

With a laugh, I shoved him. "Idiot."

But damn, I was ready—and had been since the last season after we'd lost the Stanley Cup Final in the seventh game on a power-play goal. Fifteen years I'd played in the NHL, and I was hungrier than ever to get that championship. I'd made the choice to graduate from college first, so I was twenty-one when the Blades had drafted me. Many players came right from high school or never finished college, but I knew my mother would've wanted me to have that degree.

Every hit I took, every cut from a flying stick or broken tooth from a wayward puck, was worth it, all in the pursuit of the ultimate prize: the Stanley Cup. It dominated every waking moment of my life.

Slowly, the locker room filled up with the rest of the team, and we finished getting ready. I scanned our crew. We were in a great position for the playoffs—first place in our division with 57 points, 27 wins, 11 losses, and 4 ties. Our team consisted of a good combo of rookies and seasoned players. We'd come close to the Cup so many times, sometimes I wondered if it was all a cruel dream and I was destined to be one of those players they'd talk about as good but never great. Not at the most critical moments.

"Are we ready to close it out, *mes amis*? This is our year. I can feel it, *vraiment*." Denis Bouvier's voice boomed off the walls as he strolled into the room. Our goalie, and best in the league at fending off shots on goal for three years running. Two-time winner of the Vezina Trophy, and five-time most valuable player in division playoffs. Powerful. Gorgeous. Undeniably sexy.

My former lover. Boyfriend.

Cheating bastard.

I winced, and Seb sidled closer. "You okay?"

I shrugged. Two years and *poof*. As though he'd never been there.

"It's all good." I started to slam my locker door shut but held off, closing it quietly, refusing to show how absolutely fucking devasted I still was, even after six months. Not that I had to. Seb knew it all.

Sebastian Crowe and I had been drafted together and spent four years on the Blades before he'd been traded to the North Dakota Polar Bears. But that time, plus all the blood, pain, and tears, had forged a bond not even a thousand miles could break. Seb had come home to the Blades five years ago, and I'd never been happier. I'd been best man at his wedding and was godfather to his first daughter, and he'd dragged my sorry ass to his place and held my head over the toilet after I'd downed a bottle of tequila the night I'd caught Denis naked in our bed, fucking his nonexistent heart out with Gordie McCain, a defenseman for the Illinois Icers.

"You might be our captain and the best center in the league, but you're a horrible liar, especially to me." Clearly Seb wasn't buying the bullshit I was shoveling. "Meanwhile, ignore the stupid fucker."

My smile was thin. "Kind of hard when we're on the same team. I can work with him. I've played with plenty of jerks in my time."

"Never ones you lived with." We locked eyes. "Or loved."

Unwilling to let even one of my closest friends see my pain, I brushed it off. "First time for everything. The 'golden couple' is gone." Not my choice of words, but how the league had described their most visible power-gay relationship.

Seb nodded, and we bumped fists. "Living single is the best revenge."

I couldn't help but cackle. "Spoken like a married man with two little kids."

Seb's eyes sparkled. "Hey. I gotta live vicariously, and it might as well be through you." We finished taping our sticks and checked our pads.

As close as Seb and I were, I couldn't tell him everything. I was the captain, the team leader. I had to be strong and show no cracks in the armor. I was there to build my players up and lead them on the ice.

That meant no one needed to know I sometimes still cried thinking of how Denis had packed his things and walked away without a backward glance. Abandoned again. First deliberately by my father, who never gave a damn, then by my mom, who was killed. Of course, that wasn't her fault, but I had no one left to cling to who'd tell me they'd love me no matter what. My best friend, Neil, was always there for me, but he had his own life.

Coach came in, and we quieted and sat on the benches to listen. Benson Chopard had been a superstar player in the '80s, winner of three Stanley Cups, and he'd already coached a winning team six years earlier. The Blades brought him in last season, along with a total revamp of the coaching squad, and several months later we were all still adjusting—us veterans especially as we'd been with our former coach for years. Chopard was no-nonsense, didn't put up with bullshit, but unfortunately for me, didn't appear to be a fan of the league's acceptance of gay and bisexual players coming out. He'd tolerated Denis and me, though I'd bet he was happy Denis and I broke up. That way he didn't need to think about two of his players having sex with each other.

"We're ready, are we not? Time to take the rest of this season and make it ours. The Snow Caps are a good team, but we're better. And tonight we're gonna show them. Correct?" He searched and found me. "We're leaving the trash talk in the rearview mirror. We've won the first matchup this year, so I don't want to see any of you in the penalty box for stupid mistakes and unnecessary fighting. We need to win the division."

Their center, Vlad "the Destroyer" Dostevky, and I had bloodied each other in last year's conference championship, and in the rubber game I'd been unjustly called for high-sticking, forcing me to sit in the box. My ears had rung for days from the reaming out Coach had given me. Vlad and I had met in the opening match this season, and the shit-talking had been epic. We'd slammed each other against the boards hard enough that Vlad lost a tooth, and I'd ended up with several stitches on my chin from the edge of his stick.

"Yes, Coach," we shouted, and when he and I made eye contact, I acknowledged him with a sharp nod. I understood the implication. No fuckups.

"Let's go out there and show the fans their future Stanley Cup champions."

Cheering, we trooped out through the tunnel to home end and took to the ice to warm up. My skates bit into the ice, throwing up shavings as I did sprints. There was nothing I liked more than scraping a fresh, unblemished surface, and we did drills—split teams, push rushes—while Denis took shot after shot, practicing T-moves, shuffles, and butterflies with the other goaltender, Zane Ellis. Chitty, our rookie, showboated for the early fans with displays of his cheetah-like speed. I watched him and frowned.

I megaphoned my hands. "Chitty, c'mere, now." I waited for him by the red line.

He sprayed up the ice when he joined me, and I pointed at his chest with a frown. "Save it for someone who cares, Rookie. You're gonna need your strength for the game. You'll have plenty of time for grandstanding if you win the Cup. Until that time, concentrate on what Coach says."

Chastened, he hung his head. "Sorry, Cap. Guess I got overeager."

"Remember that when it's third period. Then let them eat your ice like dust."

Happiness returned to his face. "You got it, Cap."

The fans roared as we ended our drills, and as we headed to the benches, we raised our sticks in acknowledgment. "We Are the Champions"—our intro song—blasted and brought the fans to their feet. Kind of ironic, considering we hadn't won a championship in almost twenty years, but this was New York City, and we were nothing if not ironic. I jumped the board first and skated out to center ice and faced Vlad.

"No hard feelings?"

Vlad smirked. "All good. Especially when I whip your ass tonight."

"You're gonna end up kissing it." I grinned.

The ref dropped the puck, and Vlad and I fought like demons for control. In the crowd of bodies and sticks, I managed to flick the puck toward Seb, who passed it to Peter Varhov, our speedster defenseman. He took it past center ice, and we were off.

The lead traded hands three times. The way we bitterly fought for each possession of the puck, it sometimes felt like the playoffs and not simply the second half of the season.

Third period, and the score was 3-2. My entire focus was directed at that three-inch circle about to be dropped on the ice. Less than a minute was left, and the cheering in Blades Arena was deafening. It spurred me on. Made my blood race. I wanted this win for them.

Who the hell was I kidding? This was about me. Nobody, not the shit-talking wingers or their big moose center, would prevent me from *my* goal, which was to keep it away from our side of the ice, hold the lead, and stop our rivals from scoring. Every game, every win, brought us one step closer to the Stanley Cup.

"Kiss my ass, Tremaine," Shimski, a defenseman, yelled as he tried to steal the puck and threw an elbow at me.

"Wouldn't touch you with a ten-foot stick," I called out and, skating backward, passed to Peter, instinctively knowing he'd be there to pick up the puck. With the crowd roaring, and flanked by two defensemen, he sped down the ice, passed off to Seb, who fought for control amid three Snow Caps, and smacked it to Chitty, who took a shot on goal that went wide.

"Fuck," he screamed, but I had to rein him in.

"Not the time for egos. You'll get it next time," I yelled to him. "Regroup. Let's do it now."

Once again, it was Vlad and me fighting for dominance, but I managed to slap it away to Seb. In a breakaway, he motored to the Snow Caps side, where Dumas, the Caps' right winger and one of the best in the league, caught up with him, and they fought it out with sticks and a couple of elbows thrown. Dumas got hold of the puck and sent it zipping across center ice, but the buzzer rang out before anyone on their team could attempt a shot on goal.

We won, and I dropped my stick and pumped my fist in the air. We celebrated this win as if we'd taken the Cup. The entire team filled the ice, congratulating each other while the crowd cheered and clapped. Always good to start the second half of the season with a win.

Coach clapped each of us on the back as we passed by. Everyone except me. He nodded, and his smile faltered. "Good game, Tremaine."

I smothered my response—*Don't worry. You can't catch gay*—and simply nodded with the same pseudo quirk of my lips.

"Thanks."

We met the media outside, and Seb and I flanked Coach, who fielded the questions.

"The Blades had a solid first forty games. How does it look for keeping the momentum going?" Jerry Pasquale from Channel 62 Sports yelled out.

"How did it look tonight?" Coach joked, and Seb and I exchanged grins. "Seriously? I think we have the strongest team in years. A great mix of veterans, like Rip and Seb here, two of the best in the league, and with the addition of our rookie, Chitty, we're stronger than ever in every position. Our bench is deep, as you've seen so far."

"Rip, do you agree? Are you gonna bring the Cup to New York this year?" Martin Price from *City News* asked.

"I know personally I'm ready for it."

"Any problems with you and Denis Bouvier working together?" Dara Benton from *Hockey News* called out. "Any bad blood between you two because of the breakup?"

"I'll answer the same as Coach. How did it look like it went tonight?" I joked. "It's all good. Denis and I are professionals, and I think we proved tonight that we can put our personal problems aside and play hockey. Our mutual goal is to win games, and that's what we'll do." I rose. "Thanks, everyone. Time to get out of the uniform."

We disbanded, but as I passed by another media circus, I heard Denis bragging to the crowd surrounding him.

"I fended off more shots on goal tonight than usual. I don't know if the rest of our team wasn't on their game, especially the defense, but we pulled it off. I'm sure they'll get themselves together."

I struggled against the instinct to jump in and defend my teammates and friends, but realized that wouldn't be a good look. I kept my head down and trudged on. In the locker room, the mood was jubilant and the music blasting. I stripped out of my pads and protective gear, hopped on the bike for a bit to cool off and stretch the muscles, then took a shower. The trainers checked me over for any injuries that might've popped up.

"Looking good, Rip." Dr. Mike Hutchinson, head of the medical team, finished his checklist. "You're cleared to go."

"Thanks. See you tomorrow."

"You got it."

Wearing only briefs, I headed back to the locker room. Most everyone was either with the trainers, showering, or almost dressed to go home. I opened my locker and pulled out my clothes.

"Rip?" The voice sounded familiar, and I turned around. A blond, good-looking man gazed at me with fearful eyes and a hopeful smile on his reddened cheeks. "Hi."

I thought fast and hard. Wait a sec...I knew him. "Adrian? Holy shit, it's been a minute."

Relieved, he laughed and nodded. "Yeah. A long time. I wasn't sure you'd remember me."

"Little brother Adrian? Of course I would. What's it been? Eight, nine years?"

"More than that. Yours and Neil's college graduation party."

"Damn, you're right. I can't believe it's been that long. You were just a kid." I subtly eyed him.

He sure as hell had changed from the gangly, awkward teen I'd last seen at my college graduation. A perfect, chiseled face that could've graced the cover of any fashion magazine, broad shoulders tapering to a trim, lean body... *Damn.* I'd better chill the fuck out, because this was someone I'd grown up with and considered my little brother, yet here I was, having anything but brotherly feelings for him.

His face burned bright red. "Uh, yeah. I graduated with a degree in broadcast journalism. I'm working at Channel 8 News." He swallowed. "I'm an intern with Louie Rozner in the sports department."

"Really? Wow, uh, that's...great." Apparently I hadn't learned to hide my surprised face because Adrian lifted a shoulder.

"I know what you're thinking. *What the hell does he know about sports?*"

A grin kicked up the corner of my lips. "Well, yeah, now that you said it. I thought you wanted to be a news anchor or something like that. Last I heard, you were in the middle of Nebraska? Or was that New Mexico?" When we were kids, Adrian would follow Neil and me around with a pretend microphone, trying to interview us about our practice after school or our games. Eight years younger, he'd wanted to be with us all the time. We'd tolerated him but had never paid much attention to him. Adrian had always been...there. On the sidelines. Never with his own friends. Always alone.

His smile came and went, quick and nervous. "Uh, North Carolina, but I'm home now." His shoulders drooped. "It, uh, didn't work out."

"Hey, I was close. It starts with an N. And congratulations. I'm sure Neil and Lisa are happy you're close to home."

"Yeah. I haven't seen the kids in a while, so I was happy to get a job nearer to everyone."

"That's great, but why are you here and not Louie?" I asked, instantly regretting my words at his wince. *Dammit.* Sometimes my mouth reacted before my brain had a chance to think. "Sorry. I didn't mean it the way it sounded."

His lips twitched. "It's okay. I'm, uh, filling in for him. Trust me, I know I was their last choice for this assignment, but no one else answered their phones or texts, I guess." At my raised brow, he continued. "Seriously, Louie skidded on the West Side Highway and got into a crash on the way in. He's at the hospital now. I was the only one available. The intern extraordinaire."

I grinned. "Adrian, do you even know the difference between a hockey stick and a puck?"

He rolled his eyes. "Ha-ha. Yeah. Trust me, I watched you and Neil often enough." He bit his lip. "Rip, please, I need to do this assignment, or they'll fire me. I said I could do this. I, uh, sort of mentioned I understood hockey and might be able to get an exclusive." He flicked his gaze below my waist briefly, and I didn't miss the bob of his throat as he swallowed hard. "Could you—can you put some clothes on and give me an interview? Please?"

Oh, God. I was tired, aching, and wanted something to eat and a drink. My adrenaline was crashing, and I should be getting ready to celebrate our win with my friends. But Adrian was family, the closest thing I had to one, and I couldn't let him down. "Okay, but it's gotta be quick. A bunch of us are meeting up for dinner and a celebration drink after we're all finished here." I put on a T-shirt, jammed a Blades cap on my head, and stepped into a pair of team sweats. "Let's do this."

In the area outside the locker room, a cameraman lounged against the wall with equipment hanging from his shoulder. Seeing me, he jumped to attention. "Ripley Tremaine? Whoa, you really weren't lying, huh, kid? Great game. Congrats."

I gave him my best camera-ready smile. "Thanks." Adrian stood off to the side, straightening his tie. "Ready?"

Scared as a trapped fawn, Adrian stared at me, his big blue eyes panicked. Frantic, he motioned to me. "Rip. Y-you were right. I-I don't know anything about hockey." His breath hitched, and beads of sweat popped up on his brow. I could smell his fear. "This is ridiculous. I don't know what to ask or say. I'll make an idiot of myself and get fired anyway. I shouldn't have lied. I'm so stupid. I knew I couldn't do this."

Watching him lose his nerve, a wave of protectiveness rolled through me.

"Adrian. Chill out. I'll help you. It'll be okay. Feed me questions about the trades and our rookies. Then, ask what was the turning point of the game for the team. Last, ask me what I'm looking forward to most for the season."

He chewed his lip and nodded. "Th-thanks. I thought I'd have to know statistics and how to play the game."

The cameraman snickered. "Sports not your thing, huh? I kinda figured that."

Adrian flushed and deflated before my eyes, and that pissed me off. This jackass had decided to stereotype him, and that wasn't going to fly with me. I advanced a few steps and towered over the cameraman. "Yeah? Why's that?"

The smarmy grin on his face faded. "Uh, he-he kinda mentioned it on the way here. Said he didn't know what to ask."

"Adrian, c'mere." Still pink-faced, he took a few steps toward me. "Don't worry. I don't bite." I winked at him and waited for the cameraman to get set.

"They're ready," Adrian muttered and jerked his head. "Start rolling."

The little red light came on, and Adrian miraculously changed from a nervous kid to a strong-jawed, stiff-shouldered man. This wasn't the silent little boy watching us from the stands, the whiny brother constantly asking questions, or the scared man from moments earlier.

Truth be told, he was fucking hot.

"Good evening. This is Adrian Hunt, and I'm here tonight with the star center of the Brooklyn Bladers, Ripley Tremaine. Rip, how are you feeling tonight after the win?"

"Well, Adrian, every win is awesome, but this one feels great. The Caps and Blades have a rivalry, so it's nice when we can put one in the win column."

He wet his lips, and I hoped he could follow through. "What game was most important? I mean..." His attempt to correct himself failed as well. "What do you think of…uh…"

I jumped in. "I think the most important play of the game was when Chitty stole the puck, ducked the body-check, passed to Peter, and we scored. The momentum shifted, and we dug in." I slung an arm around his neck and didn't miss the hitch of his breath.

"Thank you, Rip. Do you think your new teammates acquired in the trade have blended well with the rest of the players?" Adrian shifted under my arm, and I liked how he settled into place. He wasn't a small guy by any means, and hard muscles bunched through the fabric of his shirt. To my shock, heat blasted through me, which I immediately quashed as inappropriate. This was my best friend's younger brother. We'd grown up together. I wasn't supposed to be having dirty thoughts about him, especially during an inter-view. But with my entire focus on coming into the season strong, I hadn't thought about anything except training and our games.

"Really well, I think. We're all one cohesive unit that's only gonna get better the more we play together."

Adrian nodded, his face intent. "Uh, do you think you're going to retire after this season?"

I blinked. That wasn't one of the questions I'd prepared for. In fact, I refused to let it cross my mind. Not since my agent had asked me the same question a year earlier, to which I almost took his head off with my ferocious, negative response. I couldn't answer Adrian the same way without losing my nice-guy image, so I forced a smile and dropped my arm.

"No. Not at all. I'm only thirty-six. I've got a few more good years left, and I intend to give our fans a championship."

While I wouldn't admit it to anyone but myself, the rays of the sun setting on my career were blinding, and I wasn't quite sure what the hell I was going to do without hockey in my life. At one point I'd thought Denis and I would get married and start a family, but that dream was dead and buried.

Perhaps sensing my annoyance, Adrian put some distance between us. "Uh, sorry. Thanks for the interview, Rip, and congratulations on the great win." He faced the camera. "That was the All-Star center for the Brooklyn Bladers, Ripley Tremaine, talking about his winning game. This is Adrian Hunt with Channel 8 News."

"And...we're done." The cameraman pointed his finger at us. "That's a wrap. Great game, Ripley." With a chuckle, he turned to Adrian. "And kid—it's the Brooklyn *Blades*, not Bladers."

Wide-eyed and pale, Adrian stammered, "Oh, my God. I'm such an idiot. Can we redo it?"

My irritation over his retirement question faded, and I felt sorry for him instead. "It was live, but don't worry about it. No one will pick up on it. Heat of the moment and all that." I stretched and rolled my shoulders. "All right. I'm gonna get going."

He left first, head hanging and shoulders slumped in defeat. Poor guy. He really was out of his element. Before I knew what I was saying, I called out after him, "Adrian." He stopped but didn't turn around. "Come meet me at Slapshots for dinner later. It's only a few blocks from here."

He peered over his shoulder. "Who? Me?"

I threw him a wink. "Yeah. You owe me one for calling my team by the wrong name."

CHAPTER TWO

Adrian

Outside the arena, John the cameraman lit a cigarette and nudged me as I looked out into the street, Rip's words replaying in my head.

"So how *do* you know Ripley Tremaine?"

"*Hmm*? What?" I was still trying to recover from Rip's arm around my shoulders. His warm, heavy, very muscular arm. "Oh, he's my brother's best friend. We grew up together." No need to get into the complex dynamics of Ripley's home life and how he'd come to live with us. Especially when I didn't really understand it myself. He and Neil had always been together, in school and after, and one day, Rip had simply stayed and never left. That was pretty much all I knew.

"No shit? Whoa, that's cool." He flipped the ash on the sidewalk. "Did you always know he was gay?"

No, but I knew I was the first time I saw him in his rookie year with the Blades. My dad took me into the locker room for the season opener, and Rip stood there, sweaty and bare-chested, with a huge smile. My mouth dried, and tingles traveled up and down my body. That night I had an explosive wet dream with him as the star.

I made a face. "That's not something I talk about. He's a friend."

As if he hadn't heard me, John continued. "Sure as hell shocked me, but I guess it don't matter if he can play the game. More and more of them comin' out every day. Football, baseball...who would believe it?" He dragged on the cigarette, then tossed the butt and crushed it under his heel. "Better get going. Don't wanna be late for dinner." He pulled out the keys to the van and turned to leave.

"I'm not going. He didn't mean it. That was a courtesy invite."

John stopped and gave me a bug-eyed glare. "Dude. I'm not gay, but even I could see he was into you." He leered and waggled his brows. "Go for it. Maybe you'll get lucky."

I rolled my eyes. "Don't be ridiculous. He's like a big brother to me."

Trust me, I've been fighting these feelings for years.

"Whatever. Listen, I know you wanna get on the hard news, but Rob DeVine ain't gonna hand that over to some rookie intern whose main job is making sure the coffee urn is filled every morning."

I winced but understood John's point. Rob DeVine was a hard-ass, tough guy who barely acknowledged me as Louie's new intern. It didn't seem to matter that he and Neil were friends—I knew I'd only been hired because Neil had once worked for him and Rob respected Neil's position in the industry. If I wanted to stay and make a name for myself, it was sink or swim on my own.

"I know. But I have to begin somewhere."

"Yeah? Well, don't think that just 'cause you did the sports tonight, they're gonna take it away from Louie. He's a legend. Thirty years in the business don't disappear like that."

Sighing, I zipped up my jacket. "I don't want it. I'm not a sports person. I just want to catch a break and get noticed."

We approached the van, and John hit the key fob to deactivate the alarm. "Listen, kid. My advice? It's dog-eat-dog in this world. Use whatever advantage you can get. You know Rip Tremaine good, like you say? Get on the inside track with him. If Louie hears you got pull with a big-shot player in the NHL..." He winked. The innuendo wasn't lost on me, and my face turned to fire.

"God, no way. I couldn't do that."

"Why not? Everyone's got an angle, and if you can score with Tremaine, you'd be a golden boy. Maybe they'll give you the entertainment spot if you start dating a big shot like him."

"And do what? Spy on him? That's gross."

"Don't be naive. That's show business. Lots of reporters have started either with being besties with producers, a famous someone's kid, or banging some star. Use what you got."

With a two-finger salute, he hopped into the van and drove off. I watched the taillights recede, then headed in the opposite direction, toward the train home.

Golden boy?

As quickly as I pictured myself behind the anchor desk, I thrust the image from my mind. I couldn't do that to Rip. We might not really be friends, but I was sure he trusted me. I could never use sexuality to advance my career. Besides,

I wasn't Rip's type. He went for the hot supermodels or the famous athletes. Not nobodies like me.

Hands jammed into my jacket pockets, I stared at the traffic whizzing past and wondered how badly I'd screwed up the segment. I'd thought I was confident about my abilities, but the moment I'd seen that little red light on the camera come on...*poof.* My thoughts had turned to mashed Jell-O, my throat had dried up, and the words had refused to come without me forcing them.

Add in having to interview Rip, and I'd become a stammering, airheaded fool. The secret crush I'd had on him all through high school had been placed on the back burner when I went away to college, then moved across the country for my first job. But I'd catch glimpses of him on the sports news or on the cover of a magazine in an airport traveling for work, and those silly emotions would muscle their way into my brain again. I might not know a damn thing about hockey, but I sure as hell was a fan of Ripley Tremaine.

To say I'd been shocked by Rip's coming out speech in his second year of playing professionally would have been an understatement. Of course, I'd immediately had a fairy tale of Rip realizing he was in love with me and asking me if I'd wait for him until I was older and we could be together. All I'd been able to think of was him touching me. Kissing me.

That dream had lasted all of one month, before the stories of Rip's love affairs started to make the gossip pages. He went out with models, Olympic figure skaters, swimmers, and other sports figures who'd made the choice to wait until after their retirement to come out. Older or younger, Rip was going through every gay man he came in contact with.

Except me. Rip had obviously forgotten about my existence the moment he left home. I might've only been a teenager, but I'd been hopelessly, helplessly in love with him. I was left out of parties, sleepovers, and weekend trips to the mall and movies. I'd make excuses that it didn't matter. Eventually I'd grow up and Rip and I would meet at some point, and he'd see how I'd changed and fall in love with me.

Out of college, I'd landed a job at a local news station in the Midwest. I wanted to report coverups by local politicians, drug raids, corporations pushing out small-business owners. I had dreams of being a big-shot anchor, telling the important stories of the day with intelligence, honesty, and that touch of humor that would make me relatable and have people tuning in to hear my reporting. Silly me for thinking I could jump right into hard news, as I was stuck reporting on the latest fashions and whose Hollywood marriage was in trouble.

I'd figured I could stick it out and prove I could do it. Instead, I was out of my job as gossip reporter in one year, for revealing a major celebrity having a romantic dinner in town with an unidentified woman. We'd even had video of the two of them getting close in a secluded booth. Unfortunately for me, it turned out the woman was the station owner's wife. I was let go the next morning.

After that, I'd bounced around, trying to get my foot in the door with smaller markets—worked in Idaho and Oklahoma—none of them lasting more than a year, mainly due to budget cuts. My last job, in North Carolina, had used me as a floater, doing whatever the station manager had wanted. One day I'd be writing copy for the local lifestyle reporter, and the next I'd be at the Friday night high school football game, helping our sports reporter. All the while, I'd still yearned to cover the hard news, but each time I'd been told to stay in my lane. That I had to earn the move up the ladder to even think about transferring from essentially gofer work to news reporting.

The only time I'd get in front of a camera behind the desk was to fill in for someone if they were sick, or if it was a holiday and no one else was available. The last resort. Of course, I always jumped at the chance. It wasn't as if I had anything resembling a social life. I was twenty-eight years old, and sex was a distant memory—I might as well be a virgin. I could use—and did—the excuse that I didn't have the time to meet anyone, I was still young. It was more important to build up my career. The reality? No one was interested in me, so it worked out. Rip and Denis Bouvier had become the power couple of professional hockey, proclaiming their love for each other, forcing me to shelve my fantasy of the two of us falling in love.

And then an intern job at Channel 8 in New York City opened up, so I swallowed my pride and asked my brother to use his friendship with Rob DeVine to see if he could get me the job at his station. What they offered me wasn't any better than what I was leaving, but I jumped at the lateral move anyway. Aside from returning home to my family, New York City was one of the big markets. A chance to make a name in the industry.

It had been four months since my first day, and I could admit to myself if to no one else that I was still trying to figure out what the hell I was supposed to be doing. After I'd confided my stage-fright issue to Louie, he'd kept me in the newsroom, doing research. Anything that kept me off camera. He insisted the more familiar I'd get with the sports teams, the less nervous I'd be if or when the situation arose for me to do an interview with one of them.

Any time I spoke to Neil, he'd reassure me to give it time, that a career in television reporting didn't happen without putting in years of grunge work, yet I'd see new reporters, as young as me, get news spots. What did they have that I didn't?

But I knew: the ability to formulate a sentence without freezing over each and every word.

I slowed my steps in front of Slapshots, the pub where Rip mentioned he'd be, but then walked on by. It wasn't the space for me. Places that reeked of frat-boy, bro-dudes were never my thing, and on a night of a home team win, those hormones would be running amuck. That didn't mean I wanted to go sit alone in my tiny apartment, so spying a coffee shop, I decided to sit for a few and have a cappuccino.

Sipping slowly, I people-watched by the window. I finished my drink and bought another to take home. I paid and reached for the cup—only to have it plucked from my fingers.

"Hey," I snapped and whirled, to see Rip grinning down at me. I never felt small until I stood next to him. Two inches taller, but heavier by at least twenty pounds of pure muscle, Rip had that quality of lighting up a room and energizing the air.

God, he was perfect. Hazel eyes flecked with gold sparkled under waves of thick, dark hair that curled around his tanned, muscular neck. A scar ran through one of his eyebrows—from an unfortunate run-in with an opponent's skate blade when he'd been tripped on the ice. I'd seen that game, and my heart had almost stopped at the sight of so much spilled blood. But the scar did nothing to mar the beauty of his face. And even tonight, with exhaustion rolling through him, he was still my perfect man. The one I never stopped dreaming of.

"I told you to come have dinner with me, but I saw you through the window, walking past Slapshots."

The crowd behind us began to murmur, and Rip waved at them, "Hiya, folks. Great game, huh?"

For at least ten minutes he was besieged by fans asking for autographs and pictures, and he accommodated everyone. I finished my drink and tossed the cup, intending to leave, when I felt a hand on my shoulder.

"Not sneaking off again, are you?"

"Rip, come on, I don't belong there."

His full mouth tightened. "Bullshit. You belong wherever you want to be." Close up, I could see where bruises lay blue-black against his skin, and I spied various cuts and scrapes on his chin and cheeks. He must be hurting. The game took both a physical and a mental toll on players. "And I'd really like it if you came."

What would it be like to belong for just one night? My face must've revealed that inner longing, as Rip put his arm around me. "Please?" he whispered in my ear, sending a shiver through me I hoped he didn't feel, but that I registered down to my toes.

"All right, I'll come for one drink."

He tightened his grip on me. "Great. Let's go. The guys are waiting."

Inside the bar, I found myself sandwiched between Rip and another player he introduced me to called Chitty, a big, young, blond guy who couldn't stop talking.

"Great night, huh? I'm only a rookie, but damn, the excitement in the arena gets to me every time. It was *fire*." Between bites of his burger, Chitty gulped his beer. When he reached for another, Rip shook his head.

"Nuh-uh, rookie. Learn to pace yourself. One per night during the season." He slid my margarita to me. "You, on the other hand, can have as many as you want."

A faint smile touched my lips. "I'm good with this." Normally I drank a sweet cocktail and would nurse that until the ice cubes melted, then set it aside before I slipped away, but listening to everyone recap the game, pressed up to Rip's warm, heavy thigh, I drained the first glass, and recklessly, a second. Another appeared in front of me. Three margaritas were two and a half too many for me. My head felt fuzzy, and the room tilted a bit.

"Having fun?" Rip's husky voice rumbled through me, and though I couldn't make my lips form the words, I managed a semblance of an answer.

"*Mmm-hmm.*"

"I knew you would. It's great to see you again, Adrian. It's been way too long. You're all grown up."

"Yeah. That's me. All grown up," I repeated and licked my lips, watching his gaze drop to my mouth. I shivered with unaccustomed lust, and my head spun.

"How old are you? Twenty-five?"

Defiant but hopeful, I met his eyes. "Twenty-eight. Old enough."

"Not even thirty. Holy shit. I forgot how young you really are." The rough pads of his fingers trailed along my jaw. Desire soaked through my blood and bones, accelerating from zero to two hundred. "Young and gorgeous."

My fantasy had come to life, and I held on to this moment, wishing it could last forever.

"Well, well, *mon amour*, what have we got here? A new *petit ami*?" The mocking voice cut through my lust-soaked brain, and Rip stiffened. His hand fell away from my face, and I instantly missed his touch. Breathing heavily, I pinched my eyes to clear the fogginess of my vision and peered up at a giant of a man, golden hair flowing like a lion's mane, a smirk on his handsome face. Assessing dark eyes met mine, and I blinked. He held hands with a husky, barrel-chested man, who stared at him as if the sun rose and set in his dominating orbit. I didn't miss the crowd surrounding us with phones in the air, recording every word.

"Go away, Denis." Rip took a bite of his pasta, chewed and swallowed. "I'm busy."

Denis Bouvier. Rip's ex. The man he'd loved and lived with for years. I'd seen pictures of him in magazines and in news clips, but he was even more impressive in person.

At least physically. Denis was bigger than most, with a commanding presence that ate up all the oxygen in the room. No wonder Rip barely noticed I was alive.

"So I see. So young and pretty."

Denis's amused voice snapped my already tangled and confused nerves. "I'd better go," I mumbled to no one in particular because Rip had locked gazes with his ex. I tried to rise, but I was trapped between Chitty and Rip.

"Shut up," Rip told Denis, then tipped his head. "How's it going, Gordie?"

"Good, really good." He and Denis shared a look. "Should I tell them, babe, or do you want to make the announcement?"

"*Mais oui.* I want everyone to know, especially my closest friends." A mocking smile curved his lips, and Rip tensed as the two men looked at each other with adoration.

Fingers entwined, Gordie raised their hands and kissed Denis. "We are getting married. I popped the question, and Denis said yes."

"*Mon coeur,*" Denis murmured and nuzzled Gordie. As the rest of the team cheered their shared kisses, Rip grew stiffer. "Champagne for everyone," Denis called out.

Rip grimaced but still accepted a glass for himself and passed one to me. "Congratulations, Denis, Gordie." He tipped his glass to them, but I heard the brittleness in his voice.

I knew he had to be hurting, yet he showed grace, wishing his former lover well. I whispered in his ear, "That was sweet of you."

"I'm a sweet guy."

He took a gratuitous sip of his champagne and set the glass on the table. Feeling reckless, I gulped mine down.

Rip's fingers played along my nape, fueling a painful ache in my groin. When he nuzzled beneath my ear, I was acutely aware of Denis eyeing us. Was Rip doing this to make Denis jealous? He couldn't be drunk—he hadn't even finished half his beer. If this was his bare-minimum seduction, it worked like a charm. I was about to melt into a puddle.

"I'm glad you came," he breathed, lips tickling my ear. "Aren't you?"

"Yeah. I am. Very glad."

He nudged my cheek with his nose. "Neil's little brother. I still can't believe it's you."

"It is. All of me."

"So I see."

"I used to dream of this happening." If I were sober, I would never have had the nerve to say it, but tonight I could blame it on the alcohol.

He held my chin, and my lids fluttered in anticipation of the kiss I was so desperately craving, but my lips remained untouched, and I opened my eyes to see concern mixed with longing in Rip's face. "Adrian, I can't."

"Why?" I heard the whine of frustration in my voice. I was turned-on and close to achieving my dream. So damn close, I could almost taste it. Taste him.

"You know why."

"Neil? Is that the reason? I don't care." I touched the scar over his eye.

"I do." He twined his fingers with mine. "And I think if you were sober, you would too."

I tugged his hand close. "I am sober."

He snorted. "Yeah. I don't think so." He cupped my cheek. "It's not that simple. He's my best friend, and you're...young."

"Not that young."

A huff of annoyance escaped him. "I'm thirty-six, almost thirty-seven. My twenties are a lifetime ago for me." A gentle sweep of his thumb caressed my cheek. "Besides. You're supposed to be like my little brother. It wouldn't be right. And if Neil found out? God no. We can't do this."

It sure as hell would be right for me, but this wasn't the time nor the place to argue my point. The bar spun, and my tongue felt weird, as if it were too thick for my mouth. Before I could stop myself, my head fell to Rip's shoulder, and I sighed with contentment. Maybe Rip was right and I'd had one—or three—too many drinks. The bar had begun to empty out, and Rip squeezed my hand.

"Let's go."

"*Hmm?*" I stared up at his somewhat fuzzy face.

"I'm taking you home with me. You're too trashed to go anywhere by yourself."

In no position to argue, I let him pull me to my feet, and to my secret delight, he held me close. He steered me toward the door, and though there were plenty of people taking Rip's picture along with the other players, his attention remained focused on me.

"Are you good?" he murmured.

Was he kidding? I was floating on air, my fantasy come to life. "*Mmm.* Yeah. Real good."

He chuckled. "Okay, champ. Let's get going and get some coffee and aspirin into you." Rip waved to everyone. "G'night, folks. Hope to see you at the arena, cheering for the Blades."

We walked outside, the cool night air hitting my face. It felt so good, and I breathed deeply to stop the world from spinning. It also gave me an excuse to hold on to Rip tight. God, he smelled so good. I nuzzled into his neck.

"Rip, Rip, is that your new boyfriend? How long have you two been dating?" someone called out from the crowd of people gathered on the sidewalk. "How do you feel about your old flame getting engaged?"

"No comment. Now please excuse us." A car pulled up, and he opened the door and pushed me inside, then followed.

"I can go home myself, you know," I protested but the truth was, I felt sick and hoped I didn't throw up all over the car.

Gazing into my eyes, he covered my hand with his. "I'd feel better if you were with me."

God. Me too. If only we meant the same thing.

"All right."

It was a short ride from Downtown Brooklyn to his apartment in Dumbo, and I soon stood in his kitchen, drinking glass after glass of cold water. I popped the two extra-strength aspirin he handed me. All I wanted was to get into bed and pass out.

Way to go, Adrian. You finally get your chance, and you're a drunken mess.

"You should feel better after you get some sleep. Come." With his arm around me, Rip led me to a bedroom, and I kicked off my loafers. "Do you need help getting settled?"

"You're not staying with me?" Disappointed, my lips pulled down in a pout.

"C'mon, Adrian. We already talked about it. We can't. I'm not going to take advantage of you."

"You wouldn't be. I'm not that drunk," I lied, not revealing it wouldn't be the first time that had happened to me. "I'm all grown up, and I am not your brother. Please. Stay with me." I unbuttoned my shirt and tossed it aside.

"Adrian." He sighed. "You're way too tempting, but I can't." His lips brushed the top of my hair, and he squeezed my shoulder. "Go to sleep. I'll see you in the morning."

Without giving me a chance to respond, he left me alone and closed the door.

Even with the aspirin and all the water I'd consumed, my head throbbed, and I fell on the bed, hugging the pillow. *Dammit. I thought he wanted me.*

I can't believe I actually begged Rip to sleep with me.

A flush of embarrassment rolled through me. I squeezed my eyes shut as if that could block out how I'd thrown myself at him. God, could I have been more pathetic?

It wouldn't have mattered if I were older. Rip simply didn't want me. Guess it was another dream to add to the list of all my other ones that crashed and burned.

CHAPTER THREE
Rip

Damn, I wanted Adrian.

Pacing the living room, I argued with myself. Why was I holding back? That pretext of him being akin to my little brother was as bogus an excuse as I could come up with fast.

Adrian wasn't a kid. He was twenty-eight and a man. Neil and I were as close as brothers, but Adrian had always been in the background. All the time I'd lived with his family I'd barely noticed him. Hell, I hadn't even recognized him tonight at first.

Standing outside the bedroom door with my hand on the knob, I momentarily contemplated joining him but dismissed the thought as quickly as it came. Adrian was drunk. First, it wouldn't be right, and second, it would upset Neil. But none of that drowned out the temptation on the other side of the door, because touching Adrian had woken up the part of me that had died months ago once Denis proved to be a lying, cheating bastard.

Restless and unable to sleep, I went to the kitchen, and though I wasn't drunk, I swallowed a ton of water to keep hydrated. I had interviews with the local morning shows and sports networks, and I had to be on my game for the questions. I didn't need the distraction of sex. I'd had enough of that after my failed relationship became the subject of gossip and innuendo. I couldn't go anywhere without someone recognizing me and asking how I felt about the breakup.

When we'd split, I'd let Denis set the narrative. As far as everyone knew, we'd parted because of irreconcilable differences, not because I'd caught his naked ass in our bed with Gordon. I was too heartbroken and hurt to argue otherwise, and an ugly personal fight would've taken our concentration off the upcoming season. The last thing I wanted was for a high-profile gay relationship to take center stage. For the six months before we'd made it official and the two years we were together, Denis and I had been the face of the League's Pride Nights, and I refused to let our failure as a couple define being out in sports. We weren't the only out players, but we'd lived together, played for the same team, and on our numerous nights on the town, the paparazzi had followed us. Denis devoured attention, and New York loved us.

The league had been nothing but accepting as more players made the move to come out, but since our breakup, I chose to keep my private life just that. Private. Sure, I'd had a few flings after Denis left, but while he and several other players paraded in the press with their boyfriends,

I practiced discretion. I tried and mostly succeeded in keeping out of the spotlight. The random men I hooked up with were nothing more than a way to keep the loneliness at bay. Tonight, I'd let go in a rare public display, but funny enough, I didn't mind.

I stripped and got into bed. Tomorrow was another day, and I was ready. Adrian and I could put this bizarre night behind us and forget about it. In the morning we'd laugh over bagels and coffee, and I'd wish him well in his new job at the station. That settled, I closed my eyes, but my phone buzzed and vibrated on the nightstand. I checked the screen, my vision blurred and my head hurt, but not from the one beer and sip of champagne.

No, it was a Texas area code. Only one person called me from that part of the country, and I had no desire to speak with him. Now or ever. I let it go to voice mail, and though I wished I had the strength to simply delete the message without listening and forget it, I couldn't, and I hit the button to play the message.

"Ripley? It's me. Saw you play tonight. Lookin' good. Maybe this year'll be the one."

My jaw tensed. *Fuck.* Just what I didn't need.

"I'll try'n catch you tomorrow. Need to talk to you about some things."

Making a face, I turned the phone to silent. Whatever things my father wanted to talk about, I had no desire to hear.

Growing up, I never knew him. My parents weren't married, and seeing kids at school with a mother and father, I'd reached the age to ask why my daddy wasn't ever home. My mother had explained that he'd left before I was born and she hadn't heard from him since—no child support, no birthday or Christmas presents. After she died, family services looked for other living relatives, but no one stepped up, so Neil's parents took me in.

Color me suspicious when, in my rookie year, a man claiming to be my father suddenly popped up, claiming a relationship that never existed. A DNA test Neil's parents insisted upon proved him right, but that didn't mean squat to me. He and I might share blood, but John Carver was a stranger to me, and I had no desire to hear any tales of why he abandoned his pregnant girlfriend to raise their child alone.

Instead of giving my deadbeat dad space in my head, I chose to focus on more pleasant thoughts. Like Adrian. I was looking forward to breakfast and seeing that shy, sweet smile again.

But in the morning, he was gone. And as relieved as I was not to have an awkward face-to-face over a cup of coffee, a pang of anxiety hit me that I'd missed a chance to get to know him better. I didn't want to say good-bye.

"Idiot." I laughed and shook my head at my silliness. "Time to get your ass in gear and out the door."

"Good morning, everyone. Today on *Wake Up New York City*, we're lucky to have the star center and captain of the Brooklyn Blades, Ripley Tremaine. Rip, congratulations on last night's win," Doug Benson, the morning anchor, began, his toothy grin so bright, it hurt my eyes, but I returned it.

"Thank you, and yes. It's always nice to start out on a high note after the break."

"What do you see for the Blades for the rest of the season? Who do you think are your biggest competitors standing in the way of the Stanley Cup?"

"I think this is one of the strongest teams we've had in years. We have a great mix of rookies and seasoned players and the best coaches in the league. We all work great together and respect the hell out of each other. We'll have to continue to play with the same intensity as we have from the beginning of the season, and I'm confident we'll be in the thick of things when playoff time comes. As for competitors, the Eastern Division is tough, with the Arctics and Nordics both playing well."

"How has it been working with Denis now that you two aren't together? Any issues?" Natalie Wolf, the other anchor, asked. "It's only been about six months since you broke up, and now he's engaged."

Damn. Was this prying into my personal life ever going to end? Mustering up a nonchalance I sure as hell didn't feel, I answered with a shrug. "None at all. We're both professionals, and we're here to win games. What happens off the ice stays there."

"I guess now that you're in a new relationship, it's easier," Natalie said with a sly smirk.

"A new relationship?" Confused, I peered at her. "I'm sorry, I don't know what you're talking about."

"Last night, at a bar by the arena, where your team celebrated your win, you were seen getting very close with another man, who's been identified as Adrian Hunt, our own Channel 8 intern. Are you two dating?"

My lips pressed together. Hard. "I'm not speaking about my personal life. I'm sorry."

Natalie's head bobbed. "Oh, I understand. It's so new, so you want to keep it private."

I opened my mouth to correct her, then decided to hell with it and remained silent. They'd gotten it into their heads that they had a juicy story to follow, but I refused to give them any ammunition.

Doug gave me a big-buddy grin, as if we were friends or something. "As a celebrity, it's not easy to keep your love life to yourself." When he realized I wasn't going to elaborate, he changed course. "Do you think of yourself as a role model for gay young men who want to play professional sports?"

This was a question I had no problem answering. "I'd like to think that as more players in sports come out, it won't have to be a news story. But right now, I hope I can be an athlete that queer people look up to, and show them that anyone and everyone has the right to play sports if we want to. The game should be the focus, not a player's personal life."

"Well said. It's been great having you here today."

They wrapped up the interview, thank God. I heaved a sigh of relief that I'd dodged a bullet.

"Thanks. I brought some stuff for you both and your staff." From the bag next to me, I pulled out Blades caps and T-shirts and handed them to Natalie and Doug, who broke out in smiles.

"Wow. Thanks." They each put on a ball cap, and Doug handled the finish. "See you at the arena, Rip. Hopefully we'll be back here at the end of the season, celebrating a Stanley Cup win. Go Blades."

"We're gonna do our best to make that happen."

The camera pulled away, and we were done. I unclipped my mic. "Thanks, guys."

"Thank you, Rip. Mind if we take some promo pictures?"

"Not at all."

For the next forty minutes, I recorded promos for the station and took pictures. When it was finally over, I waited by the elevator, scrolling through my phone. Neil had sent me multiple texts, asking me what the hell was going on with me and his brother and demanding that I'd better call him ASAP.

Not yet ready for that discussion, I shoved my phone into my pants pocket. The doors opened, and two men walked out.

"Rip?"

Adrian stopped in front of me, his brows quirked. An older man waited behind him.

"Hey, Adrian, how's it going?"

"Rob DeVine, director, Channel 8 News." The man stuck out his hand. "Great to meet you. Terrific game last night."

"Thanks."

"I just watched your spot on the morning show with Nat and Doug. Good work."

"Appreciate it." Knowing how nervous Adrian was about our interview the previous night, I figured to talk him up a bit. "Adrian did a great job."

"Sure." He dismissed my words with a wave of his hand. "I'm hoping you and some other members of the team can meet with Louie Rozner when he returns, and we can do a more in-depth interview with someone who's actually knowledgeable about the game."

My gut burned listening to him negate Adrian, but when I opened my mouth, Adrian neatly stepped in, showing no signs of anger or annoyance at the put-down, although his cheeks flamed from the insult.

"I'm not sure Louie'll be in anytime soon. He's having his ankle operated on later today. But maybe you have some free time to do a video interview with him? Just let me know what works, and I can coordinate with Louie."

"Can't this week. I've got too much scheduled." Hating that I disappointed him, I pulled out my phone to check my calendar. "But late next week or the week after that, I have free spots. I can do it then."

That brought a spark back to Adrian. "Sounds good. I'll check with Louie and let you know. He might be ready to return to work."

"Maybe so," I said and crossed my arms. "But I'd rather you do the interview." I directed my attention to DeVine. "I'm sure you can arrange that?" *Fuck it.* I widened my stance, which might be a little aggressive, but I wanted what—and whom—I wanted.

"It's highly unusual. Louie's been our sports reporter for decades." A cunning gleam lit DeVine's eyes, but I remained stone-faced and held his gaze. "However, I'm sure that can be arranged, since you two are such good *friends.*"

At his insinuation, Adrian flushed a deep red, but I was used to being baited by the press and remained unbothered. "Yes, we are. We've known each other all our lives. I'm sure Adrian told you that. I feel comfortable with him."

"*Mmm.* What do you think, Adrian? Can you handle it?" DeVine's snide tone suggested Adrian was one step up from incompetent. That pissed me off. I wanted to protect him, but Adrian answered before I could intervene.

"Of course I can. Definitely." Adrian stood a bit taller, excitement brewing in his face. "But I need to run it by Louie first. I don't want him to think I'm going behind his back."

DeVine shrugged. "Louie'll do what I tell him to—that's his job. He's been at this forever, and he knows the score." He consulted his phone. "Set the time and details and run it past me first."

"Th-thanks, Rob," Adrian stammered.

"I'm doing this for the interview, not to further your attempt at a career. After this is finished, you'll still be the office intern." DeVine walked away, leaving us standing, looking at each other.

Clearly embarrassed, Adrian turned to walk away, but I put my hand on his shoulder, and he froze.

"How're you feeling this morning? Any residual effects?"

He couldn't meet my eyes. "Fine. I had tons of water and took more aspirin. Sorry I made a fool of myself."

"You didn't. We all let go on occasion. But why did you leave without waking me up? I thought we'd have breakfast together."

With a shrug, he fixed his stare on the floor. "I-I don't know. It was weird, don't you think? I figured it would be easier to leave without saying anything."

People passed us in the hallway, and wanting some privacy, I took him by the elbow and pulled him into a corner. "Why? We know each other."

"No, we don't. Not really," Adrian said, honesty filling those big blue eyes. "I didn't know you were gay until you made the announcement. You wouldn't have even known I was in New York City if I didn't show up for the interview. We haven't kept in contact since you went away to college." He shook his head. "We're barely acquaintances, never mind friends."

"Why don't we change that?" I heard myself say. "Come watch our next game, and we'll have dinner after."

Red streaks painted Adrian's cheeks. "You don't have to do this."

"What, exactly?" I was enjoying this back-and-forth.

"Pretend to want to spend time with me. Yesterday there were a lot of emotions. I understand."

The fun part faded away, seeing how serious Adrian had become. I took a step closer. "Understand what?"

Uncomfortable, Adrian licked his lips. "I, uh, just meant that with your ex getting engaged, I'm sure it must've hurt, and me being there...well, I was convenient to flirt with."

Convenient? Was he kidding? Couldn't he see how attractive he was?

"Do you think I go around flirting with random men because they're simply there?"

Adrian met my eyes, his gaze direct. "Yeah, probably."

Ouch. I pointed a finger at him. "That's bullshit."

"Is it?" Lifting his chin, he challenged me. "I've seen the articles. You're a player."

"Again—bullshit." I ran my fingers through my hair, and at his raised brows, I conceded. "Okay, maybe in my twenties I was. I'd just come out and was having a good time. But all that changed when I was with Denis. I was faithful. Happy. I liked being in a relationship." I couldn't tell if Adrian believed me.

More and more people walked the hallways, several blatantly staring at Adrian and me, their murmurs growing louder. Adrian put several feet of space between us. "I'll go make sure to get that interview set up. Do you have a PA or someone I can contact?"

"That would be me." I grinned. "I'm not fancy like that. Give me your phone." He hesitated a second, then handed it to me, and I entered my number. "And I'll see you day after tomorrow for the game, okay?"

Adrian huffed. "I didn't say yes."

"Oh, come on, Adrian. It's just a game and dinner. Plus, it'll give you a chance to get to know the sport better before our interview. And me." I winked at him. "See you at six p.m. at the arena. That's when we take the ice for practice. I'll leave your name with security at the front."

The elevator door opened, and I walked in and pushed the button. It closed before Adrian could formulate a response.

On the way down, I thought about why I was going out of my way for someone so resistant, but I remembered how every Saturday night, Adrian would be sitting with his parents, watching television. I realized now that it wasn't because he'd wanted to be home—he'd had no other place to go.

It was always in the back of my mind how damn lucky I was to have had Neil's family take me in. Even after they'd assured me I was staying, the sneaking sensation never left me that someone could come and take me away in the middle of the night. That I didn't truly belong. Abandonment and death would do that to a kid. But the Hunts gave me everything—family dinners, vacations, and holidays where I was treated no differently than their real sons. Clear as day I recalled my first Christmas with them and the stocking with my name on it up on the mantel next to Neil's, full to bursting. To this day, I still used it. I owed them everything.

With family first in mind, the least I could do was push for Adrian to score an in-depth interview. I made a note to bring Seb along so Adrian would get a two-for-one interview, which hopefully would make him look good to his news director. I knew he didn't want to be a sports reporter, but he had to start somewhere.

In the car on the way home to change for practice, Neil called again, and with a wince and muttered curse, this time I answered.

"Care to tell me what that was all about last night?" Neil asked without preamble, his deep growl bringing a smile to my face.

"Yeah, we won the game. Didn't you watch?"

"Don't be a dick. You know what I mean. Why're you messing with Adrian?"

I sighed. "I'm not. He came to interview me after the game, and I invited him to join us after for a drink. He had one too many, so I made sure he was safe."

"By getting close enough to almost eat his face? What the hell was that about? Why'd you let him get so drunk?" he snapped. "I saw some videos and pictures online. You were close enough to kiss him. Did you?"

"Jesus, Neil. Come on. No, of course not. It was nothing. Gossip. You know how it is." I tried to downplay it, but Neil wasn't a fool. "And I didn't let him get drunk. He's not a kid. He's a grown man."

"I fell asleep early but watched the replay of his interview. You put your arm around him. What was that all about?"

"I was trying to make him feel comfortable in front of the camera."

"And after I saw how cozy you two were, I called him but no one answered. Care to tell me where he was?"

I shifted in my seat, not used to being under the microscope. "He, uh, came home with me, but it's not what you think," I rushed to reassure him. "He was a little drunk, as I said, and I didn't want him to go home by himself. It wouldn't have been safe to send him in a car alone."

He snorted. "And what made him safe with you?"

Stung, I snapped at him. "Dammit, Neil. I don't deserve that. I'm not a fucking predator."

"You almost kissed my little brother, Rip," he pointed out.

My face flamed. He was right.

"I-I know. But I didn't. I stopped myself."

"You wanted to, though. Admit it."

"Listen, all this was...unexpected. But—"

"But nothing, Rip. You wanna fuck half the guys in the country? I don't care. Just keep away from Adrian."

Now it was my turn to get annoyed. "Why? I'm not good enough for him?"

"I never said that. But you're almost nine years older. Adrian's still a kid."

"He's twenty-eight, and I'm sure he's had boyfriends." Realizing that wasn't exactly supporting my point, I took a deep breath. "Look. Nothing is going on. I promise. I made sure he was safe, and that's it. He's supposed to come to the next game and have dinner with me afterward so he can learn more about hockey because he's going to interview the team later in the week. Why don't you come too? Are you still sick?"

"Lisa's got it now, so I can't leave her with the kids to go watch a game. Not if I want to stay happily married."

I chuckled as I exited the car outside my building. "I get it. So are we good? You're not going to set the dogs after me?" I waved a greeting to the doorman and headed to the elevator.

"Yeah. Anyway...I heard about Denis and Gordie. I'm really sorry. That has to hurt."

Like a fucking knife in my side, but I wouldn't admit it. Not to Neil or anyone. I needed to bury my feelings once and for all. Move the fuck on. I entered my apartment, tossed my keys, and stretched out on the couch with a grunt.

"It's fine. We're all adults. My main concern is winning games. Everything else is irrelevant."

"That's bullshit. You were never as happy as you were with Denis. You've always wanted a home, family...the works. And you'll find it. Just not with Denis."

The pain in my chest squeezed tight. Guess I hadn't hidden who I was well enough. "Yeah, sure. I know. I'd better run. Gotta eat lunch, hit the gym, and maybe take a power nap before heading out for practice."

"Rip..."

"Talk to you soon." I ended the call, refusing to allow Neil to hear my voice quiver. *Gotta keep up the farce. The captain never breaks. A leader on and off the ice.* The phone fell from my hand to the floor, and I left it there. Having Adrian coming home with me last night, and then this morning's interview, had given me little chance to think about Denis's startling news. Ghosts in the corner of the apartment mocked me—the two of us picking out all the furniture...watching training films together...making love in every room. The laughter and eventual tears. Two years we'd been together, and Denis had always put off any discussion of marriage, yet six months with Gordie and they were engaged.

Was it me?

"Fuck it," I muttered, ripped the tie off, and unbuttoned my shirt to change. "I don't need anything but the game."

CHAPTER FOUR
Adrian

I shouldn't go to his next game. Rip was only being nice when he invited me.

But I didn't have much chance to dwell on my invitation, as I spied Rob DeVine waiting outside my tiny office as I exited the elevator.

"Well?" he demanded. "What else did Tremaine want? I heard you two were talking for a while after I left."

Being the unpopular kid, early on I'd learned to hide my emotions, so it wasn't a strain to hedge the truth.

"Nothing, really. He was just briefing me on what he planned to say at the interview, the upcoming games...stuff like that."

DeVine studied me, his eyes assessing. "You know, we'd love to get a more personal side of Ripley Tremaine. As one of the few 'out' players in the NHL"–he made quote marks with his fingers–"it would be interesting to get his perspective on the league's handling of gay players, like if he feels they could do more, and what he hopes for the future–for the league and himself personally." A smirk tipped up the corner of his lips. "I'm sure you'd be able to answer that better than Louie could."

Annoyed, I worked my jaw but kept my cool. "Why? Because I'm gay?"

"Because the rumor mill has it that you two were hot and heavy at Slapshots after their last game. That's not happening with Louie for sure." He leaned closer. "Listen, I don't care who you sleep with, but if it's going to be a sports star, I'm gonna make sure the station gets something out of it."

I so wanted to tell him to take his job and shove it, but with only a few months in, it would be career suicide to make an enemy out of someone as powerful as Rob DeVine. Before Neil moved to the huge magazine conglomerate he was at now, he'd worked for Rob as his editorial assistant after graduating from college, and despite their twenty-year age difference, they'd become friends. Neil had warned me that Rob was a tough son of a bitch and wouldn't cut me any slack, but I didn't care. Truth was, I'd walk on nails to get in his good graces and get my foot in the door to the ultimate prize: anchor seat for the evening news. He was hard and unforgiving, but I couldn't deny that I was learning.

I forced a grin. "No worries. Rip invited me to their next game. I'll make sure to get you all the stories you need."

"Good man." He clapped me hard on the shoulder, sending me staggering a few steps. Already a big guy at six feet three, DeVine had let the businessman lunches get to him, and was about thirty pounds overweight. "You know, Louie is pushing seventy-five and isn't gonna be around forever."

"And you know I'm really interested in hard news, not sports."

"Pay your dues first, kid. You're an intern. Do what I tell you, and it'll all work out. Let's see how you handle this assignment."

I opened my mouth to answer him, then thought better of it and simply nodded. He walked away, and I took a seat in my chair, staring at the wall until the buzzing of my phone brought me out of my brain fog.

"Neil? What's up?"

"You tell me."

I spun in my chair. "What's that supposed to mean?"

"I heard you and Rip got pretty fucking chummy."

My face burned. "From whom? And since when do I answer to you about my personal life?"

"Since you decided to have one with my best friend," he teased. "I have spies everywhere."

I'd have liked to think he was kidding, but if it pertained to hockey and Ripley Tremaine, Neil didn't joke. He oversaw all the sports and entertainment news for his publications and had his finger on the pulse of both industries. Had he already spoken to Rip? Did he know what a fool I'd made of myself?

"Oh, come on. I had a little too much to drink on an empty stomach, and we engaged in some harmless flirting. It didn't mean anything. Rip was upset about his old boyfriend getting engaged."

"So Rip does care. Dammit," he swore. "I knew it bothered him."

"He denied it?" It surprised me that he'd lie to Neil. To me, it was obvious how deeply Denis and Gordie's announcement affected him.

"Yeah. Said it didn't matter and his main concentration was playing the game and winning the Cup, but I know him. It had to hurt. Rip always wanted a family."

Curious now, I hitched my chair forward. I was only a baby when Rip had come to live with us, and I didn't know much about the circumstances leading to him becoming a surrogate brother.

"Let me ask you: what happened with his parents? You guys were older, and I grew up with him just always...there. Mom and Dad never wanted to talk about it."

"I didn't care why he lived with us because I always had my best friend with me." A sigh filled my ear. "Rip's father was never in the picture, and his mom, Abby, was a waitress at Honey's Diner on the south side of town. We became friends at the playground and were in the weekend Pee Wee hockey league."

Annoyed, I grunted. "That's surface shit I already know. I'm talking about the real stuff. Like why did he move in with us after his mom died?"

"Because he had no one else. From what Mom and Dad told me, his father was a deadbeat and took off before Rip was even born. His parents never married. Drinking and gambling with his friends were more important to his father than anything. Mom said Abby tried to give Rip everything she could to keep up with the other kids in school. At that point Dad wasn't making much money, so she and Abby shared babysitting and would have potluck dinners the nights Dad worked at Legal Aid. After Dad made partner at the firm, Abby tried to pull away, thinking Mom wouldn't want to be friends with a single mother working as a waitress, getting by on lousy tips."

"Pride," I mused.

"Yep. But you know Mom, she doesn't understand the word 'no.' It's why after Abby died in that robbery at the diner, Mom didn't listen to the social workers who wanted to put Rip in foster care. She swooped in and took him, making the argument of what's best for the child."

"That's sad. Did he ever try to find his father?"

"Not that I'm aware. He has no idea who he is. Far as I know, Abby never even told him his name. I once asked him, and he told me he couldn't care less and to drop the subject. So I did."

"I never knew," I murmured, heart aching for what Rip must've gone through. "It must've been so hard for him."

"He doesn't like to talk about it, but yeah. Rip hasn't had it easy, and he deserves the best. Don't ever repeat this, but right from the start I didn't like him and Denis together."

Intrigued, I had to ask. "Why?"

I could almost see Neil's shrug through the phone. "Guy's too loud. Too full of himself. Everything's always got to be about him. Always looking for the camera, no matter what he does. Rip isn't like that. Professionally, he's a team player. Personally, he's sensitive. Caring."

I thought about it. "Yeah, I can see that. So you can understand why he offered me his spare room."

Neil laughed out loud. "Okay, you got me. Just be careful, is all I'm saying. Rip is vulnerable right now and might not be making the best decisions."

"And I'm not a good decision, is that what you're saying?" I rushed to finish my response. "Never mind. Look. I haven't seen or spoken to Rip since your college graduation. Don't worry. He still thinks of me as a little kid. Like a brother, he said."

"Fine. Look, Lisa's sick now, but as soon as she's better, come for a weekend. We need to catch up. I miss my baby brother, and the kids want to see their uncle."

I rolled my eyes. Neil dwelled too much on the baby part and didn't want to acknowledge that I was grown-up and capable. My desk phone buzzed. "Uh, yeah. Sure. Of course. Give them all a kiss for me. I gotta go."

I ended the call and picked up my desk phone. "Channel 8 News, Adrian Hunt speaking. How can I help you?"

"Hey, kiddo. How you doin'?" Louie Rozner's voice boomed out, bringing a smile to my face.

"Louie. How are you? How's the ankle?"

"Like crap. Broken in two places. Got twisted up when I slammed into the guard rail, and the air bag went off, it broke my nose and fractured my eye socket. I look like I went three rounds with George Foreman."

Despite not knowing who that was, I winced in sympathy. "Ouch. I didn't know about your face, only your ankle. Did they say how long you'll be in the hospital?"

"Not yet. My doctor's coming in this afternoon. Listen, I saw the spot you did with Rip Tremaine."

I squeezed my eyes shut. "Yeah, not too good, I know, but I'll get better, I promise."

"Nah, don't sweat it, you were fine," he reassured. "But I didn't know you and Rip were friends. How'd that happen?"

"Long story, but we grew up together." Hopefully, my casual answer would be enough.

"Well, Rob told me you're gonna have an exclusive sit-down with him. You up for it?"

With Louie, I felt I could be honest. "I'm not sure. I hope so."

"Listen, kid. I know sports isn't really your thing, but this could be something good to cut your teeth on."

As much as I liked Louie, I wasn't sure what he was think-ing. "How so? A simple interview?"

"First of all, never think of an interview as simple. You never know what can happen—they might drop a tidbit no one else knows or give inside info on the team. It's all how you draw the answers out of them and how comfortable you make them feel with you." He chuckled. "And from what

I heard, you and Tremaine got pretty comfy after the spot you did."

I blew out a frustrated sigh and rubbed my face. "I swear I've told this story so many times, I need to print it out. We grew up together. He's best friends with my brother."

"Uh-huh. You and him ever go out? Like on a date?"

"What? No. We're complete opposites."

"I dunno. He had a look in his eye when you were doin' your bit." He cackled. "Like he wouldn't mind gettin' a major penalty for getting too close to you. You ever hear of spearing? How about butt-ending?"

"Not you too, Louie," I groaned. "Now I know you're making this shit up."

"I swear they're real." He howled. "I'm not kiddin'. Look it up."

If there were room for me to crawl under my desk, I would've, and even knowing there wasn't, I seriously contemplated wedging myself beneath it. "Why is everyone trying to get me to hook up with Rip? It's not going to happen."

"There's no harm in flirting with the guy. Rip's a huge hockey star. Bein' with him could be good for your career. It'll get your name out there. That's all I'm sayin'. Think about it."

"Dammit. Can't a guy get ahead on merit?"

"Sure, but it's a hell of a lot easier when you got somethin' else to smooth the path. I know you wanna do the hard news, kid, but I gotta tell you, I don't see that happenin' for a while." I winced at the gentleness in his voice because he was speaking the truth from his heart and trying to let me down easy. And Louie was someone I trusted and respected. "Sterling Forest's in the anchor seat, and he's not goin' nowhere. At least for now. I know he'd like to go national at some point—all these anchor guys do."

When Louie talked, though he was a sports guy, people in the news industry listened. On 9/11, he'd been in a news van on his way to Kings Stadium in Brooklyn to do soccer interviews but had stayed in the city to give on-the-scene reporting of the unfolding disaster. He'd won an Emmy for that segment, and I soaked up every piece of advice he offered. I pinched my eyes shut and put my head in my hands.

"I know, but that's all I've ever wanted to do. I can't give it up."

"And you shouldn't. But us two work good together. And I can help you gain some confidence."

My cheeks burned at his insight. "I don't know why the camera trips me up. I'm fine until I see that light, and then…" I trailed off, unsure if I'd shot myself in the foot by showing my vulnerability.

"You're still learning. It'll happen. And don't worry if you screw up. It's all part of the learnin' process. You're gonna do good, kid. Don't worry. You're still young. There's plenty of time. Now, if you got a sec, here's how I think you should handle the interview."

I grabbed a pen and pad and started scribbling, nodding my head at his words. "Rip invited me to their next game and the practice session." I didn't mention the dinner, figuring Louie would just keep razzing me.

"Perfect. You can pick up valuable information from the players during their practice. Go early, keep your eyes and ears open for team dynamics, especially Rip and Denis. It can't be easy playing with your former lover, and now that Denis is engaged, it could make it extra tense. Might make for a good interview when the time comes."

As much as I valued Louie's help, I swore I wouldn't make my career on abusing a friend's trust.

CHAPTER FIVE

Rip

He's not gonna show.

First on the ice, getting a feel for it under my skates, I sped around the rink perimeter, all the while keeping an eye on the lower bowl of the arena. Family members gathered, and the press were up in the boxes getting ready. Part of my contract was a pair of prime seats, which I always gave to Neil for whenever he and Lisa could make the game. Tonight I'd left one for Adrian, but now it was closing on six thirty, the arena was filling up with fans, and he was nowhere to be seen.

Time to give practice my full attention. Seb and I passed the puck between us, then Peter and Chitty and Andre

Newland, another defenseman, joined, and we did a two-on-two, racing toward Denis waiting in front of the goal. Seb passed the puck to me, and I smacked it, but it sailed wide.

"*Quelle dommage, mon amour.*" Denis grinned. "Perhaps your pretty young friend is too much of a distraction, eh?"

"Fuck off and shut up. Why're you so interested in my love life? Pay attention to your own." And then I saw Adrian, an usher beside him, making his way carefully down the steps to his seat. He scanned the ice, stopping when his gaze landed on me. "And for your information, Adrian's filling in for Louie Rozner, who's hurt. Get your facts straight and your mind out of the gutter."

I left him and skated to Adrian. "You made it."

"Yeah, there was traffic. I—thanks for the ticket. I've never been to an NHL game, only the ones you and Neil played in college."

"Whole different animal. It goes fast, and you might not pick up on everything, but we can go over it afterward. You are having dinner with me."

It wasn't a question, but Adrian nodded. "Uh, yeah. And I went through stuff with Louie, so he gave me things to look for."

"Rip."

Coach had taken the ice, and I gave Adrian a quick smile. "Enjoy, and meet me in the locker room."

I didn't wait for his answer, speeding to Coach, who waited with a frown.

"This is hockey practice, not *The Dating Game*."

The hot flush of embarrassment rolled through me at everyone's snickers. "Sorry, Coach. He's with Channel 8, taking Louie's place. I just wanted to make sure he had what he needed."

"I'll bet," Denis murmured. "If not now, then later."

I spun to face him. "Fuck you. I'm getting sick and tired of your snide comments, Denis, so drop it. Now." Almost nose to nose, I glared at him, wondering how love could turn so quickly to…what, exactly? I couldn't say I hated him, but this was no longer the man who'd set my heart on fire. All I felt was sadness.

"Of course. I didn't mean to upset you. It's good to have a *friend* in the press."

"Enough, you two," Coach growled, and even Denis shut the hell up and listened. "If you can't play together, neither of you will play at all. Got it?"

Coach gave zero fucks about our personal lives. We were being paid to play hockey, not have a therapy session about our breakup.

"Yes, sir," I assured him with a steady gaze. "I'm ready for a repeat of our last game. Another win, and not only that. We want to be on top of the division and get home-ice advantage for the playoffs. Right, everyone?" As team captain, I took the job of engagement seriously. "Let's do it better."

The Miami Manatees had taken the ice on the opposite side of the rink, and I eyed them as they practiced. They were a solid team and would be looking to even the score from the last time we'd faced off.

Coach ran us through the plays, and we lined up to listen to the national anthem. We took our places on the ice, and I faced their center, Joe Carney, for the puck drop. I blocked out everything else—Denis, the pain of being so easily replaced, and even Adrian sitting nearby. I gripped my stick and waited.

Our sticks battled, but Carney took control, and we were off. He slapped the puck to his defenseman, but Seb was there and the two battled for control. Seb flipped the puck to Chitty, and he spun around and sent it flying past center ice, where I took it and sped toward their goalie. I readied my stick to take the shot when my ankle was hooked and I fell flat on my face.

"What the fuck was that?" I yelled, jumping up, facing Hooten, a grinning rookie defenseman, as the whistle blew.

"Oops, my stick slipped."

The ref pointed him to the penalty box, and though I itched to punch the smirk off Hooten's stupid face, I refrained, knowing it would send both benches into a free-for-all.

My team swarmed me.

"You okay?" Peter asked, his eyes blazing. "Fucking dickbag."

"I'm fine," I assured them all. "Let's make the most of them being a man down."

I could hear Coach shouting, and knew what we had to do. Capitalize on the penalty and score on the power play. Which we did, to the roar of the crowd.

The game was tough and physical. I got in a few unchecked elbows, and when we fought against the boards, punches were thrown. I ended up with a bloody nose and blows to my ribs that would ache for days. Yeah, I got tossed into the box, but we were leading 3-1, so it was worth it. Assholes had to learn they couldn't take a cheap shot without repercussions, especially at me. Hooten had the puck and was heading directly to our goal, our defenseman flanking him. They skated closer and closer to Denis, who came out into the crease, waiting. As much as he'd hurt me, he was still one of the best goalies in the league and as fierce a competitor as us all.

Seb stuck his stick in front of Hooten, and though Hooten tried to elbow him out of the way, Seb was too much of a veteran not to know how to handle it. The split second Hooten moved, Seb grabbed the puck and flicked it to Peter, who sent it sailing to me. The crowd screaming, I took off toward the goal, Chitty on my flank and Andre hovering a foot away from me. I passed to him, but with a Miami defenseman right there, he sent it back to me. I took the shot, and the puck slid into the net. The goal light came on.

The team mobbed me, and I pumped my fist. Fifteen seconds left on the clock, and I knew we had the win under our belt. The Manatees tried to argue Seb was offside, but that was total BS, and though they won the final puck drop, the game was over without them having a chance at a shot. The arena was rocking as we skated off the ice. I managed to catch a glimpse of Adrian, who sat in his seat, his gaze fixed on me. I broke away from my team to skate to him.

"Come to the locker room in a bit. I have to shower, but I'll let them know you're cleared."

Wide-eyed and face flushed, he nodded. "Great game."

I gave him a cheeky grin and a wink. "I know." I skated away and left the ice.

The locker room atmosphere was banging, and I sat to take off my skates, padding, and protective equipment.

"God, that feels good." I rolled my shoulders. "Nothing better than taking all this off after a game."

"Nothing?" Stripped to his protective jock and nothing else, a smirking Denis stood before me. "You must be very lonely, *mon amour*."

I couldn't deny Denis was gorgeous with all that flowing blond hair and his perfect physical shape—six feet four of pure sculpted muscle. With startling clarity, I could recall his hard body pressed to mine, but the picture that remained indelibly burned in my mind was him with Gordie in the bed we'd shared. A wave of sadness rolled through me, immediately replaced by one of anger.

"Actually, I'm happier than ever. Maybe you're the one who has regrets, since you seem to be so focused on me and my personal life." I slung a towel around my neck. "See you tomorrow."

I left him standing and went to the showers, where I soaped myself and washed my hair. Naked except for a towel wrapped at my hips, I returned to the locker room and found Adrian waiting by the front door, his eyes darting everywhere. Thank God for Seb, who approached him with a smile.

"Adrian? I'm Seb, Rip's friend. He'll be right out of the shower. Come sit here by his locker."

"Hey. I'm here." I waved to him, and relief filled his face. Seb walked by his side on his way over. "Glad you found it."

"Considering I was just here a few days ago, that's not stretching my brainpower too far."

"Ha-ha. Thanks, Seb. You guys didn't meet the other night. Seb had to go home to his wife and kids," I explained. "The girls are too little to come to games."

"Unless we reach the finals, and then I told Jolie they're gonna be here no matter what," Seb joked. "I saw that interview. It was a good one, considering I heard you were a last-minute fill-in."

Adrian remained hesitant. "Thanks. I know I made some mistakes, but I guess that's part of the learning process."

"Just like our rookie year. Gotta make the mistakes so you can improve and become the best." Seb, whose locker was next to mine, opened the door and took out his clothes. "Rip tells me we're gonna do an interview soon. Looking forward to it."

Adrian's eyes widened. "Oh, uh, wow, that's great. I thought it was only going to be Rip, but yeah, thanks."

Seb winked as he pulled his sweat pants on. "Two for the price of one, eh? Anything to keep the Blades in the media. See you tomorrow, Rip. Nice to meet you, Adrian."

Seb finished getting dressed, and I dropped my towel and took my clothes from my locker. I noticed Adrian's red face, and when I caught him sneaking a peek at me, even though I'd promised myself and Neil that Adrian was off-limits...damn, a guy could dream. He was hot as hell in his dark-wash jeans and blue shirt that made his eyes glow. Coupled with all that thick, silky, sun-streaked blond hair, and whew...I needed to get my mind out of the gutter. I reached into my locker and pulled out a jersey.

"Here," I said, tossing it to him, then stepping into my briefs and sweats. "If you're going to be at Blades games, you need to represent."

He held on to it. "But...this is your jersey." As smelly and sweat-soaked as it was, I didn't miss how he clutched it tight.

"Don't worry." I winked. "I can get more where that comes from. Let's blow this joint. I gotta eat something. I'm starving."

I made my good-byes to everyone else, and we exited the players' area and the arena. The February air brushed cool against my face, and I rolled my neck from side to side as we waited for the car. "I really should hit the gym before dinner."

"But you just played a hard game. Why would you do that?" Adrian joined my pacing.

"Believe it or not, it's a way to lower the heart rate and cool our muscles." I stopped. "What do you think? Wanna go ride a bike for a while? Unless it'll be too late for you."

He met my question with a laugh. "Don't worry. I don't turn into a pumpkin at midnight. It's not past my bedtime."

"Good. The gym in my building is perfect. Then we can order in and hang out a little, if that's okay."

"Oh, yeah, sure. That's fine with me." He seemed surprised, and I wondered if he'd been hoping to go out somewhere.

"If you want to go out, I'm okay with it. Just that I'm pretty much a homebody. The other night was to reconnect with the team after the break, but my routine is usually game, gym, food, and bed."

"No, of course, I understand."

"C'mon, the car's waiting."

Once in my apartment, I grabbed two bottles of water. "I have some exercise stuff that'll fit you. You don't want to exercise in your street clothes. Hang on a sec."

I left him in the middle of my living room and dug through my dresser, finding a pair of track pants and a Blades T-shirt Neil would wear if we were hanging out. Adrian hadn't moved from the spot I'd left him, and I tossed the clothes to him.

"Thanks. I'll, uh, go change."

On the way to my bedroom, Adrian passed by me, and at the scent of his aftershave, my body leaped with desire. But I quashed that and paced the living room, waiting. I'd made Neil a promise and couldn't renege, no matter how turned-on I was.

Keep cool. Focus on the game, not your dick.

Adrian returned, and I swallowed hard. He had a surprisingly ripped body, the Blades T-shirt stretching across his broad chest. Thin track pants clung to muscled thighs and a firm butt.

Damn. When did this happen? Adrian sure as hell wasn't a kid. He was all man.

"Ready?" My voice caught, and I cleared my throat. "Here's your water."

He took the bottle, and together we headed to the top floor of my building, where the gym was located. It was late enough for it to be empty, and for that I was grateful. I picked up a towel and hopped on a stationary bike.

"I like to ride, then do a set of light weights. Feel free to do whatever you want."

Adrian picked a treadmill from the line in front of me. He set it to a slight angle and began to run. Great. Now I was stuck watching his ass bounce. I tore my eyes away from him to concentrate on the screen of my bike. After twenty minutes, I slowed to cool down and stopped. I wiped my face and stretched for a minute before switching over to the weights. Adrian slowed to a walk and finished. He joined me at the barbells.

"Wanna spot me?" I loaded the barbell with one hundred pounds. I could press more, but it had been a physical game, and I didn't want to strain myself when we had another game in two days. "I'll do the same for you."

"It's okay. I'm not much of a lifter."

"No worries. C'mon." I lay on the bench and lifted the bar off the rack. With a grunt I pushed it up, and lowered it. I did three sets of ten reps—all the while feeling Adrian's eyes on me—then moved to a bench and did some free weights, finishing off with pull-ups.

"Done?" Adrian asked. "You don't have to rush on my account."

"Yeah. It's enough. Hungry?" I wiped my face. "I know I am."

"Yeah, definitely. I only had a sandwich at lunch."

"Let's go to my place and order. I need the protein and carbs. What're you in the mood for?"

"I'm fine with anything. Burger, salad, it's all good."

I thought for a moment. "How about some chicken and sides?" By now I was truly starving, and my stomach let out a mean growl. Adrian laughed.

"Sounds perfect."

Once we returned to my apartment, I pulled up my delivery app and found Dave's Hot Chicken. "Not the healthiest, but I'm too hungry to care right now. Take a look and tell me what you want."

I watched as he read the menu, fixated on the pink tip of his tongue caught between his white teeth.

"Rip?" Adrian's voice brought me out of my fantasy of what kissing Adrian would taste like.

"Huh? What? I'm sorry."

"I said I chose what I wanted. Here's your phone."

"Thanks." Our fingers brushed when he handed it to me, and a faint blush stained his cheeks. "I'll put the order in now. They won't take long."

Adrian took a seat on the couch. "So, uh, that was a good game. But I don't understand how you can get slammed into the wall so many times and not feel anything. If that happened to me, I probably wouldn't be able to stand for a week."

I chuckled. "Well, that's why we're the professionals. It takes practice and training." I sat at the opposite end of the sectional. "In my opinion, hockey's the most physical of all the professional sports and the most difficult. I have friends in the NFL and baseball who might disagree, but then I remind them we do it all on ice skates and they shut up."

We shared a laugh. "Yeah. I used to beg you and Neil to teach me to skate. I fell more than I stayed up."

"Did you ever learn?"

He shrugged. "Not really. No need to once you and Neil left home."

"Well, regular ice skating is different from how we play, but I can give you a few lessons. Pro hockey can be hard and brutal at times. Sometimes even violent."

"I saw that tonight up close. But you love it, don't you?" Adrian asked. "You said playing hockey was all you ever wanted to do."

Remembering those days with Neil spent on the ice, I smiled. We were both so young and filled with plans. "Yeah. I was no scholar for sure, but even if I'd excelled at school, playing professional hockey was always my goal, and the fact that I get to do what I love makes me happy." I shifted closer. "What about you? Tell me about your life after I went away to college."

"Me? Not much to tell." His laugh was quick, nervous, and didn't reach his eyes. Totally fake, and I needed to know why.

"I don't believe that. Any boyfriends? Neil always brags about you—what?" I stopped at his grimace and the roll of his eyes. "You don't believe me?"

Hurt and sadness bled through his disbelieving expression. "He's my brother. Of course he'll say nice things about me." His fingernails dug into the fabric of the armrest. "But the truth is, I-I haven't accomplished anything."

"What? That's ridiculous, Adrian. You've been working steadily since you graduated, and now you're in one of the biggest news markets in the world."

He slumped, his gaze everywhere but on me. "You know that's only because of Neil."

My brow furrowed. "What're you talking about?"

Growing visibly agitated, Adrian hung his head and clasped his hands tightly. "Neil called in a favor because he used to work for Rob and they're friendly. There's no way I'd be hired on my résumé alone."

Ouch. I felt for him, and scrambled for a way to rally his spirits. "Wait, you did well in our segment. You and your news director must be happy with that."

"Not really. I screwed up the name of the team, and I fumbled the questions you gave me to ask only a minute before."

I itched to hold him and hug away his pain. I hated to see him so down on himself, but I sat quiet, sensing he didn't want reassurance and platitudes.

"All I've ever wanted was to report the hard news, but maybe I'm just not cut out for it. I should stick with staying off camera. I'm never going to have that confidence real news people have."

I couldn't allow him to continue berating himself. "Not true. Adrian, look at me." At his dispirited half shrug, I rose from my seat to settle by his side. With his focus still on the floor, I nudged his shoulder. "Hey."

Anguished eyes met mine. "What?"

"Do you think I was always as self-assured on the ice as I am now?"

"Come on, Rip. You were Rookie of the Year, set records...I know what you're trying to do, and thanks, but it's not gonna work."

"Look, all that may be true, but my first few games? I nearly shit myself. Seriously. I spent the first intermission in the bathroom." Adrian's lips twitched, and I hurried on. "Here I was, an unknown, replacing the beloved captain, Ron Lavalier. The man was a legend. Who the hell was I, a nobody, to take his place?" Memories flooded me. "In my dreams I still hear the boos from the fans after my first two shots on goal went wide."

"That sucks. But you won them over."

"It took time. Lots of hard work, watching tapes, and talking to Lavalier himself to gain the courage to push through the negativity from the fans and my own insecurities. I'm not lying when I tell you I wanted to quit."

"Really? No way. You're kidding me."

"Nope." Fifteen years in, yet those one-on-ones with Ron Lavalier remained the most important moments of my career. A turning point.

"Halfway through my rookie year, I sat with Lavalier, and he insisted he'd had the same fears and worries. And not only his first season—the insecurity remained through every playoff game. Of course I didn't want to believe him. One of the greatest of all time telling me, an unproven rookie, that he was scared?"

"Maybe it was all to make you feel better."

I scowled. "No. That's the point. That fear was what made him stronger, the impetus to push himself harder. He refused to give in to it." I placed my hand on his shoulder. "You shouldn't either. We all have obstacles. Some real, some self-made. It's how we choose to handle them that can make or break us. Don't let the past handcuff you, keep you from the future you want."

Temptingly close, Adrian's full mouth trembled. "It's been hard doing it alone."

"You don't have to. That's what I'm trying to say."

He left the couch to pace the room. "I can't ask Neil to help with anything else. He was nice enough to get me the foot in the door by calling in a favor with Rob. The rest is up to me."

"I could help you." The words tumbled from my lips before my brain could stop them, and judging by Adrian's incredulous expression, he was as shocked as I was.

CHAPTER SIX
Adrian

I blinked, the initial urge to accept tempered by the knowledge that Rip was once again treating me like the little kid he still believed me to be.

"Thanks, but I think you have enough on your plate without me adding to it. I can handle this."

"How? You just said it's hard to do on your own. I'm offering you a chance to have someone else shoulder some of the burden."

It would be so easy to say yes. I'd get to spend time with Rip, which would be an extra bonus. But that stupid thing called pride kept me from jumping at the chance. "No offense, but what do you know about reporting?"

A grin kicked up his mouth. "I've been on the receiving end of plenty of microphones. I've learned the good and the bad. I have some tips." He nudged me. "I'm not kidding. I'd really like to help you."

"Let's say I agree." I held up a hand at his nod. "Not actually, but for argument's sake, what could you do to make me more confident?"

"First of all, this interview with Seb and me will help. And the more face time you get, the easier it'll be for you to act naturally around the camera. See, the first thing you have to learn when you're broadcasting is to forget that it's a job and make it your personality. Pretend you're hanging with your buddies."

The intercom buzzed, and Rip left to answer it while I ruminated.

Pretend you're hanging with your buddies...

That would presume I had any. I'd finished school without making any real connections. I'd thought going away to college would give me a fresh start, but instead I'd found myself even more isolated. Freshman year I stayed in my dorm room most weekends, and by the time I'd gotten up the nerve to join the Gay Students' Union in my sophomore year, most of the guys my age had already formed tight friendship circles, leaving me little room to wiggle inside. Never one to push, I'd retreated, spending my free time in the library or studying newsreels, when I should've learned the subtle art of chatting it up.

The bell rang, and Rip opened the door. The delivery person handed him the bag.

"Thanks," Rip said with an easy smile.

"Whoa, no way, you're Ripley Tremaine," the guy gushed. "Big Blades fan here. I watch the games all the time." A faded Blades cap rested on his curly hair, so he wasn't lying.

"Great to hear."

"Could I, uh, get like an autograph or a picture? My friends will freak out."

"Sure, how about both?" Rip motioned to me. "Adrian, c'mere."

I joined them, and after the kid took a few solo pictures, he handed me his phone. I took a burst of pictures, and afterward Rip signed the receipt.

"This is way cool."

Rip handed him a bunch of twenties. "Have a great night."

The young man's eyes bugged out. "Awesome, dude. Thanks."

Rip set the bag on the kitchen island and unpacked the boxes. The delicious smell of fried chicken hit my nose, and my mouth watered, while my stomach let out an embarrassing growl. Rip chuckled.

"Same, buddy. I'm starving."

We tore into the chicken, and within twenty minutes, nothing but bones and empty containers remained. I groaned.

"Oh, man, that was so good." I licked my lips and stretched. "But it's getting late, so I'd better get going. You need your rest, and I–"

"Need to think about our earlier conversation."

I crumpled the napkin in my hand and began to collect the garbage. "There's nothing to think about. I'll figure it out."

"Hey." Rip took the crumpled bags from me. "I never said you couldn't. But it's always a good thing to get help from friends. I gotta fly to Atlanta for the Arctics game, but come to the next home game. It's with the Lakes." His face remained blank. "They're the Minneapolis team. You can pick up some good quotes from the guys, plus you can watch us. That'll start giving you some ideas about the game. And you should go to a few basketball games too. I have season tickets—use one or ask Neil or a friend to go with you."

"I don't think—"

"Yeah, but I do. Look. You have to learn to be more comfortable with professional sports teams. And wait." He rubbed his chin. "I have an even better idea. Instead of sitting in the arena, sit in the box with the rest of the team. No other reporter does that. It'll be a first."

A tiny thrill of excitement shot through me. "Are you sure?"

"Yeah. Then..." I could see his mind working. "What about suggesting a sports show? Like mini talk-show segments."

"What? Me? Host a whole show? By myself?"

He squeezed my arm. "Where's that confidence I've been talking to you about? Don't worry. I'll be your first guest. And not only do I know other players in the league who'll be happy to come on, I'm friends with other athletes—baseball players, football...there's a whole network of people you can talk to. I'm part of GAINS—Gay Athletes In Sports. I'm sure plenty of players, retired *and* active, will be happy to come on and talk to you."

With visions of everything that could go wrong zipping through my mind, I chewed my lip. "You think I can pull it off?"

"I *know* you can. Tomorrow, go to Rob DeVine's office and sell the idea."

I rose to my feet. "I'd better get home. But yeah...I'll think about it. I should tell Louie too."

"Don't think about it. Do it. Let me know how it goes. And make sure you show up at the next home game. Win or lose, you'll get good sound bites."

"Thanks, Rip. You're being really nice. I-I don't know what to say."

He slung his arm around me, a comforting weight I ached to lean into.

"See you at the arena. Don't forget."

The next morning, I figured it would be best to talk to Louie prior to approaching Rob, so I got into the office extra early to call him, not only for his opinion on the idea for the show, but to find out how he was feeling after his surgery.

"Kid, how's it goin'?"

The cheerful voice gave me a moment's pause. Was I infringing on Louie's territory? He knew sports wasn't where my heart lay, but Rip's idea was a good one to help me learn to be more comfortable in front of the camera. A casual, talk-show type atmosphere might help ease my way into a more formal, behind-the-desk seat.

"It's good. How're you feeling? Are you coming home, or can I come visit you?"

"Nah. Don't waste your time. I'll be going home today or tomorrow."

"That's great. So you'll be back at work before you know it." My relief was genuine. I truly had no desire to take Louie's job.

"Well, no, see it was a little more complicated than that. As I told you, the ankle was broken in two places, plus they did some more tests and found my knee was damaged. I had to have screws put in, and they repaired some tendons. They got me doin' all kinds of damn physical therapy, so I'll probably be out longer than I first thought."

My heart sank. "Damn. I'm sorry, Louie." I was genuinely upset because Louie was no youngster and it would be a long recovery. Hearing this news made me want to stay silent. The last thing Louie needed during a difficult recuperation was to think I was angling for his job.

"Listen, kiddo. I know sports is the last thing you want."

"Yeah, but I thought it went okay. Plus, I went to the game and—"

"Adrian. I talked to Rob, and I'm sorry, but we don't think you're ready to be the full-time sports reporter in my absence."

Even Louie didn't think I had what it takes to be an on-camera reporter. It might be true, but it hurt to hear. Still, I kept my head up high. "I agree. It's basketball and hockey season. I can't do the nightly reporting on them. I don't know enough."

A sigh filled my ear. "It's got nothin' to do with your ability. You're just too green. Bryan Held was always my fill-in, and he's agreed to handle it until I can return. But you're still working here. I got stuff you need to do, an'—"

"Louie," I interrupted. "I get it." To hell with it. The worst that could happen was Louie would laugh at me and say no way. "But I've got an idea I wanted to run past you." I outlined what Rip and I had spoken about the previous night, then wiped the sweat off my brow, waiting for Louie's response.

"You know what? I kinda like it. It's like nothin' else on the air right now. And we got that Sunday spot after the news where they've been doin' lifestyle shows, but the ratings are crap. I think this'll fly. You think you can get the star power? Besides your friend Rip."

I didn't miss the subtle emphasis on the word friend but chose to ignore it. "Yeah, I do. Active and retired players. I'm sure Neil can help, and Rip said he knows baseball and football players he can call to ask if they want to be on."

"I'll bet he does," Louie murmured. "You talk to Rob about it?"

"N-no. I wanted to run it past you first. See if you thought it was a good idea and if you minded me asking him."

"Kid," Louie said gently. "You're not gonna get ahead in this industry if you're always worried about how what you do affects someone else. Even me."

"I respect you, and I don't want to seem like I'm stepping on your toes."

"Go for it. I'll put in a good word too. But lemme ask. Do you think it's gonna help get you that news spot?"

I tried to appear as nonchalant as possible. "It might. First sports, then maybe politics. Interviewing people is a good way to get my foot in the door and become comfortable with the camera."

"Yeah. So is dating a superstar. Just sayin'." He cackled, and my face burned.

"Stop, please. I told you, it's not like that between Rip and me."

"*Mmm.* Okay, I gotta go. My doctors are here."

"Bye. And thanks."

The phone went dead, and I sat staring at the desk, shoring up courage. "You're being stupid," I muttered to myself. "Just do it. The worst he can do is say no, and you'll keep doing the scut shit until something else comes along where you can prove yourself."

First I had emails to answer, but someone knocked on my door.

"Come in," I called out.

"Hi, Adrian. I'm Bryan Held. Don't think we've met yet." A tall, thin man, Bryan held out his hand with a friendly enough expression.

"Oh, yeah, hi. I spoke with Louie, and he said you were replacing him while he recuperated."

"Yeah. Tough break, but hopefully he'll be back soon. Rob mentioned Louie was planning some interviews with the Hoops after they finished playing the DC Dunks. Amazing that we finally have a few New York teams in playoff contention at the same time, plus the Kings football team that just won the Super Bowl. Makes for a busy schedule."

"Uh, yeah, sure." Who was I kidding? I barely knew that the Kings were a football team and had never watched a single basketball game in my life. "I'll get some film from production and send everything to your email."

"Perfect. Can you also make some phone calls for me? I need to check and make sure I've got my media passes set up for when I need them. Here are the numbers."

I forced my lips upwards. "No problem."

"Great, great. Thanks, buddy. Talk to you later."

Buddy? Who the hell spoke like that? I chewed my lip and got to work, and it was early afternoon before I could find a slice of time to check my messages. Rip had texted me at lunch.

Did you speak to your boss? What did he say?

Haven't had time, but Louie thought it was a good idea.

Told ya, Rip responded, adding a winky emoji.

Gathering my courage, I left my seat. Rob's office was at the end of the hall, with large windows overlooking Midtown. As I approached, his secretary, Rosalind, gave me a friendly smile.

"Hey, Adrian. What can I do for you?"

"Is he available?" At her frown, I rushed ahead. "It'll only take a few minutes if he's got something else."

"Hold on." She peered at her screen. "He's got a meeting with the news team in about ten minutes."

"More than enough time."

I must've either sounded pathetic, eager, or both because she nodded. "Let me buzz him." She spoke low into her phone, but tipped her head toward his closed door. "Go ahead."

"Thanks." I took half a second to brace myself, then turned the knob, opened the door, and entered. "Hi, Rob. Thanks for seeing me."

"I was wondering when you were going to come."

My brows knitted. "I'm sorry?"

"Sit." He pointed to the chair in front of his desk. "Louie called me."

Of course he did. Just once I'd like to think people believed I could do something on my own. "Oh. So you already know what I'm here for. What do you think?"

One thing about Rob DeVine—he was a master of the neutral face. I couldn't tell what he was thinking. "Since it's your proposal, you should tell me what it is you want."

That was fair, and I appreciated Rob wanting me to present the idea. I repeated what I told Louie, adding how the interviews could delve beyond sports, into the athletes' personal lives, charity projects they're involved with, and what they hoped to accomplish after they no longer played professionally.

"To sum up, everyone talks about the game, but I think fans would like to know the players on a deeper level. Maybe even find something relatable about them."

"And you think you're the person to do this? Why? You've never had your own show, and let's face it, your first performance wasn't stellar."

Rob had no problem laying the truth down. Inside I might be cringing from embarrassment and fear, but I'd never allow anyone to know. Not anymore. Maybe I was finally learning.

"It's because I was unprepared. But so you know, Rip asked me to come sit in the players' box for the Blades' next home game. That, coupled with an exclusive interview with him and Sebastian Crowe, will prove I'm more than capable."

"Did he now?" A crafty gleam lit Rob's eyes.

I drew my shoulders back. "We're friends. It's natural for him to want to help me."

"Yeah. Okay." He steepled his fingers together, and I held my breath. "I actually think it's a good idea. Depending on the guests you get, it could really work. But"–he put a hand up as a smile broke across my face–"first, you must get more comfortable being on camera. I'll hold off saying anything definite until I see how you do with your inter-views at the game."

"Thanks. Thanks so much. But the Blades' game? I thought about doing it more casually. I wasn't going to go with a crew."

Rob grinned. "You are now."

CHAPTER SEVEN

Rip

Sebastian leaned against the locker next to mine as we were suiting up for the pregame skate. "How was your dinner with Adrian the other night?"

My head emerged from the top of my jersey. "Fine, why?"

He showed me his phone. "I have all of us tagged on social media, and this popped up."

I took the phone and squinted at it. Adrian's blond head appeared in the corner of a few pictures. "Yeah, this delivery kid wanted some pictures. What's the big deal?"

"Nothing. Just curious why all of a sudden you're hanging out with him so much."

With a sigh, I sat on the bench. "I feel for him. Guy wants to be a reporter, and he's got a little stage fright. I'm trying to help him overcome it." The filthy dreams I had of the two of us were my secret. No one needed to know about that.

"You sure that's it?"

My eyes narrowed. "What's that supposed to mean?" I growled, but Seb simply laughed in my face. *Bastard.*

"Don't get tough with me, big guy. I'm just saying that maybe you should think about getting out there again. Dating."

"No way. Not during the season. My focus has to be on winning the games, not hooking up. I'm thirty-six, Seb. Who knows how long I've got left before the Blades replace me? You know if they're not looking now, they will be if we don't get the Cup this year. Plus, Lindstrom's a good center. More than good. And he's young and hungry to make a name for himself with the team. Something he can't do as long as I'm still the captain and center." My hand curled into a fist. "I want that Cup."

"I do too. But you understand you can have both."

"Get off my back, please." I put on the rest of my pads and picked up my stick. "Ready?"

One of the guards came in—with Adrian behind him. I grinned, seeing him wearing the jersey I'd given him. "Adrian."

"Lie to me all you want, but not to yourself," Seb murmured. "You want him."

Ignoring him, I waved them over. "Hey, Jerrold. It's okay. He's with me."

Giving me a nod, Jerrold stepped aside, allowing Adrian to come through. A nervous smile rested on his lips.

"You said it was fine to come for the game tonight, right?"

"Yeah, yeah," I reassured him. "You remember Seb?"

"Yes, hi."

"Hey, how's it going? Rip tells me you're sitting with the team tonight?"

He nodded. "Uh, yeah. Rob sent a cameraman with me. Is that okay?"

I hadn't planned on that, but I was sure it wouldn't matter. "You won't be broadcasting live, correct? Some of the guys' language can get raunchy, and I'm sure your station manager wouldn't appreciate it."

"No, he'll do the cuts in production before the eleven o'clock news."

"So we meet again, *mon ami.*" Denis's loud voice made Adrian jump. "What? Don't tell me I make you nervous?" He laughed, and I had visions of punching him in his perfect face. Denis would flirt with a puppy if it got him attention.

"Go away, Denis. Adrian is a reporter for Channel 8 News. He's sitting with the team tonight."

"Is he now? How sweet. Maybe he and I should talk. I can tell him all your little secrets." He flung an arm around Adrian's neck, sending him staggering into his chest, and I gripped my stick.

"Get your fucking hands off him."

Denis's eyes gleamed. "So protective of your reporter, *mon amour.*" He removed his arm, but I didn't miss his fingers trailing across Adrian's nape, nor Adrian's shiver. There was no denying Denis was a sexy bastard, and the thought of Adrian falling prey to his seduction made my blood boil.

"Your fiancé scored a nice goal last night, Denis," I sniped, watching his lips thin. "You must be proud he's leading the Icers so far."

"Yes, he's first in many ways. My heart being the most important."

Adrian's gaze ping-ponged between us, and deciding I needed to end this ridiculous pissing match, I lifted my stick. "Follow me, Adrian. Let's get you seated."

I'd spoken to Coach about Adrian sitting with the team and he'd agreed, but he didn't look too happy when I informed him of the cameraman's appearance.

"He's not to film me or any of the other coaches. I don't need other teams stealing our plays."

"Of course, understood."

"And next time, check with me first before making promises to friends." His glare of disapproval got my ire up.

"He's with the sports department of Channel 8, I told you. It's nothing personal."

I got Adrian settled, and John, his cameraman, set up his equipment.

"This is cool. I've got great angles here. I never had this point of view."

"Don't count on a second chance if you screw up. Remember what I said," I warned. "No filming the coaches. Strictly the plays on the ice and the penalty box. Anything else, and your station will be banned from the locker room. I'm sure your sports director doesn't want that."

"Yeah, yeah, I heard you," John said, brushing me off, but Adrian took my words more seriously.

"Don't worry. I'll make sure of it."

We took to the ice, and the Lakes came after us with everything they had. Especially me. They'd already lost the three earlier games in the season and needed to save face, so they figured smashing mine would help them somehow. I'd been elbowed, tripped, and pushed to the ice. I gave as good as I got, and the refs were kept busy handing out penalties.

In the third period and after my second major fight where I was hooked but no penalty called, I made my feelings known to Dave Hicks, the closest ref. "You gonna let them do this crap with no repercussions? That's some BS."

"Watch it, Tremaine," he sneered. "Don't be such a snowflake."

Chilled by his tone, I skated in front of him. "What the hell is that supposed to mean?"

"Step back, Tremaine," Hicks warned, standing his ground with a glare. "I'm warning you."

I smacked my stick on the ice, and he threw out his fist. "That's it. In the box. Ten minutes."

"What the fuck?" I seethed.

"You want more? I can have you tossed out completely."

By this time, Coach was yelling and the fans in the arena were booing. I knew if I lost my cool, he'd do as promised. I'd heard the rumors about Hicks and how he wasn't a fan of the league's stance on embracing their gay hockey players. In fact, during Pride, he was one of the few refs not to have a rainbow pin on his shirt, and he failed to attend any of the pregame Pride ceremonies.

Without another word, I skated to the box. Coach sent in Lindstrom as center. He was in his second year and a great backup–big, strong, and fast as hell.

"Sorry, Rip. Ref sucks." Lindstrom took off to center ice, and the fans erupted in cheers while I sat.

"Son of a bitch. He had no right to take me out. Bastard," I mumbled to myself, caught the camera pointed my way, and shut the hell up. Adrian stared at me, wide-eyed and...fearful. *Damn.* Was he scared? Of me? I forced my lips to turn upward, hoping to reassure him, but inside I fumed as Lindy scored the go-ahead goal. Still, I kept my game face on. This wasn't about me and my ego. It was about winning.

With my penalty finished, I returned to cheering fans. The Lakes rushed every puck toward the goal, and I had to admit Denis was on top of his game as he fended off multiple shots. They crashed the net, tried to draw Denis into the crease, but he was too canny for that and held them off. We battled until the last possible minute and came out on top.

Fans cheered and we hugged it out, but I wasn't happy. I'd allowed my personal life to bleed into my playing. I should've let what Hicks said slide and been the professional.

Adrian waited for me outside the locker room. "Are you okay?"

His concern was sweet. "Yeah, of course. Just another day in the life."

"What did he say that got you so upset?"

"He—" I'd almost forgotten the cameraman, who stood against the wall, several feet away from us, but still recording our conversation. Last thing I needed was to say something negative about the referees. I'd end up a target. "Nah. It was nothing important. I should've kept my cool. Penalties are part of the game."

"I guess, but you looked angry."

"I'm always angry when I gotta sit in the box." I lowered my voice. "I'll change, and we'll have dinner, okay?"

"Oh...I didn't know. Uh, sure." Pink-faced, his demeanor was nervous, yet I could see the glimmer of desire in his eyes and knew it matched my own. It was going to be a true test of wills to keep away from him.

"Good. Now come inside the locker room and get some good bites for the broadcast." Knowing John the cameraman had no issues, I beckoned to him. "Follow me."

Behind me I could hear John murmur to Adrian, "Make sure you talk to a bunch of the players."

"I know, I know. I will."

The room was hopping, and when Adrian walked in, the guys began mugging for the camera.

Adrian swallowed hard and thrust the mic into Lindstrom's face. "H-how did it feel to score the game-winning goal?"

"Awesome, but I didn't like what they did to Rip."

"Nah, no problem, man. You aced it." We high-fived.

With approval, I watched as Adrian carefully approached Peter, who flashed him a big smile. Adrian cleared his throat.

"What's next for the Blades?"

"Hopefully another win. But seriously, we're playing great, and I'm feeling good."

"If you win the division, it's home-ice advantage for the playoffs, right? How big of an advantage is that?"

"It's huge. Our fans are the best, and it's always important to start the playoffs here, in Blades Arena."

"Good luck," Adrian called out.

"Thanks, dude."

Seb leaned over to whisper in my ear. "You have to stop watching Adrian like you need to protect him. Let him make it on his own."

I tried, but I couldn't pull myself away. I knew Adrian, and he needed to see that I was there.

Adrian glanced around the room and when he met my eyes, I gave him an encouraging nod. He returned it and headed toward me, but his way was blocked by Denis.

"So we meet again, my friend. You're becoming quite the regular, aren't you?"

"You had a great game. How many goals did you fend off? It seemed like a tremendous amount."

Puffed up from the compliment, Denis grinned smugly. "I don't know the final tally yet, but if it keeps up, I may set a team record this year. Maybe a league one as well."

"What's the average shots on goal you have to take?"

"Usually between thirty to thirty-three, but this felt closer to forty."

"Wow." Adrian sounded impressed, and I hated to admit that it bugged me.

There was little Denis liked more than talking about himself, and Adrian's questions were good ones, I had to admit. Call him a cocky fuck—and I did—but Denis was correct. He was playing the best games of his career, and if we won the Cup, he was a huge part of the reason. That arrogance and self-assurance were what had drawn me to him initially. Over time, it grew tiresome, but I'd ignored it because I'd fallen in love with him.

Don't go there.

Adrian remained with Denis. "Looks like the Blades are going to have a great season overall."

"Yes. So much to look forward to. Plus, my wedding. We're going to wait until after the season ends to do it right. Maybe you and Rip will come?"

What the fuck is he talking about?

I tried hard not to be too obvious as I listened in on their conversation, but Seb called me out.

"You know Denis. He'll do anything to get attention, no matter how outrageous," Seb said. "Denis is always going to be all about Denis."

My smile was sheepish. "Busted, huh?"

"Adrian's holding his own. Give him space."

Of course Seb was right. Still, I kept a discreet eye and ear on them and couldn't help a sigh of relief when Adrian ended their interview.

"I, uh, don't know. I'd better let you go. Thanks again, Denis, and good luck with the rest of the season."

Brow furrowed, Adrian returned to me. "Was he kidding? Inviting me to his wedding? And you?"

I brushed off his concerns. "Ignore him. I'm gonna take a shower and get ready. Meet you out front in a few. You can talk to some more guys, too."

He nodded, and I grabbed my shower stuff and left him. It didn't take me more than fifteen minutes to get cleaned up and dressed, and I found Adrian outside, talking to John, their heads together, watching some film. We walked out together, and as I passed through the arena, fans asked for autographs, so I stopped. Several other players were also chatting with fans.

"I have to stop and do this."

"Of course. No problem."

My phone buzzed, stopped and vibrated again, but I ignored it. The worst thing for a player to do was ignore the people who'd waited after a long game to see them. I signed programs, jerseys, T-shirts, and posed for pictures.

"Rip, Rip." One little kid sitting on his father's shoulders waved his program. "You're my favorite."

"I am? Well, that deserves a special picture." I held him and plopped my cap on his head while his father took out his camera. A second man stood by his side, also recording us.

"Thanks so much. You have no idea how much it means for us as parents to see gay professional sports players. When Dale and I got married, we never thought we'd be fathers, but we decided to foster, then adopt, and now it's the best thing we ever did. We want Charlie to have every-thing any other little boy has."

That made me tear up. "I'm glad," I managed to get past the lump in my throat. "Thank you for sharing that with me, and have a great night."

The conversation left me emotional, which must've been the reason why I answered my phone without looking at the screen.

"Please don't hang up on me, Ripley," my father pleaded.

I covered my eyes with my hand. "What is it? I told you not to call me. Ever."

"I'm your father. Why can't you give me a chance to explain things?"

"Explain how you ran out on us? Never tried to see me? There is no explanation for that in my book."

"Please, Rip, I just want—"

"I know what you want. And I've told you before I'm not interested in your side of the story. Nothing you say can explain away what you did. I don't want to hear from you again. Stop calling me."

"You're my son, whether you like it or not. Just let me see you. Tell you the truth."

"Why? So you can play the martyr? My mother worked her ass off to give me everything and died with nothing. You think you're gonna waltz into my life and I'm gonna write you a check? That's it, isn't it? The money?" I didn't give him a chance to respond. "Just leave me alone."

I ended the call and shoved the phone into my pocket. Unfortunately, when I glanced up, I saw Adrian's sympathetic face.

"Rip. Are you all right?" He put a hand on my back, and I shrugged, unable to speak. "Let's get out of here, 'kay?"

I nodded, he put an arm around me, and we walked outside. It wasn't until we were in the car that I found my voice again.

"Sorry about that."

Adrian slipped his hand in mine and gave it a squeeze. "Don't apologize. Do you want to talk about it?"

Ignoring his question, I peered out the window. "Where are we going?"

"I thought we'd go to my apartment. We can order in. Talk."

"Adrian...I don't know. There's nothing much to say."

"I disagree." As hesitant as he'd been on camera, Adrian's voice held a take-charge edge I hadn't heard before. It hit me that the two of us were alone. I'd been so caught up in my head, I'd forgotten we'd had a cameraperson on us the whole time.

"Wait, where's John? Dammit. He didn't film the phone conversation, did he?"

"No, he stopped after you talked with the little kid and his dads, which was awesome, by the way. I told him to return to the station. Bryan will pick out the clips for the eleven p.m. sports segment. It's just you and me."

"Where do you live?"

"Brooklyn too, in Gowanus. See?" The car slowed to a stop. It was a small four-story brick building with an awning. "No doorman or fancy amenities, but I can offer you friendship and a shoulder. An ear to listen."

I mustered a half smile and followed him into the building and his small one-bedroom. He kicked off his shoes and took off his jacket. I did the same.

"Want a beer or something to drink?"

"Water would be great." I needed to keep my thoughts collected, and even one beer might loosen my inhibitions, causing me to make a foolish decision. "Nice place."

Adrian snorted and handed me a glass. "It's fine. I got lucky. It's rent-stabilized but still costs more than double what I paid in North Carolina for an apartment almost twice the size with a pool and a gym." He scanned the room. "But the location is good." He sipped his water and set it on the coffee table. "So, you're leaving for a few games?"

"Yeah. A travel day tomorrow, then two games on the road with an off day in between. Practice, of course, but I still have free time."

I'd almost forgotten how to relax and talk to someone after a game. More often than not, I'd come home and sit in front of the television, but I'd listen to the voices in my head telling me what I'd done wrong on the ice or how I'd messed up with Denis. I missed the warmth of human companionship. Being touched.

"Must be hard to always be on the go."

I shrugged and took a swig of water. "You learn to deal with it. My career in the game is relatively fleeting, so I can't complain. Hockey has given me so much."

"But you love it?"

"I couldn't imagine doing anything else. It's all I ever wanted."

Adrian's smile was wistful. "It's rare that someone gets to accomplish their dreams. You're lucky."

"You're gonna get there too. Have faith in your ability. I do." Knowing how he still doubted himself, I hoped my words would build him up.

Adrian stared off into the distance. "I don't know. I guess we'll see how they like my segment tonight. I really am trying, but it's hard. I'm not a sports buff and not into all the facts and figures. I'm sure it shows."

"So change that. You have plenty of time between now and when I come for the interview. Study the games, and if you need help, call me and we can talk about it. I'll help you, I already told you that."

"I don't know why you're bothering."

Damn, I hated how defeated he sounded before he'd even started. "Because I know you can do it. Seb mentioned to me—unsolicited—that he thought you were doing a good job." I put my hand on his leg, and he tensed but didn't move away. "I have faith in you. You need to as well."

"I'll have everything ready for when you and Seb come to the studio. So what do you want to eat?"

"Anything is good."

"Burgers and fries?"

I nodded and sat with my legs stretched in front of me as he took out his phone to place the order. The conversation with my father lingered in the corner of my mind, like a thief waiting to strike at the most opportune time.

How did the man always get under my skin? I should block his number and be done with him. Nothing he could say and no reason could be given to change my mind about his abandonment of my mother and me. Yet I couldn't take that final step. Maybe I was a coward.

"Rip?"

I'd been so lost in my head, I hadn't noticed Adrian had moved to sit beside me. "I'm sorry. What did you say?"

"Did you want to talk about the phone call earlier? I'm a good listener, and I don't repeat things."

That earlier pain choked me again. *Dammit.* Why was I so emotional? Maybe because before I'd had Denis to concentrate on, but now I was alone.

"It...it was nothing."

But Adrian was damn stubborn. "That's bullshit. Why're you lying to me?"

"I'm not. It's just...it was my father." At his brows flying high, I almost laughed. "Yeah. He's been calling me for years, and I've been ducking him. First it was for money, and I wasn't going to go down that path because I know if I feed the beast once, it'll never end."

"Oh. Wow. That's...I didn't expect you to say that."

"Yeah. Tonight he calls and says he wants to explain why he left. I'm not the least bit interested."

"I'm really sorry. I totally understand why."

"Then why do I keep thinking about him? I should be concentrating on the upcoming games and winning, and yet he's in my head." I smacked my fist on my thigh. "It's not...goddamn it. I'm sorry. I shouldn't be talking about me." I forced my lips to a smile. "You did well tonight."

"You don't have to keep it inside. I'm your friend. You can talk to me."

The buzzer rang, and Adrian huffed out a sigh. "That'll be our food."

"I'm gonna turn on the news. See what bits from your interview they used."

Adrian accepted the bag from the delivery person and set it on the table. My phone rang, and it was Neil.

"Hey, how's—"

"What the hell, man?" Neil's voice burst out from the phone, and Adrian stared at me. "You swore nothing was going on between you and Adrian."

"We're friends."

"Yeah? Well, *Out in Sports* has a different perspective."

"I have no idea what you're talking about. I haven't talked to *Out in Sports* since Denis and I broke up."

"I told you not to mess with Adrian."

"I'm not. Jesus, you're reaching. Just because we're hanging out doesn't mean anything."

"You're with him now. At this very moment." His tone was quiet. Flat. Like nothing I'd ever heard before.

"You know...I don't know when you started believing that us being best friends means I answer to you about my personal life. Because I don't. Now why don't you calm the fuck down, and we'll talk tomorrow when you pull your head out of your ass."

I ended the call and turned off my phone. I noticed Adrian bent over his, eyes pinned to the screen.

"Adrian?"

"I'm sorry," he whispered, eyes downcast, face flushed. My stomach went into free fall.

"What's wrong?"

He handed me his phone.

CHAPTER EIGHT
Adrian

My first reaction when I saw the post was to run and hide. But as I thought about it more, I got pissed beyond reasoning, and I snatched the phone away from Rip and called John. He picked up, already laughing.

"I didn't think you'd see it that quickly."

"How dare you? What the fuck did you do? I told you to stop filming."

"I don't answer to you, kid. I had some extra footage, and after I got back to the station and sent off the clips to Bryan, I contacted my friend in charge of the *Out in Sports* social-media page."

"You bastard."

"Damn, listen to you. Got a little temper there, don'tcha? I didn't know you had it in you."

"Fuck you," I spat. I'd never been so angry. Not for me, but for Rip, whose privacy had been invaded. "I'm never working with you again. How dare you sell someone's privacy like that?"

Rip had taken his phone, and his face contorted in anger. The first video was Rip on the phone, his face taut, with heartbreak in his eyes. The second was my arm around Rip and him leaning on me before we walked away. It made us look like lovers.

"Is what it is. By the way, those interviews you did were okay. Bryan was happy."

Without answering, I ended the call but had no chance to talk to Rip because Neil called me. "I can't talk right now."

"Good. So listen. I told you it's not a good idea to get too close to Rip. Why can't you listen to me? I know him."

From Rip's sadness over his brief conversation with his father, I suspected Neil didn't know his best friend as well as he thought. He sure as hell didn't know me.

"Yeah? Well, maybe not. I'll talk to you later. Bye." I ended the call and sat by Rip's side. "I'm so sorry. You know I didn't want this to happen."

"What? The rumors about you and me? Screw that." He set the phone aside, ignoring it, though I could see numerous texts popping up. "Do...did John say anything about the phone call? Do they—did he say he knew whom I was talking to?"

"No, no. He didn't say anything, and I'm sure he couldn't possibly know. And I'll never tell."

"I know. You're a good kid."

"Again? I thought we'd gotten past this crap." My lips thinned. "For the last time—I'm not a kid. I'm only eight years younger than you. Maybe when you were sixteen and I was eight it made a difference, but it doesn't anymore."

Rip didn't answer, but checked his messages, his lip curling. "Look at this. Of course Denis would be the first to text me."

He's so cute. And young. Guess you're ready to be the boss now.

"I swear," he grumbled. "It would serve all of them right if we did start dating, just to annoy Neil and make Denis jealous." He chuckled. "Even my agent wants to know if the rumors are true, but he's just being nosy about my love life. Ezra and his husband are ridiculously happy, and he wants that for all his gay clients."

Though happy for his mood shift, annoyance still swirled through me. "Yeah. Neil won't stop treating me like a little kid. Like he knows what's best for me and that's not you."

"Really?" His lips thinned. "So I'm good enough to be his friend, just not a boyfriend for his little brother?"

Uh-oh. I hadn't meant to hurt Rip's feelings. "I mean…it's only because he's so stupidly overprotective. No one would be good enough." I nudged his shoulder. "Let's eat our dinner, and maybe you can give me some insight into the players in the league? It'll help me to prepare for your interview." I unpacked the burgers and set them and the fries in front of us, then busied myself getting the ketchup, salt, and pepper. His thoughtful eyes on me, Rip sat frowning, and an unpleasant concept struck me.

"Unless you don't want to do it anymore because you think it'll cause too much gossip about the two of us and it might screw with your concentration on the game." My phone vibrated with a multitude of texts. Rip tilted his head.

"Your turn. Who are those from?"

I didn't want to check, but the flood of texts didn't stop. I groaned and picked it up. Reading the first few texts, I sighed with frustration. "Louie, Rob, and of course, Neil."

"What're they saying?" Rip had started to eat, and the words came out muffled.

I cast a despairing gaze to the ceiling. "This is from Louie: *Thought you weren't dating? Bet your ratings are going to be through the roof.* The next is from Neil: *Call me tomorrow. We need to talk.*" I saved the best—or worst—for last and winced reading Rob's text. I didn't repeat everything he said. *Glad you took my advice. See me tomorrow about the sports talk-show idea. We'll probably make it work now that you bring so much more to the table.*

If Rip weren't here, I'd probably have thrown my phone in frustration. "Uh...not much else. Rob wants to talk to me about the sports-show project." I left out the part about taking his advice since it made me sound calculating.

"That's a good thing." Rip wiped his mouth, but when I didn't respond with enthusiasm, he set his burger on the plate. "Or not? What aren't you telling me?" I didn't answer. His lips tightened and his eyes narrowed. "Adrian? Spit it out."

Heat rose through my entire body, and sweat broke out on my back, sending a trickle down my spine. The last thing I wanted Rip to discover was the desperate secret crush I'd had on him since I was a kid.

"Rob's been insinuating that if we were...involved, it would be easier to sell the show, and the ratings would be higher." My face burned. I was certain it must be bright red. I ducked my head. "I'm sorry. It's so ridiculous, and he's—"

"Hey." To my shock, Rip reached out and covered my hand with his. The rough skin of his large palm stirred a low throb in my belly, and my heart pounded. His gaze held mine, and a slow grin kicked up his lips. "Hold on a minute. Maybe it's not."

I couldn't believe what I was hearing, even as my heart leaped. "I'm sorry, what?"

"Well...everyone seems to think it's already happening, why not give them something to talk about? You and me dating. You'll get the benefit of our fake dating, helping you with the show's ratings. It can only be good for your career."

My stomach rebelled, and I thought I might be sick. "I've never been so embarrassed in my life. I'm not...I can't ask you to do that. It's not fair to put you in the position of having to pretend to be my boyfriend. You shouldn't have to force yourself." The words left a bitter taste on my tongue. If only it were true...but Rip hadn't suggested we try and date for real. He only wanted to pretend.

"I'm not that altruistic." His hearty laughter boomed in my small apartment. "You act like it's a hardship to be close to you." His fingers played with mine. "To be honest, it hurts like hell to think Neil doesn't feel I'm good enough to be your boyfriend, that he's so against it. He deserves to be played for being so angry that we might be together. Let him sweat."

"This has to be the most ridiculous thing I've ever heard," I muttered, even as my heart screamed, *Yes. Do it. You know you want to.*

"Why?"

"Because...*because*," I sputtered, "what if you meet someone you actually want to date? You're stuck with me."

He squeezed my hand. "We're in the thick of the season, fighting for the championship. When I'm playing, I'm not out looking for anyone. My concentration is solely on the game and winning the Cup. I'm not sure how many more seasons I've got, Adrian. And I want it so bad, it's all I can think of morning, noon, and night. Now that Denis and I aren't together, it's the only thing I've got to look forward to in my life."

My heart squeezed at his heartfelt words.

I'm right here, I wanted to scream. *We could be good together.*

But I couldn't put Rip in that position of refusing me. I knew he'd feel bad about it.

"Okay, what about this?" I argued. "Define our relationship. Do I stay over? Do we go out in public?"

It took Rip a moment to figure it out. "I have two bedrooms, so yeah, to make it look realistic, you could stay over when I'm playing at home. And of course we'll go out to dinner if you want, but like I said before, I'm a homebody who likes hanging out on my couch, watching television and enjoying quiet time. I'm not a clubber or a party guy. Been there, done that." He looked introspective, and I wondered if he was thinking about Denis and the life he'd lost.

"I just don't understand why you want to do this for me."

Seemingly frustrated with me, Rip carded his fingers through his dark hair. "Why not? I want you to succeed. I'm your friend."

"No," I replied with a stubborn edge. "You're Neil's friend."

"Maybe this arrangement can change that. I could use as many friends as I can get." He stared past me, his eyes distant.

Could it be true that behind the devil-may-care smile and multimillion-dollar salary that could buy him anything he wanted, there lurked a man who might be as lonely as me?

"Plus," he continued, "your family made all this possible for me." He swept a hand in front of him. "Who knows where I might've ended up if your parents hadn't taken me in?"

A lead weight bottomed out in my stomach. "Oh...so you're doing this out of a bizarre sense of gratitude. Like repaying a debt you think you owe them?" That hurt me more than anything.

But even as I spoke, he shook his head. "No. But what would it matter anyway? There's no difference. The end result justifies the means. You'll get noticed by the powers that be and get the recognition you deserve. That will help you move up the ladder and give you a chance to leverage this opportunity for a meatier role."

Dammit. I hated that his argument had merit. "I don't know..." I crumpled up the remains of my dinner, my stomach rebelling against any more food.

"Oh...wait. I get it."

"What're you talking about?" I took his trash as well and stuffed it into the bag. "What's there to get?"

"Listen." He rose from his seat to join me in my cramped kitchen area. "I'm sorry. I didn't think of the other way around. If *you* meet someone else, I'll step aside but still talk you up to the station. I wouldn't want to stand in the way of you finding a boyfriend. That's more likely."

The sincerity in Rip's eyes almost brought tears to mine, if only it wasn't so laughable. Me? Find someone better than Ripley Tremaine? "That's definitely not going to be a problem. I haven't had guys beating down my door, and nothing's changed." I couldn't humiliate myself any further and tell him I'd never had a real boyfriend, and as for the few men I'd been with, none compared to my dream of him. He didn't ever need to know.

Rip's face registered surprise. "Are you shitting me?" He grimaced when I nodded. "I mean, let's be real. Guys can be dicks."

I lifted a shoulder. "I guess so. Maybe."

He checked his phone. "It's getting late, and I need to be up early tomorrow for morning practice. I can't be late."

"Of course." He hadn't left, yet I already missed him, knowing I wouldn't see him for a while. Silly, it had only been a few days since we'd reconnected, but Rip had given me a taste of a world I'd been ignoring. Something I hadn't known I was missing but now desperately wanted to be part of.

Or was it him I wanted? Angry with myself for reverting to an old fantasy, I concentrated on my work. Rip was correct. Us pretending to be together would certainly cause a buzz. But was it the right way for me to succeed? Only time would tell. "I guess I'll see you."

"I'll call you from the road to see how it's going."

As he requested a car on his phone, we walked to the door. "I'm still not sure about this."

He squeezed my shoulder. "Sleep on it, and you'll see I'm right. There's no downside to this idea. You'll get the inside scoop to help your career, and hopefully it'll stop people from assuming I'm devastated over Denis and me breaking up."

Was he? Did Rip still think about Denis and wish they were together? His hand remained on me, and I never wanted to move. I hadn't been touched in years and I tried to remain casual, but it was an impossible task. I could only hope Rip didn't feel the tremors running under my skin.

"You'd better get going," I muttered, not trusting my voice to remain steady, and opened the door.

For one crazy second I thought Rip might lean in and kiss me. My lips tingled with anticipation. Then his face grew taut, and he backed out of my apartment. As usual, I was wrong. He didn't want me.

"Night, Adrian."

God, he couldn't wait to get away from me. I closed the door behind him and leaned against it. "Stop acting like this is anything more than exactly what Rip said. A way to get ahead. He's nice enough to want to help. You should just do what he said and take advantage of it. He'll never be anything more than a friend."

No matter how I wished he were so much more.

CHAPTER NINE
Rip

After our two away games, I was more focused than ever on making the playoffs, and I upped my training regimen. Strength and endurance were key to succeeding in the latter part of the season, and I was determined not to be outdone by the younger players.

We'd won one and lost one, and at this point, I took every loss as a personal failure. I called Adrian after practice following our return. We'd texted over the weekend, and I knew he'd seen Neil.

"How'd the visit go? Sorry I haven't been in touch more. It's gearing up toward the end of the season, and I've got commitments to fulfill." Funny how I wanted to check in with him and make sure he understood I was thinking of him. I missed seeing him and was already wondering how to fit him into my schedule.

"Don't apologize. I know you're busy. And I took your advice and watched your game, plus a few others. Oh, and Neil and I took in a basketball game Saturday night." He laughed. "I still don't have a clue what's going on, but I must admit it's more fun being at the game than watching it on the television."

"You're becoming a regular sports junkie now."

"Hardly," he scoffed, then turned teasing. "But I see the appeal. Basketball shorts and tight hockey pants."

"Oh, yeah? Watching sweaty guys running across the court or skating across the ice is suddenly your thing?" Jealousy spiked through me.

"I mean...yeah. What's wrong with that?"

"Nothing, just kidding." Not really, but I couldn't tell him that. "I've got the night off, and I was wondering if you want to get dinner."

"Oh, damn. I can't. Neil wants me to meet some people he knows that he thinks can help me. He said networking with print reporters is important, so I'm having dinner with him and someone from *Sports Weekly*. I could cancel—"

"No. Absolutely not." I didn't actually think the crossover between the two was the reason—or not all of it. Neil wanted to keep Adrian and me apart, and it pissed me off, but that was a conversation for Neil and me. "Good for you."

"Yeah, but maybe another night this week?"

"I'll let you know. Tomorrow we have a home game, and then we go to Tennessee and Vermont. Playoffs are coming up, and I usually sequester myself and study training films and hit the gym more."

"Oh." He sounded as disappointed as I felt, but as much as I wanted to see Adrian, I couldn't afford to slack off at this crucial point of the season.

"I guess I'm being a bad fake boyfriend," I joked.

"I'm still not sure about this. I really hate lying to people."

The distress in his voice was real, and I decided to tread lightly. "Come on, Adrian. We're not hurting anyone. We're friends now, and you know I enjoy talking to you. It's refreshing to be with someone who isn't caught up in hockey twenty-four seven. I'm glad we're getting to know each other."

"Me too," he whispered, and I struggled to keep my word to focus solely on hockey and not this sweet man who'd fallen into my life like a shooting star.

"Maybe we can meet for a coffee or hang out a little. Carve out time during the day to see each other? I don't know..." Fumbling wasn't something I was familiar with—on the ice or in my personal life. Being this tentative around a man was shocking. I'd never had trouble finding sex; I'd had my share of wild hookups when I was younger. Instinctively, though, I knew Adrian was much less experienced and wouldn't appreciate a man with an ego. And after Denis, I'd lost my swagger. My past was something I'd never given a second thought to, but now it made me cringe.

"Not something I can easily do. My schedule during the day is quite hectic."

I hadn't considered that. Too wrapped up in my own issues. "Yeah, I'm sorry. Well, we can talk at night when I'm finished with my game. You can tell me how your day went."

"Oh...yeah, that'd be nice. But Rip, you don't have to do all this for me." His words came out on top of each other, rushed and breathless.

"Maybe I'm doing it for me." Making myself vulnerable freaked me out. I'd never done that with Denis or anyone else I'd dated in the sports world. It wouldn't have occurred to me. Even with Neil, I never opened up about my fears of growing older, becoming slower. Easily replaceable. With Adrian I could be me. The me I once was before the spotlight shone on my every move.

"Call me later, okay?" Adrian asked. "I've got to go."

Each night I was away, Adrian and I ended up speaking. I coached him on hockey stats, and then we'd get on FaceTime, where I'd make him practice asking questions. One night he seemed particularly down.

"What's wrong?"

"Nothing," he replied, but I could read his dejection in the downward tug of his lips.

"Adrian...come on. Tell me."

"It's stupid. I overheard Bryan talking to some of the reporters on staff, and he called me his gofer. It made me realize that's really all I am."

I winced and quickly thought of words to help ease his hurt feelings.

"Assistant to the sports director isn't a gofer. And soon to be host of a Sunday night sports show. Don't let it get to you."

"It's hard," he answered glumly. "The only good thing was that I heard the news anchor, Sterling Forest, say that Bryan's lucky he has someone as thorough and with a work ethic like mine working with him. I didn't even know he knew who I was."

"See? You're making an impression."

"Yeah. Forest is well respected in the news world. I've seen him in the elevator, and he just nods. Pretty intimidating."

"Well, it's obvious he's noticed you. So that's a good thing. Keep doing what you're doing."

"Thanks. I'm trying."

Aside from our conversations, I spent my time at the gym and at practice, and the dedication showed. We won all three games that week. I looked forward to coming home and seeing Adrian for our interview. The night before I was due in the studio, I called him.

"You ready? I know I am."

"Uh...yeah. I-I think so."

From his hesitation, I doubted the truth of that answer. "You've been studying the info I gave you? Watched the games?"

"Yeah. Yours. It's just hard to pick it all up on the television screen—offsides, icing, what each position is supposed to do. I don't know if I'll ever be able to understand it all."

"I wouldn't worry too much. Plenty of teams don't act like they know the rules either, from seeing them play." I thought my joke was funny, but apparently Adrian didn't appreciate my sense of humor, as he didn't join in my laughter. "Seriously, though, it's an instinct you pick up from time on the ice. You learn the rules as you go, and how to bend or break them. Sort of like newscasting. The more you do it, the more comfortable you become."

"I just don't want to sound stupid or fumbling."

"You won't. Tomorrow, pretend it's you and me talking on the phone or over dinner. Don't think about the camera."

"Thanks, Rip. I know you're busy, and you don't have all this time to babysit me."

"I'm not. It's not a big deal."

"It is to me. I'll see you tomorrow."

The call ended, leaving me wondering who'd cut down his confidence tree to a stump.

Not on my watch.

In the news studio, the audio tech clipped on my mic, and we ran a sound check. I didn't speak to Adrian because I could see from his rapid breathing and how he kept running his hand through his hair as he spoke to Rob DeVine that those nerves we'd worked so hard to keep at bay were eating away at him. He shook his head vehemently, but Rob stood his ground and pointed his finger in Adrian's face. They came to some agreement—or rather, DeVine had made his wishes known and Adrian capitulated and would do as told.

Nothing I could say or do would help him, but even if he asked me questions I didn't want to answer, I would. Seb nudged me.

"You sure he's gonna be okay? Looks like he's about to heave."

I hated to agree with him, but Adrian's pale face didn't bode well. "I think he'll be okay once we start. Tell a funny story or something to break the ice."

An evil grin crept over Seb's face. "Oh, good."

I groaned. "You're gonna make me look like a fool, aren't you?"

Eyes dancing, Seb shrugged. "Maybe, maybe not."

That morning, as we arrived at the station, I'd decided to let Seb in on the plan Adrian and I had cooked up.

"Listen. I want to tell you something. About me and Adrian."

Cackling, Seb slapped his knee. "I knew it. You're together. I said to Jolie last night I knew it was gonna happen sooner rather than later. I like it. He's a nice kid. Might be good for you to be with someone out of the game."

Denial had sprung to my lips, but then Adrian had joined us, and the final audio checks were made before I could explain. For now, though, it was more important to make sure Adrian was going to be okay.

"You'll be great." I squeezed his arm, and I could see the denial in his eyes and increased my grip. "Remember everything we practiced this past week. You've got this."

The production assistant made one last adjustment to our mics, and Gerrard the cameraman called out, "Three, two, one." The camera light turned on, and music swelled in our earpieces. Adrian shifted in his seat and blinked.

"W-welcome to *Playing the Field*, the new show where I bring you insight and information on all your favorite athletes, from football to baseball, hockey to basketball, and everything in between. Today for our inaugural show, I have two of the Brooklyn Blades, Captain Ripley Tremaine and All-Star winger Sebastian Crowe. If you watch hockey, you know the Blades are in the end run leading up to the playoffs and hopefully the Stanley Cup."

Seb waved. "Great to be here. Thanks, Adrian, for inviting me."

"Yeah," I joined in. "Happy to be your first guests. Great concept for a show. Feel free to ask us anything."

"That's right. Personal or private." Seb winked at me, and I knew I was about to take a shot at my pride for Adrian's sake. "I've got a funny story to break the ice...so to speak."

"Tell us, please," Adrian urged. "I'm sure the viewers will love to hear it."

"It's about my best buddy Rip and a little mishap with his skates as a rookie. Turns out he'd tied the laces of his skates together by accident, and when he stood up to walk, he fell flat on his face."

I groaned as Seb relayed the story, and Adrian laughed, his eyes darting to me to see my reaction, but I grinned and shook my head.

"Is this true, Rip?"

I pretend-glared at Seb. "Oh, yeah. I was nervous, what can I say? Matter of fact, the whole team called me Trip for months. Until I broke the number of goals scored by a rookie, won Rookie of the Year, and was named the youngest captain in Blades history." I smirked. "So I'll take the ribbing. I think I've outgrown that nickname."

"Considering your record, I agree. This question is for both of you. What's been your most exciting game and time on the ice in your career so far?"

I stepped up first. "Definitely my first game as a rookie. All my hard work and dreams came down to that moment. But also winning the division title and getting to play in the Stanley Cup Finals the first time. I'll never forget it."

"I gotta second what Rip said," Seb agreed. "There's something humbling about stepping out on the ice for the first time."

"Did you both know you always wanted to play hockey? When did you think you might have the talent to go all the way to play professionally?"

"Growing up near Lake Placid, we learned to skate before we could walk. You know that, Adrian." He winced, and I wanted to kick myself. Adrian had no affinity for the ice. He spent more time facedown on the ice than standing up. I rushed to continue. "But I always wanted to play hockey. It was hard as a child 'cause it was just my mom and me, and after she died, I moved in with your family. Your parents recognized my talent and helped me tremendously. Hockey was going to get me a college scholarship." The wobble in my voice shocked me, and Adrian put a comforting hand on my forearm. "If it wasn't for them, I don't know what I would've done. I owe them everything." "They love you and never doubted your talent."

I fell into the pure blueness of his eyes, and everything else faded away. "My mom once told me if I want something bad enough, to fight for it. Do whatever you can to make a dream happen. It's why she worked double shifts at that run-down diner where even the roaches wouldn't visit. I knew it wouldn't be easy being a gay man in professional sports, but with friends like Seb and a great team like the Blades behind me, I never felt like I didn't belong."

"We have to take a break now, but we'll be right back with more from Ripley Tremaine and Sebastian Crowe of the Brooklyn Blades."

Drained and unexpectedly emotional, I settled in my chair and blew out a breath. A glass of water was pressed into my hand.

"Here you go," Adrian murmured. "Are you okay to continue?"

"Yeah, definitely. You're doing great." No lies there. Adrian was handling himself like a pro.

Seb patted me on the shoulder. "Everything good?"

"Yeah. I'm fine."

"Ready to go on, or do you need more time?" Adrian asked, and my smile was wry.

I had to remind him it wasn't up to me. "I think when the commercial is over, that's it, ready or not."

"Just want to make sure. Is it okay to continue with that line of questioning?"

I nodded as the music came on again. "I'm good."

Adrian chewed his lip. "I'd, um, I'd like to continue with what we were talking about before the break. Your sexuality. Have you ever felt discriminated against because you're gay? I mean...has it been hard for you in the league being an out player?"

A question I knew to tread around lightly. "I've never regretted my decision to come out as a professional hockey player. And the Blades organization as well as my teammates have been nothing but supportive. I can't control how people feel, but personally, I've never had any problems."

Untrue. However, it wasn't something I'd reveal to anyone. But Adrian proved surprisingly insightful and probed deeper.

"Is it true that some fans have blamed your sexuality for the Blades not winning the Stanley Cup?"

Ouch. That was unexpected, and I jerked my head to meet his steady gaze. I understood these were the questions that people tuned in to hear, and I gave him credit for not shying away.

"I don't like to dwell on negativity and ugly words. But yeah, some people think they have the right to come into my direct messages and write things they'd never dare say to my face. I delete, block, and move on. I have zero time or tolerance for bigots and fools. So many great athletes came out after they retired, and I don't fault them for waiting, especially when people misbehave. The focus should be on the game, nothing else. But to answer your question, it proves the point that sexuality has nothing to do with your ability to play professional sports."

Seb spoke up. "Rip deserves to be judged on his skating alone, not for anything else. And for that, he's the best of the best. A definite Hall of Famer."

"Thanks, buddy." Surprising tears burned my eyes.

Maybe figuring it was time to give me a break, Adrian turned to Seb.

"What about your family, Seb? You have two young children. Does your wife come with you on the road?"

"Well, Jolie's a trooper. She doesn't travel with me now because the girls are too young, but she used to when we were first married, and she's made good friends with some of the other wives on the team. We love being part of the Blades family."

"Have you ever felt pressure to be at home more?"

Seb's brow furrowed in thought. "I'd like to, and she knows that, but we discussed everything before deciding to have children and concluded it was worth the time away now, to give us a better future."

"How did you two meet, and was your wife always into hockey?"

"Oh, absolutely not." Throwing his head back, he laughed out loud. "Jolie was a sports novice and had never watched a hockey game until we met. She worked as a sales associate, and we met when I had to buy a suit for the ESPYs."

"I'm sure she's a pro now. Does she like to skate with you?"

"Not at all. Hockey is my thing, and reading is hers. She has her book-club friends. But she's my number-one cheer-leader and promised me the girls will learn to skate. I can't wait to take them out on the ice."

Adrian consulted his note cards, and I could see the muscle jump in his jaw. "Uh, Rip, you recently broke up with your boyfriend of two years, Denis Bouvier, who's the Blades' goalie. Do you think being on the same team might affect your playing this season?"

I'd been asked this question often enough to have the answer prepared. "Not at all. Denis and I are professionals. Our mission is to win games and ultimately the Stanley Cup. Nothing will keep us from our objective."

Adrian bit his lip and flicked his gaze to mine. I could see the struggle in his eyes, and he huffed out a breath. "Are you seeing anyone right now?"

I could take the easy way out and simply say no. But the more I saw Adrian and we spent time together, the more I liked being with him. Did he honestly need me?

Maybe not. But given all our conversations, I was more than a little curious to see how far Adrian would go with the charade.

"Yes. I am."

"Really, dude? Holding out on your best friend?" Man, that twinkle in Seb's eye annoyed the fuck out of me. He was enjoying my personal life way too much. "Who is it? I'm sure your fans want to know."

Adrian cleared his throat. "I don't think Rip should have to reveal his new relationship if he doesn't want to."

A noble statement, but Rob DeVine paced behind the cameras, and I could see the storm brewing in his dark expression. If Adrian didn't come up with something big and juicy, DeVine was going to rip him a new one and take away his big chance, even though the interview was going well. Screw what Neil and everyone else thought.

Taking Adrian's hand, I leaned in and kissed his cheek. "Don't be so shy, babe. I don't mind."

The scent of his aftershave swirled around me, and it was a good thing I was aware of the camera, as I wanted nothing more than to tangle my hands in that thick golden mop of his and kiss the living hell out of that trembling mouth.

"But—"

"It's okay," I soothed before facing the camera. "Adrian and I grew up together, but he was younger and I never paid him any attention. But now? The age difference doesn't seem to matter. We've reconnected, and..." I lifted a shoulder. "The rest is private. Between the two of us."

"That's great news," Seb said with a grin. "I'm happy for both of you."

The cameraman signaled that we had less than thirty seconds left. Visibly shaken, Adrian licked his lips, and the sweat on his brow gleamed in the overhead lights of the studio.

"Uh, I, uh, this has been *Playing the Field* with guests Sebastian Crowe and Ripley Tremaine of the Brooklyn Blades. I hope you enjoyed the show. Let us know your thoughts on the station's website, Channel 8 News dot com. Good luck to you both in your quest for the Stanley Cup."

The studio lights dimmed, and Rob DeVine motioned furiously to Adrian, who jumped out of his seat. I watched as DeVine spoke with a big smile on his face, and Adrian listened, nodding. I didn't like fooling people, yet I still firmly believed this would help him.

"So I wasn't wrong," Seb murmured. "I could see it right away."

"It's not what you think," I answered. "He did well, don't you think?"

"Not what I think? You said you two are an item. And yeah, he did. A little nervous in the beginning, but overall it was more than decent for a first show."

I checked my watch. "I promised Adrian we'd have lunch after the interview. Wanna join us?"

"Are you kidding me? And be a third wheel?" Seb snickered at my glare. "I gotta get home, finish packing, and say good-bye to the girls. I'll see you at the airport."

"All right. Catch you later." We bumped fists, and while I waited for Adrian to finish, I signed a few autographs and took some pictures with the production team. My phone buzzed, and seeing texts from Neil pop up, I ignored them, but there was one call I didn't plan on ignoring.

"Brody Martin, how the hell are you?"

Brody, superstar tight end, and his husband, Devlin Summers, the former iconic quarterback of the Brooklyn Kings, had become good friends of mine when we formed GAINS. There were over fifty members, retired and active players of all professional teams. In addition to being on the board and their sports reporting jobs, Brody and Dev had a weekly podcast called *The Huddle*, and I'd been on it a few times.

"Good, man, how's it goin'?" Brody's soft southern accent played in direct contrast to Devlin's fast-talking New York speak.

"Going good. Just finished taping a new sports show coming to Channel 8, and then we're heading out for some away games."

"Life of a busy player. Listen, Dev and I were wonderin' if you might wanna come on *The Huddle*–talk about your run for the Stanley Cup and the rumors swirling about this new relationship you're in."

"Are there rumors?" I made a face. God, I hated this publicity nonsense.

"Well, after those pictures..."

I winced. "Yeah. I mean, it's all pretty new."

Brody said, "People love to talk, especially when it comes to pro sports and queer relationships."

I huffed out a sigh. "Yeah, well, people need a new hobby."

He chuckled. "If it makes you feel better, it wouldn't be all about you and your new boyfriend. Like I said, we'd talk hockey, heading into the playoff season..."

"And maybe what it's like playing with an ex?" I was pretty sure Brody was too nice a guy to come right out and ask, but I knew that sooner or later I'd have to talk about it.

"If you wanna. People are interested in that kinda dynamic."

Adrian and DeVine had finished, and DeVine was on his phone. With cautious steps, Adrian made his way over to me, and I was much more interested in what he had to say than talking to Brody.

"Yeah, sure. Why not?" An idea sprang to mind. "Why don't Adrian and I both come on? He can talk about his new show, and I can talk about me."

"Great idea. Even better. You're leaving for a road trip, so how about next week?"

"Sounds good. Send me the details."

"Catch you later, Rip. Thanks."

I ended the call to Adrian's curious expression. "That was Brody Martin. He played football for the Brooklyn Kings and wants us to come on his podcast. I said yes because it would be great press for you and the station."

Adrian chewed his lip and carded his fingers through his hair. "I'd have to check with Rob."

"I'll do it."

"Wait," he said, attempting to hold me back, but I shook him off.

"Rob," I called out, and before Adrian could object further, I left my chair and crossed the room. Adrian followed at my heels. "Rob, got a second?"

He dragged his gaze from the phone. "Yes?" His smile was sly. "So the rumors were true, then."

I ignored his innuendo. "Listen. I got a call from Brody Martin. He wants Adrian and me on his podcast, *The Huddle*. I figured it would be good publicity for the station and the new show. Agreed?"

"*Hmm...*" His sharp brown eyes assessed Adrian and me. "I like it. Adrian, you don't have a problem with it, I'm sure."

"Uh, n-no. I'm fine. It'll be okay."

Figuring Adrian wouldn't have the nerve, I had to ask Rob what he thought about the segment we just did.

"I thought Adrian did a great job with the interview, don't you?"

"You did, *hmm*?" His brows drew together. "He was pretty nervous."

Adrian wilted a bit, so I stepped up for him since I knew he wouldn't defend himself. "Yeah, maybe. But it went smoothly. He asked good questions."

"I guess we'll see how the ratings go when we air it. If they're high enough, we'll schedule it for another slot. Have you thought about who you'd have as a guest if we do decide to give you another show?"

"Not sure yet. I didn't want to make inquiries—not without knowing there'd be another."

"Smart. No need wasting people's time if it all goes belly up and no one watches. Let's hope it makes the cut. Hopefully people will tune in to see you interview your new boyfriend. I'll let you know." Without another word, he left us standing together in the empty studio.

"Rip..." he began, and I could see he was looking for a way out, so I took him by the hand and pulled him out of the room and down the hall until we reached a secluded area.

"Stop knocking yourself. It went great, and Rob is being a dick because he can."

"I didn't want to ask any questions about us, but Rob insisted."

I put a hand on his shoulder and squeezed. "I was prepared. Now let's go get that lunch and give people something to talk about for real."

Attempting to set Adrian at ease, I told him funny stories of my mishaps and screwups during my first season in the league. The fact that I was named Rookie of the Year was irrelevant, and I minimized it for his benefit. With his sparkling eyes and flushed cheeks, I had to remember we were simply friends playing a game of attraction and desire.

Café Fiorello was a Lincoln Center institution, and I knew at lunchtime it would be a scene. Not a place I'd normally choose, but I wanted people to see Adrian and me. I held his hand and tangled our fingers together as I put the last bit of chicken parmigiana in my mouth and sighed with appreciation. "Damn, that was good. Listen, the show came off great, and this podcast with Brody and Devlin will help you attract viewership. They have a big audience."

Adrian had finished his spaghetti and meatballs, but he still tensed every time someone came by the table to ask for an autograph.

"You still don't think I can do it on my own?"

The light in his face flickered, and I hastened to answer before it got snuffed out. "Yes, you can. But let's face it, you're still an unknown. You need people to know who you are. Don't you think doing this will get more eyes on you? Get your name on people's lips? I've watched enough of these shows to know that sometimes it's all about popularity and who people want to see."

"I guess. It just feels weird to pretend."

Funny thing was, I really liked talking to Adrian. He wasn't starstruck by my fame, and he listened to what I had to say. Unlike with Denis, there was no one-upmanship with who was more of a fan favorite. I was going to miss Adrian on this road trip.

Seemed like I wasn't pretending the boyfriend thing all that much.

CHAPTER TEN
Adrian

I knew this was going to happen.

The charade wasn't going to work.

Not because Rip couldn't fake it. He was the perfect pretend boyfriend.

The problem was me. I was enjoying myself way too much. I didn't have to fake it.

Our lunch was...fun. I knew Rip was trying to put me at ease, and he succeeded. I started out tense, believing everyone in the restaurant was wondering what a gorgeous man like Ripley Tremaine, the superstar hockey player, was doing with a nobody like me, but at some point I forgot all that and simply enjoyed our conversation. He didn't treat me like that tagalong kid anymore.

Rip paid the bill and took my hand, holding it tight. "Time to go to my place to pick up my luggage and get to the airport."

"I can't. I've got to get stuff together for Bryan for the evening sports segment."

When we walked outside on Broadway, a car pulled up. Rip slid an arm around my waist. I froze, and he leaned close to whisper, lips touching my ear, "I guess we'll say good-bye here."

As it had been the other night, having him in close prox-imity set my heart pounding. My breath came in short pants. "Okay. Have a great trip."

A wicked grin tipped up his lips. "Try to miss me a little." He ran his nose across my cheek, resting his mouth on the edge of mine. "I'll call you."

Shaking in his arms, I could only nod, and his eyes glowed fire.

"You're really gorgeous, Adrian. I hope you know I'm not pretending when I say it."

Were those words real or to build up my confidence? Rob and Louie would say it didn't matter. Go with the flow and use it to my advantage. I put a smile on my lips.

"Sure. And you're pretty amazing yourself." Over Rip's shoulder I spied a cameraman and curious people with their phones out. "People are taking our picture." He nuzzled my neck, and turned-on as I was, I still had ques-tions. "How did they know we'd be here? They don't just hang out, looking for people, do they?"

"I might've called someone to come and get a few shots of us. The pictures will push the ratings for my appearance on your show."

A bit of my joy dissipated, knowing this was truly a pretense, yet having Rip's hard, muscular body pressed to mine left me a quivering ball of need. I clung to his broad shoulders. "Th-thank you. For everything." My grip on his jacket grew tighter, and I swayed closer, but he released me and stepped away. Eyes glittering, his fingers trailed along my cheek.

"Adrian...I have to go."

Without another word, he climbed into the waiting car and was gone. A chilly wind blew, and I put my head down and walked toward the subway to return to the office.

Rob had been happy with the interview and ecstatic at Rip's revelation of our relationship. *"Gonna be great for ratings. You didn't do half bad."* Not exactly the most ringing endorsement, but better than him saying *you sucked.*

At the office, I met with Bryan. I'd come in early to go through the schedule and choose the clips for the early news. He was going to the Hoops game later, and I'd made sure to have all the stats he'd need for the eleven o'clock show. When we were finished, Bryan directed his best-buddy, chummy grin at me.

"Heard you had good interviews with that show you're doing."

My smile was faint. "Yeah. It went okay." I rose from my chair.

"So. You and Ripley Tremaine, huh? He's a great player."

Maybe he was trying to be friendly, but my head wasn't into it, nor was I about to confide in someone I barely knew, who considered me nothing more than his gofer. "He is. I'd better get going. I've got some phone calls to return and stats to gather for you. I'll make sure production has all the clips ready, and I'll go over your script for the six o'clock news."

He let me escape, and I sank into the chair behind my desk in my office. I checked my voice mail, and there were emails from strange men, some wanting my number, some wanting to know what Rip was like in bed...in vivid detail.

A few tried to attach pictures, but our anti-porn software blocked them. I deleted them, but the fact that this attention was solely from those social-media posts proved Rip was correct. Linking us together was getting me noticed, only not in the best way.

I took a moment and wondered what Rip was doing. Had he gotten on the plane? Should I call him, or would that seem weird since we were faking it?

The phone on my desk rang.

"Newsroom, Adrian Hunt speaking."

"Mr. Hunt, this is Jay Monroe from *Out in Sports*. I was wondering if you had time to meet me today for an interview. I know it's short notice, but I'm hoping you can fit me in."

"*Out in Sports?*"

Why would they be calling... *Oh. The Ripley Tremaine effect.*

"I'm pretty tied up for the rest of the day, but—"

"Well, I was thinking more like after-work drinks? With Rip away, maybe you have some free time?"

"Uh...I guess." Alone, and yet my face still burned, knowing people thought Rip and I were together. Intimate. Heat flushed through me.

If only...

"Good. You're in Brooklyn too, right? How about Barbalu on Bergen St.? They have nice wine and cocktails."

I'd never been, but then again, I'd never been anywhere. In the time I'd been back, I hadn't had a date or made any attempt at being social. Work had my complete focus. "Sure. I get off around six."

"Say, seven? I'll make the reservation and meet you there."

"Okay. See you there."

I hung up and debated for a moment before texting Rip.

Someone from Out in Sports called, and we're meeting for a drink. What should I say?

I didn't expect him to answer immediately, so I dove into my pile of work, arranging Bryan's schedule and checking with the film crew about the clips for the evening news. My phone vibrated, and I hoped it was Rip, but instead Neil's name flashed across the screen. I squeezed my eyes shut for a second. I knew what was coming, and I could only avoid it for so long.

"Hey. How's it going? I'm busy, so it'll have to be quick."

"Getting a little bossy, are we?"

"Ha-ha. But seriously, I've got stuff to do with Louie out, and I'm still learning and finding my way."

"Yeah? What way is that? To Rip's apartment?"

My jaw clenched. "I'm not discussing my personal life with you."

"Adrian, come on. Just listen to me for a minute."

"Do I have a choice?" I shot back but huffed out a sigh and relented. "Fine. What is it?"

As *if* I *didn't know.*

"I'm all for you dating and having fun. You're in the business, so I expect you to meet public figures."

"Gee, thanks for the approval I wasn't asking for."

Either Neil hadn't picked up on my sarcasm or he'd chosen to ignore me—most likely the second as he was always in big-brother protection mode.

"There's nothing wrong with you having fun with athletes, although I wasn't aware you liked the jock type."

I'd been away for over six years, and while I loved my brother and never doubted he loved me, we weren't close. And Neil certainly wasn't someone I'd confide my most secret desire to.

"Well, now you know," I answered lightly. "I'm a single gay man enjoying life in the big city."

"But Rip—"

"Is my business. Please, Neil. Don't go there."

His *hmph* of dissatisfaction filled my ear. "I don't want you getting hurt, but I'll respect your wishes. Let's talk business. How did the interview show go?"

Was I surprised he'd already heard of my new project? Not at all. "It went fine. I think Rob was happy."

"Oh, he was. Called me and said, 'Your little brother knows the score.' What'd he mean by that?"

"Not a clue," I hedged, anxious to change the subject. "I've got to come up with some names for my next show, and Rip said we'll be on a podcast...*The Huddle*?"

"With Dev and Brody? Nice. They're good people and have a huge following. It'll certainly be good publicity for your show. That's great, Adrian. You're covering all the bases and really jumping into this with everything you've got. Great work."

"Thanks." While his approval warmed me, it wasn't my hard work. It was all Rip. "I'd better go. I've got lots to do."

"Wait. Adrian." Neil sounded hesitant. "I want to apologize to you."

"What for?"

"I know we've never been close, and that's on me. I'm older, and I should've paid you more attention."

My cheeks burned with humiliation. "I'm not your responsibility. Then or now."

"I know that. And I'm not saying it out of obligation. I love you, and not because I have to. I'm proud you've worked so hard to accomplish your dreams. And before you say I helped you get this job, so fucking what? You're my brother, and I'd do anything for you. It's a hard world. Everyone needs help."

"You didn't," I whispered, overcome by this confession from Neil, whom I always believed to be the ultimate corporate man and rarely showed emotion, outside of his wife and kids.

He snorted. "Let me set you straight. Lisa's dad knew the head of the station and got me an interview after I graduated. Rob hired me, and yeah, it all worked out, and I got this job on my merit, but if you think I didn't have help initially, you're wrong."

Stunned, I rubbed my face. "I-I didn't know."

He chuckled. "Not exactly something I broadcast. Look, you've picked a tough, competitive world to work in. But I don't want you to ever think you don't have my support. You do. I'll always be there for you. I love you."

I brushed the wetness from my eyes. "Thanks. I love you too."

"I think you'll knock it out of the park. Think of this as a stepping stone toward your ultimate goal. Give it all you've got to make it succeed."

"I'm trying, but it's not that easy. I'm doing things I never imagined."

"Wait a sec. Is that why you and Rip are dating?"

Neil always was too smart for his own damn good, plus I was a terrible liar. "Uh, well, Rip suggested that if we said we were dating, it would ramp up interest in me, so people would want to watch the show."

"Son of a bitch." He laughed, loud and hearty. "I don't know whether to punch him or shake his hand."

"What?" Surprised he wasn't biting my head off, I breathed a sigh of relief as well. I didn't want Neil angry with me, especially when we'd aired our feelings and were on this new, tentative ground of friendship, along with the bond of brotherhood.

"As much as I hate to admit it, he may be right," Neil said. "Fans will be curious, as will the sports community. Rip's a star in the league, and that, together with his status as one of the major faces in hockey's Pride events, makes him one of those athletes who naturally attract media attention.

Being his new love interest—God, I can't believe I'm actually saying that about you and Rip in the same sentence—will also put you in the spotlight. Lots of eyes on you." He paused. "You sure you're ready for that?"

"No," I answered honestly. "But I think I should try. Don't you?"

"I'm not sure. But this is your life, your choices. See? I'm treating you like a friend, or someone who can make their own decisions."

My lips twitched. "And I thank you. I'd better get back to work. Thanks. I-I appreciate the call and the conversation."

"Don't be a stranger."

"I won't."

The afternoon flew by, and I finished all my tasks a little early. The temperature had dipped, and a chilly wind stung my cheeks as I walked down Seventh Avenue toward the train. It was that in-between time in the city—the holidays long gone, while the promise of spring remained a tantalizing few weeks away. A cold resignation was set in everyone's faces as we all hurried to our destinations. I wished I could go home and stay there, eating hot-and-sour soup and General Tso's chicken. I wanted to go out for dinner and make small talk with a reporter like I wanted to have a root canal.

My phone buzzed, and seeing Rip's name on the screen, my pulse skyrocketed. The cold and wind forgotten, I smiled and leaned against a lamppost.

"Hi. Where are you?" I checked my watch.

"Just got to the hotel. How's it going? How was your day?"

I couldn't deny the rush of pleasure his call gave me. Foolish, I knew, because it was all a farce, but a guy could hope.

"Did you get my message? About the interview?"

"Just reading it now. We had turbulence and the Wi-Fi was out."

Which meant he contacted me on his own and not because he was answering my question. My heart did a double-time beat of happiness, but I squashed any excitement immediately. Rip was simply following our action plan and acting as a good boyfriend. A *pretend* boyfriend. I had to remember that.

"I'm getting on the train to go meet him. What do you think?"

"Think about what? You're gonna talk about the show."

I rolled my eyes. Could he be that dense?

"You know that's not why he wants to meet me. It's an excuse to get to the real story of you and me."

"Yeah? And? That's what we planned."

Sweat broke out over my body.

"What should I say? I don't know how far we're taking this."

"Take it as far as you want," his husky voice rasped in my ear, and my body thrummed at the imagery of Rip and me having sex. Making love.

I bit my lip and fought for control.

"Which is what?"

"You tell me, Adrian. Listen, I gotta go. Talk to you later."

The call ended, and I continued on my way, down the stairs and hopping on the train.

Deciding to play it by ear and not get too worked up about the interview, I took a deep breath and pushed open the door of Barbalu. The hostess led me to the table where Jay Monroe sat. He rose to his feet as I approached.

"Adrian? Nice to meet you."

"Same."

We shook hands and sat across from each other. Jay was older, around my father's age, and dressed in a beautiful suit and designer tie. He wore a thick gold wedding band,

and a thin Cartier love bracelet peeked from beneath his sparkling-white shirt cuff. His silver beard was trimmed short, and bright-blue eyes behind silver-rimmed glasses held warmth. I felt easy in his presence, but Rip had warned me that reporters were always looking for an inside scoop and I should be on my guard to expect probing questions.

Before either of us spoke, the server approached. I ordered a glass of Pinot Noir, and Jay ordered a Scotch and soda.

"Why don't we get right into it?" he said, and I braced myself. "We know you and Ripley Tremaine grew up together. When did you reconnect and decide to take your friendship to the next level?"

I wet my lips. "Well, I guess it was the night of the game with the Snow Caps? That first game of the second half of the season? Louie Rozner got hurt, and I was called to step in."

"Yeah. We were covering it. And the rest is history, as they say. Tell me a little about yourself."

I went through my rsumé—leaving out the embarrassing parts about getting fired and freezing up on camera—while he took notes on his tablet. The frequent sips from my water glass eased the dryness in my throat. We ordered dinner, and I ate too much bread, nervous that I wouldn't know what to say.

"When I heard that a position at Channel 8 News opened up, I jumped on it, hoping I'd get to come home. That's about it. I landed a job working for Louie Rozner, a legend as you know. And as I said, Rip and I reconnected that night Louie got hurt."

"Fate." He pinned me with a direct, unblinking gaze. "How is Rip handling being on the team with Denis? Has he mentioned any tension between them? Are you concerned about the two of them being together so much?"

My smile was faint. "No. First of all, remember Denis is engaged. And Rip and I are so new."

"Have you dated other professional athletes?"

My lips twitched. "No. I haven't dated much. Been busy trying to build up my career."

"You're originally from New York?"

"Yeah. My parents live in Florida now, but my brother and his family are here, so I wanted to come home."

"And now there's Rip."

My cheeks burned. "Yeah. But...my work and personal life are separate."

A deep chuckle rumbled from his chest. "Do you really think so?"

"I'm hoping." My chin tipped up. "I want to be known for something else besides being Ripley Tremaine's boyfriend. That's why I'm starting a show called *Playing the Field*, where I'll talk to players and try to let the audience get to know them better."

Jay tapped away on his iPad. "That sounds interesting. So something more personal?"

"Yeah. And not only hockey, but baseball, football, basketball—I plan to have athletes from all the sports. I think fans will enjoy that. It'll be on Sunday night."

"I'll make sure to watch it."

"Thanks." I thought I gave a good shpiel, and hopefully he'd plug it in the article.

"So about you. Were you always a hockey fan?"

"No, not at all, although I watched my brother and Rip play all through junior high and high school. And I've kept track of Rip's success through the years."

"Did you have a crush on him when he lived with your family?"

Damn my tendency to blush so easily. "No. I was eight years younger. He probably thought of me more as that annoying little kid always tagging after him and my brother."

"When did you first realize you were gay? Did you know Rip was gay when he was a teenager?"

Jesus, Jay was tossing out these questions like the automatic pitch machine at the batting cage my dad used to take me to. And now, like then, I was a little overwhelmed.

"Uh, I...about Rip, no, I didn't know he was gay. From what I remember, he always dated girls. I came out to my parents at fifteen. Rip was already playing professionally, but I don't remember if he'd come out." I chewed my lip. "Someone's sexuality shouldn't have anything to do with their job. Rip is a great hockey player no matter whom he loves."

Jay glanced up from the screen. "He's the best of the best. Youngest team captain the Blades ever appointed. But he's been playing it hard and rough for almost fifteen years, and I can imagine he might be coming to the point where he's thinking of his next steps. Has he mentioned what he plans to do after he retires?"

A sneaky question and one I knew—from when I'd asked it—would upset Rip.

"We haven't discussed anything about that. He's concentrating on winning games. That's all I know."

"I heard you and Rip were at Fiorello's this afternoon."

"Yeah. A good-bye lunch since he left for the airport right after."

"Must be hard to separate so soon after you got together."

"It's okay. I'm plenty busy with work."

Jay cleaned his plate, then excused himself to use the restroom. My phone rang, and seeing Rip's name gave me a ridiculous rush of pleasure.

"Hi. You're at the hotel?"

A little out of breath, he stretched, groaning in my ear. "Not yet. On the bus. I'm ready to crash. I hate flying."

"Well, you can rest now. I'm still with *Out in Sports*, but we're wrapping it up. The reporter asked if you were thinking of retiring, but I shut him down."

"Good. Fuckers," he growled. "How's it going otherwise? Don't forget to plug the show."

"I did. When will you be home?"

"Miss me already?" he teased, and I couldn't help smiling. Yeah, maybe it was all for show, but I still enjoyed talking to him. I didn't have many friends, and I knew instinctively I could trust Rip.

"Yeah. Definitely." I could keep it light and easy even if the truth was, I wished he were the one with me.

"Dammit," he swore.

"What's wrong?"

"My father. He called again. Third time today. Bastard isn't leaving me alone."

I didn't know what to say and watched Jay approach. "I–I'd better go. The reporter is coming back, and I don't think you want me talking about your father in front of him."

"No, 'course not. I—can I call you later? I know it's silly, but you're the only one I've told about him."

Something twisted in my chest. "Yeah, sure. Text me later."

"Thanks, Adrian. That'll help."

"Bye."

Jay took his seat. "Everything okay? You look a little red-faced."

"No, I'm good." I slipped the phone into my pocket.

"Was that Rip?"

No sense in hiding it. "Yeah. He just called to tell me they're at the hotel in San Antonio."

"Are you going to fly out to see him?"

The idea hadn't crossed my mind. "N-no. Why would I?"

Jay shrugged. "Just curious. It's the weekend, so I thought maybe you'd want to have a little getaway and see him play." He raised his hand. "Check, please. I have to get home and take out the dogs. It was nice meeting you, Adrian. Refreshing, actually."

Amused, I watched as he handed the server his card and signed the receipt. "Why's that?"

"You're not the usual type—after a star for the attention or money. I hope it works out between the two of you."

"Thanks."

We shook hands and parted at the door—me to walk home, Jay to get into the car waiting for him. On my way home I passed couples walking together, on their way to dinner or finished and heading home. The ache to belong, to be touched, grew with each step until it hammered at my brain.

Do it. Yeah, it's crazy, but you know you want to.

Maybe if I'd stopped to think, I would've realized it was a silly idea, but I pulled out my overnight bag from under my bed, threw some clothes inside, and within minutes headed out the door to the car waiting to take me to the airport. At LaGuardia, I headed directly to the gate, having bought my ticket online. I scanned my boarding pass, and the ticket agent smiled at me.

"Enjoy your flight to San Antonio, Mr. Hunt."

CHAPTER ELEVEN

Rip

"Move. Faster, *faster*," I yelled, directing my teammates. "Try and stop them from getting past you."

I slapped puck after puck at the defensemen speeding at me. We'd been practicing, getting the feel for the ice prior to this game with the Strikers. Behind me, Denis and our other goalie, Zane, were doing splits and taking turns fending off shots on goal.

"Back in the box," Coach called out to us, and we collected the practice pucks and skated toward him. When we were all together, he waited for us to set our sticks down.

"We've got a nice three-game streak going, and I want to see that extended. The Strikers are hot now, and we need to be prepared for them. They're tough."

We nodded to each other. "They sure are," I said. "Especially since we've split the season so far this year. They want to win the last matchup."

"Let's not give them the chance. Keep your asses out of the penalty box and your eyes on the puck. Nothing else should be on your minds but winning this game. Got it?"

For some bizarre reason I felt as though Coach's words were directed at me, and it pissed me off. I'd been nothing but laser-focused on the games ahead, watching films during the flight and studying our playbook. I'd taken only a few minutes to call Adrian before we got to the hotel, to make sure he'd done okay with his interview, but the entire morning, my concentration had been solely on practice. I didn't even have my phone turned on.

"Let's do this," Coach was saying, "show them who's the next Stanley Cup champions. All right? Play it smart."

Idly, I scanned the arena—and blinked. Hard. I rubbed my eyes.

"What the fuck?" I whispered, a grin curving my lips. "I don't believe it."

Seb, tightening his skates, glanced up from his crouched position. "What's wrong?"

Not a damn fucking thing because sitting two rows behind the penalty box was Adrian, wearing my Blades jersey. Looking straight at me with those big blue eyes that had held me entranced during our lunch. I hadn't stopped thinking about that afternoon.

Who're you kidding? You haven't stopped thinking about him since that first night at Slapshots.

I had no idea when he'd arrived, but he was here now, and the electricity that seemed to always spark between us sent a shock through me.

Seb peered into the stands. "Is that…"

"Yep. Adrian."

Seb's grin was broader than mine. "Can I presume you had no idea he was coming?"

"Not a clue." I raised a hand to acknowledge I'd seen him, and he graced me with a shy smile in return.

The lights turned on, and with one final glance at Adrian, I took to the ice with my team. Having Adrian there energized me, and I was ferocious in my practice, stealing the puck from my teammates, taking shots on goal. I was ready and wished the game were that night instead of the next day.

"Looking pretty good," Coach said. "Now go get some rest. Tomorrow we'll watch the films and do a light morning skate, but you better be ready to rip their asses a new one when it counts."

I stripped off the pads and protective equipment and joined the other guys riding the bikes to cool down. After I took a shower, I dressed and sat next to Seb, who was tying his sneakers.

"I know you wanna be with Adrian, but we've got to go to the hotel."

"I know, I know. I just want to talk to him. He came all this way just to see me. It's only right."

"Coach won't like it. He'll get pissed at you."

"Tell me something new." I took out my phone and saw a text from Adrian. He was waiting outside. "I'll be right back."

Seb laughed and shook his head. "Tell me again how it's nothing."

"Shut up." I flipped him off and pushed through the doors. I immediately spotted Adrian at the far end of the hall, and I headed directly to him.

"What're you doing here?"

Looking shy and a little nervous, he ran his hand through his hair. "I, uh, it's the weekend, and I had nothing to do…"

"So you thought you'd travel halfway across the country for a hockey game?" I teased.

"No. I wanted to see you. I mean...see you play." He stumbled, and I couldn't help myself. I put my hand on his cheek.

"That's the nicest thing anyone's ever said to me." I leaned down and brushed my lips to his. "I wish I could hang out and talk, but I have to go back to the hotel with the rest of the team. Where are you staying?"

"At the Marriott."

A wide smile tugged up my lips. "Wow. What a coincidence. So are we. I'll see you there, then. Meet me later, and we can have a coffee at the restaurant. Okay?"

Wide-eyed, he nodded, and I left him to return to the locker room. When I checked over my shoulder, he remained standing, his fingers touching the spot where I'd kissed him.

The rest of the team poured out through the double doors, and I was surrounded by them. Adrian swiftly left the hall in the opposite direction, and we got on the buses to the hotel. I took out a couple of things from my suitcase before lying on the bed to stare at the ceiling, and there was a knock on the door.

I pushed off the pillow and answered it. Seb breezed in. "What'd Adrian have to say?"

As close as Seb and I were, I wasn't about to tell him what Adrian had told me. I yawned and stretched, the muscles of my sore ribs pulling tight.

"Not much, but I thought it was really sweet of him to come."

"Oh, I agree." Seb's grin was wicked. "Where's he staying?"

"At this hotel. Funny, right?"

"A riot." Taking a seat in the club chair, Seb stretched out his long legs, arms folded behind his head. "So lemme ask you. What're you doing here with me?"

"You know we have curfew. Coach will kill me if I break it."

"Plenty of the guys are at the bar downstairs." Seb's eyes twinkled. "You've got an hour. Move that pretty ass."

For whatever reason, I was nervous, but I pulled out my phone, and after hesitating only a second, I texted Adrian.

Meet me in the restaurant now? I can't stay late.

I chewed the inside of my cheek, waiting.

Be there in a minute.

I jumped to my feet. "I'll see you in an hour. Thanks, Seb."

"No problem. I'm gonna call Jolie."

"Tell her hi from me." He followed me out and returned to his room.

With my phone and key card tucked into my pocket, I shut the door behind me and headed down the hall to the elevator.

In the lobby I followed the signs to the restaurant and spotted Adrian on his phone in a booth. He looked up, and that shy smile hit me like an elbow to my gut. I was becoming used to him. I liked seeing him.

"Hey. Get settled in okay?" I asked, sliding into the booth.

"Yeah, I'm fine." He scanned me, frowning. "Your face...-doesn't it hurt? It looks worse tonight than it did right after the game the other day. How do you play so soon after all that fighting?"

I touched the fresh gash above my eye and winced. My face and body bore the scars of all the years I'd played. Bruises had blossomed all over my body, and my knee had taken a hit that might require taping. Truth was, I ached everywhere. "You know, I don't even think about it anymore. The fighting...it's just part of the game. It can get dirty and ugly sometimes, but we can't let ourselves be intimidated."

Doubt shimmered in Adrian's eyes. "I guess I never realized how bad it was in professional sports. I don't remember that happening when you and Neil played in college."

The server came and we both ordered coffee, and Adrian also ordered a cranberry muffin.

"Fighting isn't allowed at the college level. We'd get thrown out and suspended from future games, so it's not worth it. It's an intimidation tactic in the pros."

"I'm surprised they allow it at the professional level, since so many little kids come to the games."

"Hey." I reached across the table, took his hand in mine, and squeezed it. "I'm sorry it upsets you, but there's not much I can do about it. I'd rather talk about you coming all this way to see me."

That cute blush I liked painted his cheeks pink. "Well...I had that interview with the guy from *Out in Sports*, and he kind of got me thinking that a real boyfriend would want to spend the weekend watching his guy play. And it was only a plane ride away, so it made sense. I hope my being here doesn't distract you from playing. You don't mind, do you?"

Around the restaurant, people watched us surreptitiously, and I figured now was as good a time as any to get the gossip going. I laced our fingers together and met his eyes, smiling into their blue depths.

"I'm so glad you're here. My only regret is that I can't spend much time with you. I have breakfast at nine in the morning with the team, the game with the Strikers in the afternoon, and come home on Sunday."

"Oh." His disappointment was obvious.

I played with his fingers. "We could have dinner after the game tomorrow, spend time together then."

He blinked. "Really?" At my nod, he grew shy. "I'd love to. I have to get home on Sunday too. Early enough to catch the show."

I grimaced. "Damn. I forgot. Our plane leaves in the afternoon, but I should make it by that time. We could watch it together."

Adrian's hopeful face was sweet. "I-I'd like that."

His phone buzzed, and glancing at the screen, he made a face. "Sorry, it's Louie. I have to answer. Louie, hi. What's up? How're you feeling?"

I sipped my coffee, and caught several people staring, I waved them over. "Hey, guys. Yeah, it's me. Want a picture?"

About five men approached, and I took photos with them and autographed jerseys, books, and whatever else they gave to me. When I was finished, Adrian wore a funny expression.

"What's wrong?"

"Nothing. Somehow, Louie found out I was here."

I chuckled. "Louie's got friends everywhere. Someone at the arena probably saw you with me after practice and reported back."

"Yeah, well, he said I should cover the game. Our affiliate here will send me a cameraperson so I can shoot my report, and I'll just send it to the station."

Our server approached. "Can I get you anything else?"

I took the check and gave her a twenty. "Here. Keep the change. Thanks. Let's go, Adrian."

He stuffed the rest of his muffin into his mouth and chewed it. "Okay, but—"

"No buts. Come with me." I held out my hand, and after a moment of hesitation, he took it. I led him past the rambunctious drinkers at the bar, where some of the team was hanging out and mingling. In a secluded corner, I found a small sofa, and we sat side by side, Adrian's hand still in mine. I faced him, our legs touching.

"We talked about it. This is the way to get you noticed. Nothing's changed."

Liar. So much has changed, and you're afraid to admit it.

All the time we were spending together made me acutely aware of how long and dark his lashes were, a startling contrast to his golden hair. Or how he smelled so warm, like cinnamon and vanilla. Light-brown stubble dusted his jaw. My jeans grew tight.

I wanted Adrian, and it had nothing to do with helping him succeed. I wanted to kiss him.

"I'm not so sure." I cupped his cheek, and his eyes widened, his mouth falling open slightly. How had I never realized how fucking sexy he was? "We'll figure that out later. But right now? I'd like to kiss you. Is that okay?"

CHAPTER TWELVE
Adrian

Unable to speak, I nodded. I must be dreaming, but Rip touching me, all that heat soaking through me, was as real as it got. My heart pounded as Rip's mouth settled over mine. I didn't care that we were in a public place where anyone passing by could see us. All that mattered was his warm, hard lips demanding my submission, and I opened beneath him and sucked his velvety tongue. This was Rip. Not the superstar hockey player on the ice, whom fans loved and cheered, but the man I'd crushed on since I was a teenager.

Strong fingers tangled in my hair, and Rip anchored me to him, taking me apart, breath by breath, until I almost swooned.

God, I was on fire. My lips tingled, and I fell into the storm of desire brewing in Rip's golden-flecked eyes. I drew in air, took the initiative, and touched my lips to his. A wisp of a moan broke free, deep from his chest. It was the most sensual sound I'd ever heard, and I traced the bones of Rip's face, taking care not to touch the fresh scrapes and bruises.

Our gazes locked, Rip held my chin and kissed me a second time, even more desperate and needy than before. I spun out of control at his touch. It was as if no one existed but the two of us. I couldn't remember the last time I was kissed, but either way, it was nothing like this. Rip owned me, took me apart and put me back together, whole but not the same. Never the same again.

"Adrian," he whispered. He gentled his kisses, slower and more deliberate, but by this time, I was flying high and couldn't move. "We'd better stop."

"Wh-what?" I was woozy from desire and could've stayed there all night in our little private cocoon.

"I'm only human, and you're way too tempting." He continued to slide his fingers through my hair, and I understood why a cat loved being petted. I could've purred with contentment from his touch.

"It's okay." My face burned. "I—you can come upstairs with me." I imagined us naked together. In bed. Rip on top of me, that hard-muscled body pressing me into the bed. Thrusting. Taking. I grew lightheaded with desire.

"I can't."

Disappointment flared in my chest. "Oh, yeah, of course. So...I, uh, guess I'll see you after the game."

"Yeah. You sure will." He smiled against my cheek.

With reluctance, I pulled away and gazed into his flushed face. "We're still friends? This is all just for my show, right?" I asked, hoping he'd say no.

He blinked rapidly. "What? Oh, yeah. The show. Right, right. We're friends. This is all for show."

Dispirited, I hung my head. Already Rip was withdrawing. He shifted away and raked the tangled hair off his brow.

Rising to his feet, Rip held out his hand. "Ready to go? We can ride up in the elevator together."

"Sure. I'm tired."

Side by side, we walked to the elevators, and I could hear the raucous laughter from the bar area. The doors opened, Rip walked inside, and I followed.

"What floor?" He held out his card to the scanner.

"Nine."

"I'm on fifteen."

We stood in silence waiting for the elevator to stop. I didn't want to wait for him to speak, to hear excuses why he kissed me and how it wouldn't—or couldn't—happen again. "Night, Rip. See you after the game tomorrow afternoon."

I pulled out my key card and entered my room. I sank onto the bed and stared at the ceiling. My fingers skimmed my swollen lips, and I replayed every delicious second of that explosive kiss.

He's lonely, and he knew I was willing. It doesn't mean anything.

And even this late at night, I got a text from Neil.

You're in San Antonio for Rip's game?

I didn't want to answer but knew he'd keep bugging me until I did.

Yeah. I'm covering the game with our affiliates.

I waited, knowing Neil would have more to say, and I wasn't disappointed.

You said it's not real, but isn't this taking it a little far? Traveling halfway across the country?

I could only imagine what Neil really wanted to say and held off because he didn't want to have an argument. I pressed my lips together.

I'm doing what I need to do. That's it. I'm going to sleep. Good night.

Now if only I believed my own story. After Rip's kiss, I was more in love with him than ever.

It was an ugly game. Like the Blades, the Strikers were on top of their division and third in points in the league. I lost count of the number of times I covered my eyes to keep from watching the fights. Tensions ran high, and in the end, the Blades lost.

Knowing Rip would likely be in a lousy mood, I stayed away from the locker room and returned to the hotel. I showered, changed from my jersey, and settled in, waiting to hear from him about what we were doing for the evening but then decided to take the initiative for once. I made a reservation at the steak restaurant in the hotel, which I'd read was one of the best in the city.

It was close to seven when Rip texted me.

Just got to the hotel.

I answered him immediately: *I'm ready anytime you are.*

I might not be the best company.

Athletes, like performers and other creatives, tended to base their self-worth on their public performances. My job tonight, therefore, was to play the good boyfriend and lift Rip out of his funk. Of course, if we were truly dating, my method would be decidedly sexier than a good steak dinner.

Did I dare? We'd already kissed, and I sensed he'd been as turned-on as I had. If we were two consenting adults, why couldn't we have sex? There'd be no expectation on my part that Rip would fall in love with me, and I could finally put to rest the silly crush I had on him. I'd built up such a fantasy of Rip being the perfect lover, the reality couldn't possibly live up to the hype.

I waited in the hotel lobby, noticing several Blades players commiserating over drinks. My attention was drawn to the corner table, where Denis was sitting with a group. He finished the contents of his glass and caught my eye. A grin spread across his face, and he licked his lips. Heat prickled through me, and I broke eye contact.

"Sorry. I had to wait for the elevator." A little out of breath, Rip put a hand on my shoulder, and noticing the group in the bar, leaned in close. "I'm really glad you're here tonight." A kiss I knew was meant to be quick turned slow and deliberate, and I held on to him, my tongue daring to slip into his mouth.

"Adrian..."

My name on his lips, all rough and strained, set my blood on fire. I did that to him. Me, Adrian, who'd never had a date in high school or college, was turning on one of the sexiest men in sports.

"What's wrong?"

His arm tightened around my shoulders. "Nothing. You're just making it hard."

"Is that a bad thing?" I slanted a look up at him and could see the indecision in his eyes. I didn't want to be the cause of more problems, weighing him down.

"Maybe. I'm not sure. And that's the problem. I can't think about anything but the game right now. We lost today, and I'm pissed about it."

The moment vanished, and I brushed a light kiss to his cheek. "Let's have dinner, and you can tell me all about it. I'm a great sounding board."

"Are you sure?" Doubt was written in every furrow of his brow. "I'm...angry."

"There's no other place I'd rather be. Come on. I have reservations at the steak house here. It's supposed to be excellent."

We walked into the dimly lit restaurant, where I'd asked for a corner table so we could have privacy.

Rip ordered a Scotch, and I chose wine. After we gave our order, I reached out and took his hand. "Talk to me."

He chewed on a piece of buttered bread. "It's not just one thing. I mean, obviously, we lose games. But Coach took me out more than usual, and I'm just wondering if he's planning on Lindstrom taking my position. Which doesn't make sense during a playoff race, but I can't help thinking something's going on."

"If you'd played more, would you have won the game?"

He shrugged. "Guess we'll never know. And I'm not saying Lindy isn't good. He is. But he's only had two years in the league. I've had more than fifteen. That should count for something."

Morosely, he chomped on the crusty bread and stared into space. Several patrons recognized him, and he put on a smile.

"I'm sorry," I said, wincing at my thoughtlessness. "I should've realized you probably wanted to be alone tonight. We should've stayed in."

He covered my hand with his. "No. It's good." His frank gaze captured mine, and my breath caught. "I'm glad you're here, Adrian."

"Me too."

Our food came, and it was delicious. Rip seemed to be in a better mood, and I even got him to laugh at my story of the mishap that got me fired from my first job.

"She was practically sitting on the man's lap, and they were kissing. Like, tongues down each other's throats."

"And you didn't know she was the boss's wife?"

As devastated as I'd been at the time, I could joke about it now. "No. I just remember when I saw it was the mayor, I figured it would be a good gossip piece. Like, *Who is this mystery woman with the mayor?*" So I took a few pictures with my phone, and we ran with the story. You couldn't see her face, but the station manager recognized her dress and hair—I mean, she was his wife—and called me in at the end of the day and fired me."

Rip toyed with my fingers. "That's not fair. It wasn't your fault."

"I guess, but he had ultimate control at the station. And I was young and easily replaceable."

"Young, yeah." Rip held on to my hand. "Replaceable? I'm not so sure about that."

The air vibrated between us, and a yearning grew in my core, blood beating thick and heavy in my veins.

"Rip," I whispered, and I saw a reflection of my desire in his eyes. My pulse spiked. He wanted me.

"I'll get the check," he rasped and scanned the restaurant for our server.

A man, tall and tattooed, with a weathered face and hazel eyes, walked to our table. His boots clanked on the wooden floor.

"Ripley?"

Rip froze and slowly withdrew his hand from mine. "Who are you? What do you want?"

"I'm John Carver. I heard you were here. C'mon, son. I just wanna talk. Can't we at least try that?"

Son? Oh, my God. This was Rip's father.

"Don't call me that," Rip growled. "I'm not your son. And no. I'm busy, and I don't have time."

"I drove almost five hours from Dallas just to see you. I'm sure your friend will understand." Carver gave me a perfunctory glance.

Rip rose, anger blazing from his eyes. "Don't dismiss him. I didn't ask you to come. Nothing you can say can ever change the truth. You walked out and left my mother to raise me alone. I blame you for the fact that she had to work nights at that crappy diner. That's why she's not here to see me."

"Rip, let's go." I grabbed his hand, and he held on to me as if flood waters threatened to tear us apart.

"I wanted to," Carver started explaining, "but—"

"But what? You had better things to do? Finish a six-pack? Put another bet on the horses or the game?"

Rip shook with anger. I'd never seen him so emotional, except for the last time his father had called.

"Rip," I whispered. "It's okay. I'm here."

His grateful smile, trembling at the corners of his mouth, almost broke me, but I held on strong. I heard him draw in a steadying breath.

"It wasn't like that," Carver went on. "I–I know I made mistakes, but you're my son, dammit." His voice echoed in the hushed restaurant, and Rip paled.

A murmur rose around us, and I tugged at Rip's hand. "We should go. This isn't the time or place for this."

Carver pinned me with a fierce glare. "Who are you to tell us anything?"

Rip jabbed a finger at Carver. "Don't you dare speak to him like that. Or at all. He's more my family than you'll ever be. I've got nothing to say except you and I might share blood, but that's it. Now stay away from me."

We strode out of the restaurant and into the hotel lobby, Rip still holding my hand in a death grip.

"I'm so sorry, Rip."

Rip kept quiet, and I didn't push, knowing there was nothing I could do to help him. Walking through the lobby, I saw Rip's teammates were still hanging out at the bar, including Denis. Absolutely not the place for Rip to be, so I steered him toward the elevators.

"Let's go upstairs."

With a sigh, he stopped and leaned against the wall. "I'm all right. You don't have to babysit me."

"Is that what you think I'm doing here?" Breathing heavily, I met his eyes. Every cell in my body yearned for him, and it must've shown in my eyes. I couldn't deny it any longer.

Before he responded, the doors slid open, and a couple of guys walked out.

"Whoa, Rip Tremaine. Tough loss."

Rip's smile was faint. "Yeah."

"Can we get a pic?"

I held the elevator and watched Rip pretend to be okay. He joined me inside, and the doors slid shut.

God, what a life, where no matter how bad you hurt, both mentally and physically, you needed to pretend for the fans. When did he get the chance to be himself? Suddenly I remembered the young Rip tearing across the frozen lake in town, Neil whooping with laughter behind him. We were all so innocent then. A fleeting golden age we'd neither understood nor appreciated and which was now lost forever. It brought tears to my eyes.

"I should go to my room, and you to yours, Adrian. We said this was only for show." His gaze was fixed straight ahead, and I nudged him.

"What about that kiss?" We were almost at my floor, so it was now or never. My face burned. I'd never been so pushy, but I'd never wanted anyone as bad as I did Ripley Tremaine. This might be my only chance.

"I shouldn't have." He met my eyes. "But—"

"No buts." Where I got the courage to say these things, I didn't know. I laid my fingers across his mouth. "I know this was supposed to be for show, but I want to be with you. And I think you want me too."

CHAPTER THIRTEEN
Rip

We didn't speak, and Adrian didn't get off at his floor. Instead, he followed me to my room, and I locked the door behind us. He remained close—I could hear his quick breaths. My heart pounded when I turned and he stood there, hesitant yet with his chin up and his eyes steady on mine. That nervous, shy kid had faded, and taking his place was a man. I rested my hands on his shoulders. God, he was sweet, and I couldn't forget how he'd stood by me tonight with my father. I couldn't imagine Denis even caring.

"We had a plan. Pretend to be lovers to help you get your footing and give you some name recognition to help your career. Taking it any further would complicate things."

It physically hurt to leave him, but I walked away, kicked off my loafers, and sat on the couch. Still avoiding him, I propped my head in my hands. "It's been a long day, and I think we should both take a step back until our heads are clear."

He should only know how I fell asleep every night. Wondering what he'd feel like next to me. Wishing he were under me.

He followed me to where I sat. "It's already complicated, and I know exactly what I'm doing. You do realize Carver made your relationship public? People now know he's your father."

I lifted a shoulder. "Big deal. I'm not such a mega super-star that anyone will care. I'm just another fucking hockey player."

Adrian sat beside me. "You're so much more than that. A great friend. You help so many charities. And by coming out while playing professional sports, you've touched count-less lives. You are a *very* big deal."

I barely heard his words. "Why did he have to come? Why can't he leave me alone?" When I was six and crying because I didn't have a father, I'd needed him. Thirty years later, I was fine on my own.

"I'm not telling you what to do, but maybe it would be good to talk to him or listen to what he has to say so you can get it out of your system."

Adrian's words brought me up short.

"Talk to him? And listen to his lies?" Frustrated, I ran my hands through my hair. "What purpose will that serve?"

"Closure. He obviously wants to talk to you."

My smile was grim. "More likely he wants to borrow money. Talk is cheap, but his debts probably aren't."

"So? Let him say what he wants, and you can walk away. But I know if I had any questions, I'd want the answers before sending him away forever."

It was as if our roles were reversed and Adrian was the wise, older friend giving advice to the younger, insecure me. This was the first time I'd opened myself up, made myself vulnerable. And I was fucking scared to death.

"I-I can't do this right now. We're in the middle of a run for the Cup. I can't afford a distraction from that goal."

"Tell Carver exactly that—you'll be willing to talk to him once the season is over and you win the Cup."

My lips twitched. "You've got it all worked out, don't you?"

"No, I don't." He brushed the hair out of his eyes. "But it's what I think is best for you. And that's all I care about." He ducked his head. "I mean, you said it...we're friends, aren't we? And friends help each other."

"You've helped me. Maybe you're right. It would be like an exorcism. Should...should I text him and say what you just told me? That I'll talk to him after the end of the season?"

Again, I leaned on Adrian, and as was becoming more common, he helped me. "I think that would be best. You get to play the rest of the season without him popping up and distracting you, and he knows you're agreeing to meet with him."

Emotionally drained, I didn't think and reached out to hug him. "Thank you. I appreciate your help so much."

"You're welcome," Adrian said, his face in my neck, his voice muffled.

My lips touched his hair, and he trembled. "About what you said in the elevator..."

"I meant it, and I understand that we can have sex and remain simply friends. Nothing more."

God, it was so easy to slide from temple to cheek, his skin rough with late-night stubble. Our mouths met, and I cupped his cheeks, holding him steady as I took him in a kiss that left no doubt where we were heading. I should say no. I was older. More experienced. His brother's best friend, and I'd said nothing would happen between us. But none of that mattered when Adrian returned my kiss with the thrust of his tongue. I sucked on it, and he slanted his lips over mine, twisting his fingers in my hair to lock me in place while he took control. His dominance left me breathless and shocked to the core. This wasn't shy, sweet Adrian. He was taking me with him on a discovery of the type of passion I'd never explored.

"Yeah, that works."

Greedy with a hunger that exploded through me like a fire waiting to be unleashed, I sucked his tongue, licking and biting. I pulled apart his shirt, hearing the buttons rip away from the fabric but not giving a damn. Dark-golden hair swirled across his chest and led down below his slacks. I undid the tab and clawed at the zipper. Adrian's cock bulged, and I rubbed it, watching him squirm. His skin flushed, chest heaving, swollen lips gasping, red and wet. I almost busted loose myself.

"Rip, *Rip, please,*" he groaned, and my dick throbbed. "Please. I want…"

"What, baby? What do you want?" At my words, his cock jerked, and the wet spot grew larger. "My mouth on you?" I traced the outline of his heavy cock through the thin cotton. "Is that it? You want me to suck you?"

His eyes flew open. "Yes. God, please."

I drew his pants and briefs past his hips, letting them fall to his ankles, devouring the reveal of his naked flesh. His dick was thick and long with a leaking head I couldn't help pressing a kiss to. Sticky precome flowed out, and I lapped it up.

"*Mmm,* so sweet and hot. You've been hiding your gorgeous self, haven't you? And now it's mine." I traced the reddened crown with the tip of my tongue and gave it a brief suckle. When I grasped him at the root and took him fully to the back of my throat, a strangled cry burst from his gasping lips.

"Fuck, Rip. Yeah, yeah. Don't stop."

I couldn't even if I'd wanted to. And I didn't. Beneath me, Adrian quaked and shook, his fingers clawing at the fabric of the couch. Sweat gilded his face, and his hips thrust hard and fast. I sucked him, teasing the veins running along the length of his shaft.

"*Mmm*, so good." I hummed and slid a finger past his taint, up the crease of his round ass.

A keening sound burst from his lips. I was transfixed–Adrian was wild and beautiful as he released the tension from his tightly wound body, coming hot and bittersweet, then lying boneless and twitching under me.

His eyelids fluttered, and he reached out with his hand. "Rip, let me."

I shucked my pants and briefs and lay next to him. As if he knew my body, his hand moved warm and firm on my aching dick, his touch expert in wringing out an orgasm that broke me to pieces.

"Oh, baby," I moaned and turned his chin toward me. Our lips met as he pumped me to completion. Warm come spread between us, but I held him close. He rested his head on my chest, and I played with his silky hair. The connection between us was impossible to break, and I covered his hand with mine.

"We should shower."

"Uh-huh," Adrian murmured. "We should."

"Come on." I sat up and slipped my arm around his waist. On shaky legs, we made it to the bathroom, where we soaped each other, rinsed, then dried off and fell into bed. I thought I'd be wide awake, but I didn't remember a thing after laying my head on the pillow.

The following morning I awoke before Adrian and spent an inordinate amount of time ogling his naked body. He was beautiful—long legs, broad shoulders narrowing to slim hips. Full, kissable lips pouted in his sleep, and his hair lay in a messy tangle of waves.

It would be damned nice to wake up with Adrian every morning. The heat of our attraction was undeniable, but it wasn't only about sex. I could talk to him—in fact, it was refreshing to spend time with someone not into sports. Pleasure could be achieved in ways other than games won and goals scored. Maybe it was time I thought about winning at life instead of a winning season.

His lashes swept up, and I met those pure blue eyes with a smile. "Good morning."

Pink suffused his cheeks. "H-hi. Is it late?"

"Nah. Not even seven." I lay next to him. "You sleep well?"

"*Mmm*, yeah." He stretched, muscles rippling under his skin, and my throat dried. "Really well."

He was too fucking tempting, and I needed to taste him. I kissed him, sucked his tongue, and he moaned, his hard dick poking me, smearing sticky wetness on my thigh. I took us in my hand, and with steady, hard movements rubbed up and down. My thumb played over our sensitive heads, and Adrian groaned. The scent of our sweat rose hot and thick.

"Come on, that's it," I encouraged. "Give it to me." He spurted through my fingers, and I grunted and came, spilling on Adrian's stomach. We lay panting as thoughts whirled in my head. Why not take it further? Our friendship was growing every day, and sexually? No doubt we were compatible. With a grin, I wiped the sweat from my brow. Adrian turned me inside out, and I wanted to explore that excitement.

Adrian sat up and pushed the damp hair out of his face. As if he'd made a decision, he straightened his shoulders. "I just want to say, I know you're not interested in a relationship, and I'm not either, but I'm not sorry about what happened between us."

My thoughts of a possible future died an ugly death. His words hit me like a punch to the gut, but I'd learned long ago not to show emotion until I was alone. So I kept my face neutral and nodded.

"Me neither. It was fun."

Adrian's eyes lowered momentarily. "Yeah...fun." He smiled at me. "All for show, like we said originally. Now that we've been together—"

I didn't want to hear the words I knew were coming. I'd already had my guts ripped out by Denis. Losing Adrian wasn't a risk I was willing to take.

"You're important to me, Adrian. It's only been a short time since we've reconnected, but the reality is, we've known each other forever. I don't want to screw up our friendship. We can leave it as something that happened here, and that's it."

When he didn't respond, I left him lying in the bed and took a shower. I'd hoped to spend some more time with Adrian, but now I wasn't so sure that was his plan. And seeing my father in person had upended me. I still hadn't come to grips with it. That had to be why I suddenly needed to cling to Adrian. He'd been there with me, and he was the only person who knew my father existed.

Finished with the bathroom, I saw that Adrian had left the bed and gathered his clothes. I pulled out my clothes and dressed.

"I can shower in my room if you want," he said with downcast eyes.

Acting like strangers after sharing such intimacy seemed foolish. "Adrian, come on. Emotions ran wild yesterday. We got carried away, but nothing's changed between us."

"I guess you're right." Relief shone in his eyes. "I've got this new show to concentrate on, and you've got the playoffs coming up. We're both adults who can handle our business. Plenty of people remain friends after...you know..." He turned pink.

Damn, he was cute, and as much as I was hurting, I couldn't be angry with him. "Agreed." I put a hand on his shoulder and fought to restrain myself from encircling his nape and pulling him close. "The most important thing is our friendship."

The air crackled between us as our eyes met, and something painful twisted in my chest. I was lying, but if Adrian was determined to keep it light and easy, I'd do what he wanted.

He chewed the inside of his cheek and gave me a sharp nod. "I agree. Pretend boyfriends but real friendship."

"That sounds about right to me. Especially now, I think we can pull off the boyfriend gig, don't you?"

I didn't miss that blush I was beginning to become addicted to. "I hope so."

The team plane was leaving at three, and Adrian's an hour later. We didn't have much time to spend together, and there were still some things I wanted to hash out between the two of us. I tossed down my coffee and called for the check. Adrian had barely touched his breakfast.

"Ready?"

Adrian's brows rose, but he took my hand, and together we left the restaurant. I didn't miss Seb's smirk or Denis's narrowed gaze. Didn't people have their own lives to think about instead of inserting themselves into mine?

"What's the rush?" Adrian asked as we walked outside. "You seemed like you couldn't wait to leave."

I shaded my eyes against the sun. "Well, I have to leave the hotel for the airport no later than one with the team, and when in Texas, we need to see the Alamo. Don't you think?"

I heard my name called. "Rip?"

Shit. Last night I'd gotten so caught up in Adrian, I'd forgotten to text my father to leave me alone until after the season. John Carver stood waiting in the parking lot. He waved at me, and still holding Adrian's hand, I walked over to him. "What're you doing here again?" I demanded, wondering if he was following me around town.

"I was hopin' now you might have a minute to hear me out."

"Well, you were wrong. I have to pack and leave. And if you don't stop following me, I might have to get a restraining order. For the last time, leave me the hell alone."

"Rip, please. Just lemme talk to you."

"I don't have time. My plane leaves in a few hours." I refused to look at him. "Don't call me anymore either." I made a show of taking out my phone and blocking his number. "I should've done this years ago."

Grief and pain clouded his weathered face, but I was determined not to let it sway me. I stared straight ahead.

"One day you're gonna talk to me." He strode off.

I couldn't imagine that would ever come to pass. Because he'd never been there. After school I'd sit in the diner to do my homework while my mother worked, the smell of grease from the grill embedded in my clothes and hair no matter how many times I showered or asked her to wash my shirts and jeans. Hating the men who flirted with her or tried touching her. Wishing I could be with her on the weekends instead of spending all my time with Neil—not because I didn't want to be playing hockey with my best friend, but because I knew how hard she worked to give me a new stick or better skates, and we didn't get to see each other enough. I wasn't one of those kids who rebelled against authority. My mother sacrificed her needs for mine, and in the end she died trying to be the best mother she could. Alone.

Adrian peered at me.

"You okay? You're all red in the face."

Get your shit together.

"I'm good, I promise." Blocking John Carver had lifted a weight from my shoulders.

We made our way to the Alamo, where we didn't have time for a tour but took numerous pictures. It was quick and fun, and for a brief moment I was able to banish all thoughts of hockey from my mind. Being with Adrian freed me from the constant strain of the upcoming schedule and how many games were left to play. It was rare I had time simply to enjoy life. I was too busy comparing myself to younger players who might replace me or thinking about that damn Stanley Cup championship.

Back at the hotel, we separated to pack. I didn't have much, as my equipment was already en route. I wheeled my carry-on to Adrian's room. He opened the door, and I saw his suitcase open on the bed.

"The team bus is here, so I gotta go. I just wanted to say good-bye."

Adrian had changed into a sweater for the cooler weather in the city. "I, uh, guess we'll talk when we're both home? The show's on tonight."

"Yeah? We could watch it together."

"Oh, yeah. That'd be nice." He bobbed his head and gave me a brief smile.

"Let me know when you land," I said in a vain attempt to prolong our time together. Why was he acting so standoffish?

"Sure, okay. Uh...safe flight." He closed and zipped up his carry-on.

"Yeah, you too."

Without thinking, I brushed my lips to his, and before I knew it, my tongue pushed into his mouth and I was kissing him with a deep, fierce intensity. Adrian's arms wrapped around me, and I was seconds away from walking him backward toward the bed.

"Ahh, *l'amour.*"

Hearing Denis's snide remark was like a douse of ice water over me, and I braced myself. Dancing dark eyes met mine.

"Go away, Denis. Don't you have anything better to do than watch me kiss my boyfriend?" Adrian stayed within the circle of my arms.

"Boyfriend happened very quickly, *non*? I recall we didn't make our relationship public for months."

I was about to respond, but Adrian beat me to it.

"You're getting married. Why do you care anymore what Rip does and with whom?"

CHAPTER FOURTEEN
Adrian

Denis's brows winged high. The lingering assessment he gave me set my skin crawling.

"*Hmm.* The boy has claws."

My face grew hot with anger. "I'm no boy. And there's no reason for you to be rude to Rip. From what I heard, you were the one who cheated on him."

Denis's face tightened, and he stormed away. Rip cupped my cheek with a smile. "You were pretty hot defending me."

I rolled my eyes, then frowned. "Was he always this much of a jerk? I honestly can't picture the two of you together. You're so different from him."

"It's complicated. I thought we were compatible, and I overlooked things that bothered me because it didn't seem important at the time. Like his ego. Denis believes he's the best, and that kind of self-confidence can be sexy. Or at least it was for a while. But Denis had to be the best or first in everything. I swear I once caught him measuring his dick to see if it was bigger than mine."

My jaw dropped. "You're kidding me. How childish can you get?"

Rip smirked. "Just for the record, mine is bigger."

I huffed. "Not a fact I needed to know."

Rip snickered and checked his watch. "Shit. I gotta go." He caught my mouth in a quick kiss. "Remember to call me tonight when you get home," he yelled out, halfway down the hall. He turned the corner and disappeared from sight. I skimmed my fingers over my lips.

Rip was gone, leaving me to wonder why he'd kissed me as a real lover, and why he wanted me to call him later. I closed my door but didn't return to packing. Instead, I lay on the bed and stared at the ceiling, reminiscing about the night we'd shared and this morning. That glorious, delicious night where he'd awakened me from the sleep of loneliness, followed by a morning of joy and pleasure such as I'd never known existed.

"No use sitting here. I'd better get my ass moving. No private plane home for me."

I finished packing and wheeled my suitcase to the lobby. I'd checked out online, and I was debating whether I should get something fast to eat at the coffee shop before I left, or maybe a muffin to take with me, when I felt a tap on my shoulder. I turned to see Rip's father, John Carver. My face must have not been welcoming, as he took a step away from me.

"Hello. You do recognize me, don'tcha?"

Wary, I nodded. "Yes. You're Rip's father. He left already."

"I know. I'm here to talk to you."

I put up a hand. "No. I have nothing to say."

"Please? Can you just listen to me?"

I pulled out my phone to check the time. "I have to go. My plane leaves at four."

"It's not even two. Please? Rip won't listen to me."

"What makes you think I will?"

The resemblance between father and son was strikingly apparent—both had high cheekbones, an angular jaw, and the same wide hazel eyes.

"Because I've got nothin' else to lose. All I want is for you to listen to what I gotta say."

Feeling guilty, as if I were betraying Rip, I motioned him to follow me to the corner. I pulled my suitcase along, and we took seats opposite each other. "Go ahead."

He clasped his hands over and over, but I sat quietly, giving him time to quell his nerves. Wetness glimmered on his cheeks, startling me. Still, I waited, and he blew out a harsh breath.

"I'm not here to plead my case by tellin' you I was a great person. Me and Abby, Rip's mother, we were two young kids who fell in love, but where she was strong and worked hard, I was the hothead. If things didn't go right, I blamed someone else for my mistakes." He pinched his eyes for a moment, then straightened his shoulders. "I started gamblin'– small-time shit at first, but fell deeper in the hole, and soon it was my paycheck. Eventually that wasn't enough. I borrowed money, and when I couldn't pay it back, I robbed houses, stole things...anything I could get my hands on." He coughed, and I girded myself to avoid feeling any sympathy toward him, the way I would for anyone with an addiction.

"None of this explains why you left her alone," I said, determined not to let his story sway me. Each time Rip spoke to his father, he came away worse than before. My allegiance was to Rip. "She was young and was going to have a baby."

"The loan sharks threatened me, and I knew I'd never be able to get ahead of the interest rates. They wanted me to get into more and more dangerous shit, so I left. Ran out on Abby without a word and made my way south. I got to San Antonio and decided it was far enough and stayed. I never knew she was pregnant, not until years later when I heard of this kid drafted into the NHL with the name Ripley Tremaine. Ripley was Abby's mother's maiden name, and Abby's last name was Tremaine. I thought it was too much of a coincidence, and when I saw he grew up where we once lived, I figured he had to be my kid."

"You do look alike."

"I never woulda left if I knew she was pregnant," he insisted, and I grimaced.

"I'm not sure I believe that. You easily walked away from someone you supposedly loved to save your own skin and disappeared. Never once cared to contact her."

He lowered his gaze to his tightly laced fingers. "I-I know I was wrong. But I did what I thought was best."

"Yeah," I said. "For you. No one else. Certainly not Abby, whom you claim you loved."

"I did love her." He made a fist. "I did."

"Then why wouldn't you ask her to go with you? You saved your own ass and to hell with anything or anyone else. And when you knew your son was going to be rich, you decided it was okay to show your face."

"I was wrong, okay?" he burst out, loud enough to turn the heads of other patrons sitting nearby. He rubbed his face and hitched his chair closer. "It was a mistake to ask for money. But I was younger and stupid back then. I just want Rip to understand I didn't walk away from him or his mother voluntarily. If I'd known I was going to have a kid..." Weary, he shook his head, but I pushed him.

"If you had, what? Would you have taken Abby with you? Raised your family?"

He hunched his shoulders. "I-I dunno."

The conversation was going nowhere. "What is it you expect from me? This all happened long ago. There's nothing I can do."

"Can you...do you think you can get Rip to speak to me? Maybe if he listens to what I gotta say, he won't be so mad."

While I understood why Carver wanted a relationship with Rip, I still questioned his motivation. "And so what? Let's say he forgives you. What do you hope to accomplish?"

His face was incredulous. "What're you talking about? I'll have a son—my son." Carver's jaw worked hard. "You don't get it."

"Get what? Make me understand it, then. Why do you really want to be his father? Have you changed?" That lingering silence told me everything. "I've had enough. And I have a plane to catch."

Shoulders hunched, he didn't rise or offer any more words to convince me otherwise. Maybe he'd used up his practiced speech, or I'd hit a nerve. Either way, more than anything, I wished I were with Rip to help him find clarity in the muddy waters his father had churned up.

Suitcase in hand, I walked away and found a cab idling outside. My phone buzzed.

About to take off. Come to my place tonight to watch the show?

I should've said no, but I typed: *I'd be better watching it alone, picking up all the things I did wrong.* My finger hovered over the Send button.

Don't be stupid. You made it clear you're just friends. Nothing's gonna happen.

I deleted the text and answered instead: *I'll try.*

No answer—not that I expected one since he was probably in the air—and I reached the airport, becoming busy with my check-in. I boarded my plane and settled in for the flight home. Aside from a few bumps, it was uneventful, and I breathed a sigh of relief when I finally entered my apartment. I lay on the couch for a moment of quiet, which of course meant my phone rang.

"Hi," Neil said. "Have a nice weekend?"

"Yeah."

"You're not going to tell me anything, are you?" he grumbled.

"What's there to tell? You know I'm a pretty private person. I'm not used to all this attention." Even if Neil and I were closer, I still wouldn't talk about my sex life with him. Having it on public display would take some getting used to, at least until it ran its course and Rip and I no longer needed to pretend.

"Social media had you everywhere with him."

There was more behind those words, but I wasn't going to pick a fight with my brother about this game Rip and I were playing. We were building a friendship alongside the pretend, and I didn't want to risk knocking down what was already there.

"We're friends. That's more important than anything."

"You're right. Have I told you how happy I am you're home again?"

Tears threatened, and I wiped my eyes. "Maybe I can come over next weekend?"

"Yeah. We'd all like that."

"Talk to you soon."

I ended the call filled with happiness and checked my watch. Nine forty-five. If I left now, I could make it to Rip's before the show started. I picked up my phone and shoved it into my jacket pocket. When I opened the door, Rip exited the elevator and slowed his steps. My stupid heart gave a jump for joy.

"Wh-what're you doing here?"

"I wasn't sure you'd come. And I really wanted to watch the show with you. You worked so hard, and I wanted to see the end result. I know it's gonna be a success." Surprisingly shy, he raised a shoulder, his gaze fixed on mine. "So I figured I'd come here."

I couldn't help my smile. "Considering I was going to you for the same reason, I think that'd be okay. I-I'd like that."

He came in and set his duffel on the floor. I raised a brow, and he blushed. "I brought some sandwiches, figuring you probably wouldn't have anything here and it's late."

"You're very thoughtful," I murmured, wondering what else was inside.

"I've been known to be." That cocky grin appeared, and I rolled my eyes.

"I have some beer in the fridge if you want."

"Just water. I need a clear head for morning practice." He dug into the bag and pulled out a paper bag. "Turkey and roast beef. I had them put the mustard and mayo on the side since I didn't know what you liked." His eyes twinkled. "That's me being thoughtful again."

Dammit. It was too easy to fall for this homey togetherness. But I was under no illusion Rip was my boyfriend. We'd decided to be only friends. Both of us had too much going on in our lives to dedicate time to a relationship.

"I agree." At that moment, my stomach chose to growl loudly, and Rip laughed out loud.

"Let's dig in and turn on the TV. I don't wanna miss it."

I took the sandwiches from him and got some plates while he found the remote. The last ten minutes of the news was on, and I handed Rip his sandwich and water.

"I wonder if they'll give me a good lead-in to the show," I mused, and ate without tasting as I stared at the screen.

" 'Course they will," Rip declared and took a swig of water. "Wait and see."

As always on Sunday night, the news ended with the sports segment, and Bryan had attended the Hoops game and interviewed several of the stars after their win. The clip of him at the game switched to the studio shot, and he faced the camera.

"It was great fun to talk to the Hoops, and we all hope you'll stay tuned for a new show that's premiering tonight, right after the news, hosted by Adrian Hunt, sports intern and boyfriend of the captain of the Brooklyn Blades, Ripley Tremaine. Tune in, and I hear you'll get some insight into their relationship, as well as an interview with All-Star winger, Sebastian Crowe."

"Ooh, I know I'm looking forward to it," Paula, the weekend anchor, gushed. *"Adrian is just the nicest person, and I hear he and Ripley Tremaine grew up together."* She sighed. *"So sweet that they've been reunited all these years later."*

I choked on my beer. "For fuck's sake. It's an actual interview show, not that hookup reality nonsense. Next thing you know, they'll be wanting us to kiss on camera."

"Don't let it get to you." Rip kicked my bare foot with his socked one. "*Shh.* It's coming on."

The theme music they chose was pretty catchy, and I leaned in close, heart pounding as my name flashed across the screen: *Playing the Field with Adrian Hunt.* The camera panned the three of us, then came to rest on me.

"Damn, you're hot," Rip murmured. "I'm one lucky guy." His foot rubbed mine.

"You're ridiculous." But I didn't pull away.

My phone started buzzing, but I ignored it to watch the show. Rip kept one eye on the TV and the other on his phone. He frowned and grunted, continually pressing the Delete button. A few messages earned a grin and a head shake.

At the commercial, Rip took another bottle of water I handed to him. "It's looking good. I know you, so I picked up on the nerves in the beginning, but as the interview went on, you did better."

"You really think so?"

"I know so. Come on." He patted the space next to him. "Sit next to me for the second part."

I told myself he was being kind, but I was glad Rip was here with me. It was nice to have someone who'd tell me the truth. I sat next to him, and he put an arm around me. I side-eyed him.

"Is this how you sit with all your friends?"

He winked. "Only the cute ones. Look. It's back on."

During the interview, when onscreen Rip took my hand and kissed my cheek, admitting we were seeing each other, I caught Rip eyeing me, and his grip tightened on my shoulder. Again, both our phones began to vibrate like crazy, but we ignored them. I settled against him, content and amazed that this was my life. I had no idea how long my luck would hold, but I was happy to bask in the glow for as long as it lasted.

We sat quietly, watching the rest of the show, until the final credits rolled. Rip picked up the remote and turned off the set.

"That was great. You nailed it. I'm willing to bet Rob will be thrilled when the ratings come in."

"With him you never know. I'm just hoping he won't nitpick too much."

"People like him need to find a little fault in everything to justify exerting control. Agree with him and then wait for your fan mail to come. That and ratings are what'll eventually get you in that anchor seat. Because I'm damn sure there's gonna be nothing but positive feedback."

His hair brushed my cheek, and our shoulders touched. If I turned my head, our lips would touch.

So I did.

"Adrian," he whispered, that gravelly voice sending my heart into overdrive. Rip captured my face between his hands, and his mouth moved across mine, our tongues playing together, hot and sweet. Fire and honey. My hands found his hair, and I pulled him close.

"What're we doing?" I kissed his rough cheek, his eyelids, his jawline. I was drowning in his scent, his taste. My cock throbbed, and I wanted to bury myself in his heat.

"Damned if I know," he answered, returning my kisses with a fervor that let me know he wasn't playing the game we'd put into motion. "But whatever it is, I don't wanna stop. Do you?"

If I said yes, Rip wouldn't push me and we'd stay friends, pretending we were dating. But this weekend, having tasted the forbidden fruit, I wanted another bite.

"No. I don't."

A slight grin tipped up the corner of his reddened lips. "I brought supplies. Just in case this might happen." He ran his nose down my cheek. "But don't for a second think I expected this."

"Well, I'm not saying no."

He took my hand, picked up his bag, and we walked to the bedroom, where we shed our clothes and lay naked on the bed. He hovered above me, his thick, beautiful dick rising between us. I ached for it. My eyes fluttered shut for a moment, imagining Rip pounding into me. Wrecking me. Making me feel.

"Please," I whispered.

"You are so gorgeous." A large, rough hand smoothed over my body, stopping to cup a butt cheek. "Perfect."

Our rigid cocks brushed each other, each skin-to-skin touch sending a lick of fire through my blood. I couldn't stop trembling, and maybe Rip took that as a sign of fear because his touch ceased.

"No," I cried out, then kissed him hard, leaving us panting and breathless. "I've wanted you for years. Don't stop."

Rip held my gaze, and I waited.

CHAPTER FIFTEEN
Rip

I'd always believed I was less than because I was the poor kid, the one who'd gotten his clothes from the Goodwill and had lived with someone else's family because he'd had no one else to take him in. Maybe that was why I'd hopped from man to man, never allowing myself to get close, figuring they wouldn't want to know the real me. Even with Denis, we'd rarely gone beyond the hockey stats or what event we'd go to. I'd fallen for his charm and all the sex appeal oozing from his pores until I'd discovered it hadn't been reserved for me.

With Adrian, it was different. He asked questions and delved into the person I was aside from hockey. And having finally met my father, old wounds peeled open that had never properly healed. I knew Adrian would want to be by my side to help, but now I needed him for so much more.

"Rip?" He propped himself up on his elbow. "What's wrong?"

I pushed the hair off his brow, gazing into his beautiful eyes. "Nothing." Refusing to allow anything to ruin this moment, I leaned in and pressed a kiss to his lips, feeling them soften under mine. "How could there be when you're here with me?"

Adrian's naked body lay hard and hot next to mine, and I skimmed my hands over the firm planes of his chest and shoulders. My mouth took his, my tongue demanding entrance. Our kisses grew lingering, silk stroking velvet, and a moan broke free from deep in my chest.

When I brushed my fingers into the cleft of his ass and touched his hole, he groaned and widened his legs. "More," he begged. "More." His breath stuttered, and his hands clutched my hair.

Pleasure-pain streaked through me, and his needy cries mingled with my gasps. I ached to have him and couldn't stop touching him, kissing him. Shivers ran down my spine as I stroked his skin, loving the sounds my touch coaxed from him.

Watching him come apart, something shifted within me, cracking the shell I'd placed around my heart after Denis left.

"It's been so long," he whispered. Moonlight played off his luminous eyes, and my heart lurched at his confession.

"Let me love you." I kissed his lips, his jaw, and moved lower, nipping at the pulsing vein in his neck before biting and sucking his nipples. Adrian writhed beneath me, the smell of his sweat, cologne, and precome creating a heady cocktail for my senses. I slipped my tongue along the length of his shaft to circle his balls and raised his trembling legs, exposing his tight hole.

"Rip," he panted. "I want…"

My fingers played with his crease. "That? You want that?"

He shook his head. "More." He ducked his head, and I could barely hear his soft, hesitant voice. "Y-your mouth. I've never…"

It dawned on me what he was asking, and I dipped my head. When my tongue slid past his rim, Adrian's hips lifted off the bed, his hands twisting the sheets. I held his thighs apart and licked, while he keened.

"Baby, I could spend the whole night playing with your sweet ass, but I gotta get inside you."

Eyes burning, Adrian worked his dick and nodded. "Yes, yes. Please." The slick sound of his hand moving on his hard length spurred me on, and I jumped off the bed to get the lube and condoms from my bag. I'd already loosened him up with my tongue and was anxious to feel his tight ass wrapped around my aching dick.

It had been months for me, which must've been why my hands trembled a bit as I rolled on the condom. Over-anxious, I eased past the ring of muscle and sank into the pure perfection of Adrian's body. Liquid fire engulfed me as Adrian clasped my cock, drawing me deep. He was made for me, and we moved in sync, a rhythm I'd never grow tired of. I was complete. Where I was meant to be.

Home.

I thrust gently, then with increasing vigor until I was pistoning into his willing body with a force and determination I normally reserved for skating.

"More," he begged. "You're splitting me apart. I need it."

"I've got you, baby." I pushed his legs up to his chest to heighten my penetration, and Adrian wailed, his eyes rolling back in his head as his body arched off the bed. His dick spurted out streams of come over his belly and chest.

My cock swelled and throbbed, held tight in his hot passage. Every stroke in and out of him sent a surge of electricity through me. I was on top of the world, strong and invincible. There was no time for me to breathe—my orgasm barreled through me, and with one final pump, I exploded. My heart hammering, I collapsed on Adrian, covering his sweat-soaked body with mine.

A minute or an hour might've passed—I'd lost all sense of time—before I was able to move again. As gently as possible, I pulled out, got rid of the condom, and joined him in the bed. Adrian's eyes glowed, and I couldn't help the smile that curved my lips. I took his hand.

"How do you feel?" I lifted his fingers to my cheek, needing our connection.

"I don't think I have words to describe it." Shy now, Adrian bit his lip. "I know I'm not that experienced, but—"

"*Shh*," I comforted him, then kissed him, unwilling to let him diminish what happened between us. "It was perfect. *You* were perfect."

It didn't surprise me that he hadn't been with many men. Someone like Adrian didn't give his body away easily.

"Can I tell you something?" I whispered.

"Of course."

I rolled to my side so I could gaze into his sweet, open face. "I'm realizing now, after learning more about you and being with you these past few weeks, that maybe I'm not all that knowledgeable in matters of the heart." At Adrian's dubious expression, I cupped his cheek, brushing my thumb over his full bottom lip, still swollen from my mouth. "Adrian, you can live with someone and never know them. Have sex and not feel anything beyond the physical release."

"Is that what your life's been like?"

Instead of answering, I kissed him, a long, leisurely press of lips and silken dance of tongues. I couldn't imagine a time feeling Adrian's warm body under mine wouldn't drive all thoughts out of my mind other than the need to touch him and be touched. Even hockey came in second to him.

"Yes. Filled with people but always alone. Lovers eager to share my bed but never willing to learn what's in my heart."

Adrian rested on my chest. "I hear your heart. And I understand what you mean. Sometimes I feel the same. Like I'm walking through a crowd, but no one sees me. Or I speak and no one listens."

His silky hair slid through my fingers. "I see you, Adrian. And I hear you."

We lay quiet for so long, I was falling into that dreamlike state between sleep and wakefulness, but I was brought to wakefulness as Adrian spoke.

"Rip...I don't know if I can keep doing this."

A chill ran through me. "Doing what?"

He sat up, the comforter pooling in his lap. "I told you I wasn't really good at pretending. That's especially true when it comes to being physical."

I joined him, sitting upright against the headboard. "Talk to me. Tell me what you're feeling."

"Caught."

His answer surprised me. "Caught? That sounds negative, and I thought what happened here tonight was positively fucking awesome."

His face was hauntingly sad. "That's the problem. It was...but it's not real. And if we keep doing this"—he waved a hand between us, casting his gaze downward—"I'm afraid I might start wishing it was."

"I thought you didn't want anything serious. You said that in San Antonio."

A tiny smile flickered. "I-I lied because I thought that's what you'd want."

Be still my fucking heart because the way it banged double time, I knew what I had to say. If I didn't, Adrian would pull away, and that fucking terrified me.

I licked my suddenly dry lips. "Wh-what if I feel the same?"

Dubious eyes met mine. "You don't have to say that."

I shifted to the center of the bed so I faced him. "I'm not. Maybe we're even more in tune than I thought." This was not a conversation for the dark, so I leaned over and switched on the bedside lamp. "I think we need to talk."

"Isn't that what we're doing now?" He winced at the light in his eyes, but I didn't miss the defeated droop of his shoulders.

"No. You're telling me what I'm going to say as if you already know, when the truth is, I'm still not sure." I took a breath. "Adrian, sometimes things happen when we least expect them, or when we aren't looking. I definitely wasn't looking for a boyfriend or someone to love because I firmly believed that Denis ruined my trust in relationships. I was content to have sex just to get off."

Adrian's cheeks turned pink.

"My focus was and had to be solely on hockey. Anything less, and I wasn't giving it a hundred and ten percent."

"You're playing amazingly well—the best of your career, I've heard the sportscasters say."

"I think so. But maybe it's because I'm happy. Finally. I have someone in my corner who grounds me. Someone I can talk to about anything and be myself with."

Adrian shook his head. "C'mon. You have great friends. Neil, Seb...they know you better than I do."

"In certain respects, yeah," I admitted. "But I never told either of them about my father. Or how hurt I was about Denis cheating on me."

"Why? I don't know Seb well, but Neil would understand. He's like your brother."

"We don't get deep into the really personal stuff. Seb helped me after I found Denis with Gordie, but I'm his captain and I have to show that I can put aside my emotions, no matter what. I don't want anyone to think I can't handle my shit. I can't afford to appear vulnerable."

"I'm not sure I agree with that," Adrian mused. "A true friend understands. Maybe you need to give him more credit. And even so, Neil would be there for you, no questions asked. You can't deny that. You two have always been attached at the hip."

"It looked that way, didn't it?" I rubbed my chin and sighed. "Guess maybe I'd always been somewhat of a faker because I never told him everything. Don't get me wrong—I love Neil, and I would take a bullet for him. But some things are better left unsaid. Even to the best of friends."

Adrian put a hand on mine but said nothing. Waiting for me to say what I'd kept hidden all my life.

"I want you to know everything." I turned my palm up and laced our fingers. "About how even though your parents took me in and cared for me like I was your brother until I left for college, I still woke up every morning wondering if that would be the day I'd be taken away. How no matter how much I love your mother and everything she's done for me, I still miss my mom and wish she were here." It might be long ago, but the pain of what I lost haunted my every step, no matter what glory I'd accomplished.

"I know that feeling. On the outside looking in. Not that it was your fault or Neil's, but it was like that with your friendship. There was only room for the two of you and no one else. I was the tagalong. It was you and Neil, and I always came in second." He lowered his gaze.

"Not with me." I reached out to take his hand. "Not anymore. I'd like to put you first in my heart."

"But we only did this as a way for me to get noticed at my job," he protested. "It's not reality."

"And it worked, but in the meantime, nothing has to change." I smiled encouragingly. "People already think we're together. Maybe we did such a good job because we're not faking it."

But Adrian remained unconvinced. "Neil thinks we're still putting on a charade. I don't like lying to him."

It figured. I had to fall for a guy with values, but his innate goodness was what made Adrian so special. In a world where every day people judged me by statistics and what they saw on a screen, I'd allowed Adrian in, under my armor, past the mask.

"Just for a little while. We only have a month or so until the playoffs. Once that's done, we can tell him. But please. I need you to stick by me now. Be the real boyfriend you're pretending to be."

His full lips twitched. "Do you know how ridiculous that sounds?"

I crawled to him. "Nothing's ridiculous when it comes to how I feel about you."

"I guess we can try. I wouldn't want to upset your rhythm."

That twinkle in his eye brought me as much joy as a game-winning goal, and I couldn't refrain from kissing him over and over, leaving us both breathless and shaking.

"Baby, you are my rhythm. The rhythm of my heart."

Suddenly, Adrian pulled away, a solemn expression replacing the one of pleasure.

"I have something to tell you. I hope you won't be mad at me."

CHAPTER SIXTEEN
Adrian

Instinctively, I knew Rip wouldn't be angry, but I still felt I had to say it.

His smile was tender. "I doubt I could be mad at you, but talk to me. Tell me what's wrong." At my hesitation, he brushed the hair off my brow, his face filled with concern. "Please?"

"Okay." I sighed, resigned. "After you left, I was down in the lobby, and your father approached me."

In a second, anger and pain replaced the hazy after-glow of sex and peace between us. Rip flipped up the covers, jumped out of bed, and started getting dressed. He'd pulled on his briefs and sweats, but I put a hand on his arm.

"Please? You said you wouldn't get angry. Don't you want to hear what I have to say?"

"No, because I know." Rip yanked the sweatshirt over his head, struck a pose, and lowered his voice to mimic Carver. "*You don't understand. I love Rip. I wanna be his father so bad. It doesn't matter that I ran out on his mother and left her to carry the burden all by herself.* Did you know..." His voice cracked. "Did you know she ran away at seventeen to be with him and she was only twenty when he left? He was four years older than her. What kind of man leaves a woman alone with no support? I'll tell you—a selfish bastard."

My heart broke, and I put my arm around him, feeling him shaking. "I know. And I'm not disagreeing with you. I told him it wasn't up to me to talk you into seeing him. And I asked him if money has anything to do with him wanting a relationship with you."

Rip nodded with approval. "See? You understand. So why would I be mad at you?"

"Because..." I chewed my lip, the information I was about to reveal torturing me. "I found out something you don't know."

Growing agitated, he threw his hands in the air. "What, Adrian? Spit it out already."

"There might not be a legitimate reason for your anger at your father. Carver told me he left because he had a gambling problem and was in debt to loan sharks who threatened his life."

"And?" Rip lifted a shoulder. "I mean, okay, that's scary, but he was more concerned with his life than my pregnant mother's."

"Except..." I chewed my lip, knowing how the hurts of the past still tormented him. Would telling him really change anything? But he deserved to know the truth. "He didn't know she was pregnant. Maybe she found out after he left or she knew but hadn't had the chance to tell him, but he swears he had no idea she was pregnant."

His angry face paled under the dark, late-night stubble, the news sending an obvious shockwave through him. He put his hands over his face, and all I wanted was to hold him close and tell him it would be all right, but that was impossible. Decades of hurt couldn't be swept away by a few words or kisses. Several moments passed before he raised his gaze to meet mine, and his eyes were wet.

"Why should I believe him? Do you? And even if it's all true, I don't care. He still left a young woman alone to fend for herself and never once contacted her in all the intervening years. Why didn't he ask her to come with him? Maybe she would've wanted to start a new life as well. The least he could've done was call her and let her know what happened to him, but when I asked her, she said she never heard from him."

"I don't have all the answers. I'm sorry." I put my arms around him. "All I want is to give you some peace."

"You do," he whispered. "And you have nothing to be sorry for. I'm glad you told me."

"I'll never keep secrets from you." I yawned against his neck.

"Let's go to bed. You've had a big night, Mr. Television."

"Silly. You must be exhausted as well."

A wicked grin curved his lips, and then he kissed me, activating the desire I'd kept smothered all these weeks. I wanted him again, and from the thick bulge in his sweats, Rip's thoughts were in sync with mine.

He pushed me onto the bed, and I tried to resist. "I should check my messages. Rob might've called, and I'm sure Neil—"

"Later." Our arms and legs tangled, and he pulled me on top of him. "Much later."

The next morning, we drank our coffee standing by my small breakfast bar. "How do you feel today?" At Rip's slow, wicked smile, I shook my head, but I couldn't stop the flush of pleasure heating my blood. "Stop it. I'm not talking about the sex."

He nudged my nose with his. "Why not? It was incredible, wasn't it? Yesterday." He licked a wet path down my neck, and I shivered. "This morning."

Growing weaker by the moment, I sidestepped his seduction. "Yes, of course. How can you doubt it?" I could still feel him, and I'd have to figure out how to carry the ache of that pleasure-pain all day.

"I don't. You turned me into someone I don't recognize."

I wanted so desperately to believe him, but that old devil of insecurity still sat firmly ensconced on my shoulder. "When I was in college, I used to imagine..." I waved my hand. "Forget it. This is silly."

"Stop." He slipped his arms around my waist. "Nothing you say is silly. Tell me what you used to think about," he urged, holding on to me. "Let me in."

"I-I never thought of myself as passionate. I was shy and awkward, especially with men I found attractive. And if anyone tried to talk to me, I'd stutter and end up saying something stupid." All those memories of my futile attempts at school to make friends came rushing back, and I wanted to sink into the ground. "It was awful. After trying to go to parties a few times, I gave up and stayed in my dorm or went to the library."

"I'm sorry."

"It's not your fault." I forced a smile. "It wasn't much different from high school, so I was used to it. But I'd imagine what it would be like with you." My voice dropped. "I wanted you to be my first, despite knowing that was impossible. You were already playing hockey, and you were a star."

"Who was it?" he growled. "Who was your first?"

I squeezed my eyes shut. "It doesn't matter."

His lips moved against my ear. "Everything about you matters to me. You'd better get used to it."

I turned in his arms to face him. "It was my twenty-first birthday. I was lonely, and though Neil and my parents called to wish me a happy birthday, no one else on campus knew. I was alone, sitting in my dorm room, listening to music, so when Kevin, my RA, came to my room with a little cake and beer, I was happy. Someone had thought of me. Of course I invited him in."

Rip's eyes blazed with anger. "You got drunk?"

"You already know I'm not much of a drinker." I shrugged. "But no. I wasn't drunk. I knew exactly what he was doing, and I wanted it."

"You had sex with him."

I faced him with defiance. "Don't judge me. You don't know what it was like. I was so lonely. He kept telling me I was sexy, that he'd always thought so. And I believed him. I wanted it to happen. I wanted to know what it was like."

God, could I sound any stupider? A naive boy.

Rip massaged my shoulders, and I settled in his arms. There was tenderness in his touch as he caressed my face. "Baby...that's not the way it should be. I'm so sorry." His jaw hardened. "He took advantage of you, the bastard."

"I guess, but I was okay with it because I felt like I'd finally been included in the special club. That someone wanted me."

"It's not okay. Was he at least decent to you after? Did he take care of you?"

I refused to sound as naive as I'd been that night. Kevin had cleaned me up, but I'd woken up alone. We never spoke about it afterward.

"Yeah, it was fine. No great love affair, as you can imagine." Now that I'd bared my soul, I wanted to know about him. "What about your first?"

A faraway look settled in his eyes. "Hockey camp. I was sixteen. Jeff and I sneaked out of our bunks and went to the locker room. Got it on in the showers. Fumbled our way through it." He laughed at the memory. "Once I was in college and playing, you might not believe it, but it wasn't so easy for me either. I never knew if the guy was into me because he liked me or because I was a hockey player. And our coaches were always on our backs about concentrating on the game and not girls." Absently, he stroked my stomach. "Guess they didn't think there were any gay hockey players, but we managed to find each other. I wasn't into the party scene because I knew if I got caught, they'd take away my scholarship. I didn't want to upset your parents after all they'd done for me."

"They would've helped you no matter what. I hope you know they love you as if you were their own son."

"Considering what you and I have been up to, I'm glad I'm not."

That brought a smile to my face. "I'm glad you're not either."

"But honestly, I guess maybe that's why I always went with other athletes—they could relate to my world."

My heart sank. He'd just voiced my greatest fear. "That makes sense. You want to be with a person you have some-thing in common with."

I tried to pull away, but he held me close and smoothed the hair from my face, kissing me slowly, softly. "Don't. Because that would be you. I know you care about me, the person. Not the hockey player. It wouldn't ever matter to you if I played hockey or worked at a desk job. We grew up together, we shared the same values and want the same things."

"What do you want?" I had to ask.

"The same thing everyone else does. To be happy. Loved. I want to feel safe and know that my home is my sanctuary. The place where I'm free to be me."

We stood in my small kitchen with the early morning sunlight brightening around us. Rip's encouragement gave me all the safety I could've ever hoped for, and I knew I could now make it on my own and forge my path because I'd been given the strength of his friendship.

"I'd better get going. Might as well get in early and see what Rob has to say about the show."

"Have you checked your messages?" Rip scrolled through his phone. "I have three missed calls from Neil."

"I've got two." I wasn't about to mention the all-caps texts where Neil asked me point blank if Rip and I were sleeping together. "You still think we shouldn't tell him the truth? I know you want to wait, but I hate lying."

Rip set his mug on the counter. "I know you do. And if it matters that much to you, tell him, but like I said, I have to concentrate on the game right now."

"I guess it can wait a few more weeks."

He cupped my face. "Don't think you're not important to me, because you are. It's just–"

"Hey, stop. It's okay. I'm not worried you're putting me second. Even I understand what the last few months and weeks of the season mean."

He pulled me into his arms. "Has anyone ever told you you're the best fake real boyfriend ever?" His warm mouth hit mine.

"No," I answered when I could breathe again. "You're the first." The scariest thing was that I wanted him to be the last.

He pressed another kiss to my lips. "I gotta get to practice. We have some big games coming up, and I intend to win them all."

"Of course. I understand." I returned to the sink to wash the breakfast dishes, but I sensed him lingering. "What's the matter?"

"What about tonight? If you can't make it earlier because of work and you have to miss some of the game, I'll have a ticket waiting for when you do come. You can see as much as you can, and then we'll leave together."

Could I be any happier? Dishwashing liquid be damned, I put my arms around him. "I'd like that. A lot. I'll try to make it so I can see most of the game. It just depends on how the day goes and what Bryan needs for the sports segment tonight."

"As long as you come home with me, that's all I care about."

We finished up and left. Rip took a car, but I walked to the subway, even though he said he'd have the car take me to Midtown. If we were going to make it work, little things like that would have to get ironed out. He might be a millionaire, but money wouldn't hold power in our relationship.

I made it to the office, and my phone rang as I was about to sit at my desk. "Adrian?" Rosalind sounded brisk. "Rob wants to see you."

"I'll be right there."

I set my bag on the desk and did an about face. Rosalind tipped her head when I approached. "He's waiting."

"Great." I hoped I wasn't going to be sick all over the floor. I knocked and winced at his stern "Come in."

Was it brusquer than usual? Was he mad? I hadn't screwed up. I knew that for a fact.

He was sitting when I entered and didn't stand to greet me. Should I take that as a negative sign? I kept quiet and waited.

"Take a seat, Adrian. I assume you got home early enough to watch the show?"

"Yes. And I thought it went very well."

"You did, *hmm*?"

I lifted my chin. "Yes."

He smiled. A real, actual curve of his lips, startling me. I couldn't recall seeing him not snide or condescending to me. "I did too. I'll admit you surprised me, in a good way. You have to work on your opening a bit, but that will come with practice. The more shows you do, the easier it will become."

"Practice? More shows? So you're going to keep it? *Playing the Field* is going to be a regular Sunday-night slot?"

"I'm not promising anything yet. I'll need to see the ratings and have a meeting with Ed Riley, the station manager, but I can't see a reason why he'll feel any differently than I do."

Of course it would be unprofessional to do a happy dance in my boss's office, but I couldn't contain my elation. "Thank you. I'm going to work really hard to make sure it's a must-watch."

He played with the pen in his hands, and I could see something else weighed on his mind, so I waited, barely breathing.

"I know you think I've been tough on you, and maybe I have. Do you know why?"

I hadn't expected this kind of conversation with Rob. It seemed almost personal, and we didn't go beyond surface stuff—good mornings and good-byes, ratings and schedules. But I'd grown in the few months I worked here.

I started out as a nervous little grunt, scurrying through the halls, fearful of being noticed, but now I wasn't afraid to stand up for myself. Make my voice heard.

"You were testing me. To see how far I'd let you push me before I pushed back."

His lips kicked up. "Bingo. To succeed in this world, you need to look everyone in the eye and tell them you're the best at what you do, even if you're not. To believe you're ready."

"I am ready, and I'm going to prove it to you with this show."

"You'll be able to prove it in other ways as well. We want to send you to follow the Blades' playoffs."

"Me?" My brows drew together. "What about Bryan? He's the sports guy."

"We need him here in the studio to do the sports." Rob frowned. "Are you saying you don't want the assignment? Frankly, it could give you the edge as to whether the station decides to go with your show or not. You need the airtime."

I recalled Louie telling me how I should stop putting other people's needs ahead of mine. I wanted to be with Rip more, and this would be the perfect way to achieve my goal. And hearing that Rob was in my corner was pretty damn important.

"I'll do it. Thanks. You won't regret it."

"Make sure of it."

CHAPTER SEVENTEEN
Rip

After leaving Adrian's apartment, I made it to Blades Arena well before the nine thirty practice time. It gave me time to relish the quiet of the locker room, smelling fresh from the cleaning crew. No pungent scent of too many bodies, sweat and cologne, and no equipment and pads littering the floor and benches. I taped up my stick and didn't feel like waiting for the rest of the team. The empty arena echoed as I sped down the ice. Division flags of past wins hung from the ceiling, and I skated past the jerseys of the Blades' retired greats: Lavaliere, Stepnik, Barnes, Kozlov. Some Hall of Famers, all All-Stars. Some had achieved that Stanley Cup win, and I wanted into that exclusive club.

"Rip, what the hell?" Seb skated to me, followed by the rest of the team. "Where'd you disappear to last night? I texted after Adrian's show, but you never answered."

I had no chance to reply as Coach waved us all to the box. "Good to see the captain setting the example for the rest of the team. I don't have to tell you that the Alpines are division rivals and only ten points behind us. The key is possession, pressure, and persistence. Keep on their asses, and don't make any mistakes. They're fast, eager, and have a lot of young talent."

My jaw tightened at his emphasis on the word "young." He wasn't wrong, yet it made me more aware than ever how fleeting my time might be with the Blades.

"But we have what they don't. Experience." I met Coach's gaze, then scanned the team and nodded with determination. "This isn't the first time we've been here, and I'm confident our veterans will lead the way."

On the opposite side of the ice, the Alpines were getting in their morning skate as well. They were an exciting team with some great prospects, but Coach was right—we knew what it was like to be in a playoff race. This was our year, and we were hungry for the championship. As happy as I was with my new relationship with Adrian, I had to put all thoughts of him out of my mind and channel all my effort to my team. I raised my stick.

"Coach knows what's up. We need to stay on their asses, force them to make errors and turn over the puck. They have a lot of rookies, which means they're not used to everything we've got. We're gonna push them to the limit, have defensemen press them from both sides. This isn't a time to make records or think about personal goals. We have one mission: win the game."

The rest of practice went smoothly, and I spent the day getting stretched, having a massage, and doing a light workout. I took a power nap, listened to some music, and returned to the locker room to get ready for the game. Much as I wanted to know how Adrian's day went and how the preliminary ratings for the show ranked, I had to compartmentalize everything else in my life that wasn't this upcoming game.

I walked with my team through the tunnel, and we took to the ice. As always, being on my skates sent my pulse into overdrive. I loved it, and the rush of adrenaline pouring through my veins heightened my awareness.

Fans had entered the arena, and we split up and skated to them to sign autographs and take pictures. I didn't see Adrian, but I was surprised to see Neil making his way to one of the seats I had reserved, and my gut tightened. I finished taking pictures with one group of fans, and skated to him.

"Hey. Great to see you. Been a while."

He cocked his head. "Yeah, well, you've been busy."

I hefted my stick. "Just a little. I'd better go. Gotta do last checks."

"Good luck."

For the first time in decades, talking to my best friend left me uncomfortable. Maybe that was to be expected because of my new relationship with Adrian, but I couldn't concentrate on Neil's feelings, or even Adrian's.

The game was as predicted—fast, furious, and physical. For each push we made, the Alpines shoved back. We capitalized on drawing their goalie into the crease, and I scored twice and Peter once on a spectacular shot. They figured to try our own play with Denis, but he was too wily to fall for that trick and smothered their attempts.

Our forechecking game was working double time, and they tried to send the puck to their wingers, but we'd watched enough films of their games and were more than ready for it. I smashed into their defenseman, face-planting him into the ice, and Seb stole the puck, taking it down ice with Chitty on his heels.

"Yes, to your right," I screamed. Chitty was there to receive Seb's pass, and he threaded a shot right between their goalie's legs a second before he butterflied.

In the end, we won 4-2, and I was fucking wiped. I headed into the tunnel and saw Neil and Adrian sitting together. I didn't know whether to be happy or concerned, but my body hurt too much to care. My knee had taken a solid bang when I was tripped, and the fights against the boards left me with aching ribs. As always, we had to do the press meet, and it was the same questions every game. At this point I felt like they might as well put a cardboard cutout of me with a tape recording playing the answers.

"Do you think this will be the year the Blades will win?"

"Who do you see as your biggest obstacle to get to the final?"

And a question was directed to me from that weasel reporter, Martin Price, who made his living writing hit pieces on New York teams.

"Rip. You took a hard knock to the knee. Will you be one hundred percent for the next game?"

Fucker. But of course I smiled. "I hadn't noticed. So I guess it's not a problem at all. I *am* a hundred percent."

"Do you think it'll hold up in the playoffs?"

"Definitely."

"Any thoughts of retiring?" he asked, and I narrowed my eyes.

"Not me. How about you?" The rest of the media circus in the room laughed, and I rose to my feet. "I need to change, so if you'll excuse me, I'll let Seb and Coach answer the rest of your questions."

I hated throwing Seb to the wolves, but if I didn't leave, I might have been tempted to grab a stick and smack Price on top of his shiny head. I left them sitting and headed to the physical therapy room. I shucked my protective equipment, and our trainer, Gustav, worked on me. I groaned and rolled my shoulders as he dug into a hard knot. He tsked about my knee, rubbed some smelly shit on it, and wrapped it.

"How bad?" I held my breath in anticipation of bad news.

"It's strained, but we'll ice it, then apply heat. That should help you. Hard game, huh?"

"You know it." I grunted and sighed when he draped heating pads over various parts of my body. Twenty minutes later I stretched and stood, testing my knee. "Feels better." I clasped his hand. "Thanks, man. You're a miracle worker."

"Come early next time, and I'll stretch it before the game and wrap it. In the meantime, don't strain it."

I gave him a thumbs-up and headed to the locker room.

"Listen up," Coach called out. "That was a good game. You all came out hungry and anticipated their plays. I liked what I saw. Tomorrow be here at nine thirty for practice, then films on the Defenders. We have two days until that game, and I want us primed and ready."

"Yes, Coach." Tired as I was, I rose to my feet. "Remember that the Defenders are second in the Western division, and though they beat us at the end of last season, it was only by a goal. They're gonna be gunning for our asses, but we'll be ready for them, right?"

"You bet."

"Definitely."

"Damn straight."

A hot shower revived me, so by the time I was dressed and ready to leave, I felt alive and awake. A gaggle of fans waited at the exits, and I signed their programs, hats, jerseys, and took photographs, well aware that Neil and Adrian waited on the periphery of the crowd. They seemed to be getting along well enough, as both had smiles on their faces. I waved to everyone and tossed my cap to a little girl.

"Night, everyone. See you in two days. Come cheer us on."

Finally free, I joined them, and Neil's relaxed expression faded, replaced by a wariness I'd never seen, at least toward me.

"Hey," I said. "Great game, huh?"

"You were amazing," Adrian gushed. "Two goals." Perhaps realizing he was overenthusiastic in his praise, he pressed his lips together.

"Thanks. Are you up for something to eat? I'm starving." I directed my question to Neil, since I fully intended on spending my dinner and night with Adrian.

"I ate before the game, but I'll join you anyway if you two don't mind a third wheel."

Adrian's cheeks flamed, but I kept it casual. "Sounds good."

We ended up at a diner a block from the arena. "Best burgers in Brooklyn," I informed them as we slid into a booth.

"I only had a yogurt and granola bar for lunch, so I'm hungry." Adrian took the seat opposite mine, and Neil sat next to him.

The server appeared immediately. "Hey, Rip Tremaine. Great game. I'm betting on the Blades to get the Cup this year. The team's on fire."

"Thanks a lot. I think so too. I'll start out with a pitcher of water and a bacon double cheeseburger with fries. Adrian?"

"Um, a cheeseburger and fries, please. Water's fine for me too."

"Just coffee for me, please," Neil added.

"You got it, guys."

She left us, and we sat staring at each other. I wasn't about to speak first. If Neil had something on his mind, he'd tell me eventually.

"What're you doing?" he finally asked after we'd held a staring contest for a minute.

My hand tightened on my glass. "Meaning what? 'Cause I think I'm sitting here waiting for my food."

His lips thinned, turning white. "Cut the crap. You told me this boyfriend shit was all a farce. But from what I've seen, it doesn't look that way."

"Lemme ask you something. For argument's sake, let's say Adrian and I are really together. It's obvious it would bother you. Why?"

Always one to say what he meant, Neil blew out a harsh breath. "Look, I love you like a real brother. But you and relationships don't have a good track record. I'm looking out for Adrian too."

"Whoa, wait a minute. Hold up. Denis's cheating is my fault?" Hearing it from Neil's mouth hurt almost as much as Denis walking out on me. Of all people, I'd thought Neil would have always been on my side. In the end, it looked like I could only count on myself. A nudge to my foot brought my attention to Adrian, and he smiled at me and shook his head. I was wrong. I wasn't alone. Not anymore.

Making a fist on the table, Neil grew angry. "Where the hell did you get that from? No, of course not. I always thought he was a smug fucker and hated how badly he treated you because you deserve so much better. I know what family means to you."

Speaking of family...with all the tumult of the past few weeks, I'd never told Neil I'd met my father. I'd never even let him know I knew he existed. A year ago, I probably would've called him right after my father confronted me in Texas, but now it was Adrian I automatically turned to. Still, Neil was my best friend, and this was one of the single most important events of my life. I wanted to share it with him and get his opinion.

"There's something I've been keeping from you," I said, and watched his eyes dart to Adrian, then again to me, his face hard as if he were readying for battle. "It's got nothing to do with Adrian. Years ago, someone showed up in my life claiming to be my father."

Neil's eyes popped out, and his jaw dropped. "You're shitting me. And you sure it's him?"

"Yeah. I had him take a DNA test, and we're a match."

Stricken, Neil raked his hand through his hair. "Goddamn, Rip. I-I never expected this. Why didn't you tell me this before? You shouldn't have had to be alone through that." I winced at the betrayal in his voice. "I thought you trusted me."

I couldn't tell him that his parents knew and he didn't. "I'm sorry. It wasn't that at all. I trust you with everything. You're my best friend, my brother in every way. But you and Lisa just had a baby, and I guess...I didn't want you to think less of me."

"Never," he insisted. "I could never think less of one of the most important people in my life."

Our friendship was strong, and I knew we'd be able to move past this once we aired it all out. For the first time since we sat down, I could breathe easy.

"Thanks," I whispered. "Over the years he's called me. In fact, that photo of Adrian with his arm around me that showed up on the Internet was right after he called me. Adrian was simply comforting me when that cameraman took those pictures."

"That piece of shit," Neil muttered.

"When we were in Texas, he approached us at a restaurant, insisting he wanted to talk to me, but I had no use for him. I told him to get lost. Instead, he came after I'd left to try and get to Adrian instead."

"And he had a lot to say." Adrian filled Neil in on their conversation, which, I hated to admit, still left me with more questions than answers.

"What do you think I should do?" I asked Neil.

"Oh, man." He sighed. "That's a question for Mom. I'm sure she'd want to know. Have you said anything to her?"

I shook my head. "No. I wouldn't want her to think I wasn't happy with her and your dad as my family. I couldn't love anyone more as my parents."

Shocked, Neil protested. "No way would they ever think that. They'd both be so happy for you to have a connection with your blood relative."

"Blood doesn't always mean better."

Neil's gaze shifted from me to Adrian, then back to me. "I lucked out in both."

I lifted my chin. "I know I did. I've never been happier. Ever."

"With Adrian? All of a sudden, you're interested in nice guys?"

I had no desire to let the conversation spiral. I had too much to lose, professionally and personally. Somehow, I had to convince Neil to table his concern for Adrian.

I pinched my eyes shut for a moment before answering. "Whatever is happening between Adrian and me is between us. We're both adults, and we don't need your permission for anything we do. But come on, man. I'm in the middle of a playoff race, and it's at the wire. You, more than anyone else, know how important this time of year is. Please...I'm sitting here begging you not to distract me with this. Not now. After the season is over, we can sit and talk. Friend to friend. Brother to brother. Just not now."

Our food came, but I waited to hear what Neil would say.

Instead, Adrian jumped into the conversation.

CHAPTER EIGHTEEN
Adrian

"Neil, you're my brother, and I'm grateful you and I are becoming closer, but I really resent you interfering in my life under the guise of protecting me."

He started to sputter. "I'm only—"

"I haven't finished." I met his eyes, and his jaw snapped shut.

"Okay, sorry."

"For years, you and I saw each other on holidays or when I'd come home for the kids' birthdays. You know nothing about my personal life—if I've had boyfriends, bad breakups, or had my heart broken."

Chastened, he hung his head. "I'm sorry," he whispered. "I was so wrapped up in my own life, I left you out there without a safety net. But we're gonna change that."

"I can smile about it now because I'm past it, but yeah. I can't lie. It would've been nice to have someone to lean on or talk to. I didn't have many friends."

Guilt was written all over his face. "I was always there if you needed me. For God's sake, Adrian. You should know that."

"Should I? Why? Even now, you want me to blindly listen to you. Take your word as gospel, no questions asked. I don't hear you listening to me. But if you thought for a moment about what you're saying, you'd realize that maybe you're wrong."

"So you and Rip are together?"

Frustrated, I slapped my hand on the sticky table, sending my silverware flying. "That's not the issue. Stop obsessing about what Rip and I might or might not be doing and concentrate on what we're asking of you."

"Which is what? I'm still not sure."

"Respect our privacy. Think about our work, because that's what we'd like to talk about. You barely asked me anything about the show, except with respect to Rip."

"I-I figured you'd tell me if anything was wrong."

"What about if it went right?" Rip glared at him before turning to me. "I want to know. What did Rob say? How were the ratings?"

Breaking eye contact with Neil, I gave Rip the full force of my joy. "It was the highest rated premiere they'd had in three years." Late in the afternoon, Rob had called and given me the news. "The network head loved the format."

"Yeah, baby." Rip whooped. "I knew it. Didn't I tell you that you crushed it?"

"You did, but—"

"But you still doubt yourself, don't you?" Neil broke in with the heat of anger. "I can see it in your eyes. I thought the show was terrific, and I'm not just saying that because you're my brother. Also, don't think I'm using my friendship with Rob to push you ahead. Yeah, I helped you get your foot in the door, but all this is your accomplishment. And I have no doubt it's only the beginning."

Hearing Neil's confidence got me emotional. "Thank you."

Neil frowned. "I don't get why you have so little faith in yourself. Considering it was your first show, you handled the questions like a pro, and you're only gonna get better. I'm really, really proud of you, Adrian. I can't understand why you didn't succeed at the other jobs. I think you're a natural."

I met Rip's eyes, and he gave me a tiny nod of encouragement. Funny how having the gift of Rip's friendship and support gave me a strength I wasn't aware I possessed.

"I never told you, but I didn't leave my other jobs voluntarily. It wasn't because I wanted to try different markets." Out of sight, under the table, Rip ran his foot over mine, and his touch gave me the strength to tell the truth. I set my jaw. "I screwed up. Bad." I ran down the list, and with each mistake, it was like a weight lifted from my chest. Where I once cringed and would beat myself up for my stupidity, I now could learn and move on without letting it crush me.

"Crap, Adrian. I'm sorry." Neil's lips twitched. "But I gotta say, that must've been a kick in the balls to Calvin Connelly."

My brow furrowed. "You knew my news director at KABL?"

"I've met him a couple of times throughout the years. A real putz." He snickered.

Rip took a big bite of his burger and gave me a wink. For the first time, I felt like I belonged in the inner circle he and Neil had created.

"Yeah, he was. I swear he was a homophobe—that's why he stuck me with the gossip and fashion news. He believes that's all gay men are good for. He always thought he was a superstar athlete because he played college hockey."

Rip poured some water into his glass. "Well, we all know that's not true. Bet Neil could whoop his ass."

"No shit. I'm pretty rusty, though. I haven't played in months," Neil remarked and finished his coffee. "When the season's finished, we should get together. Have a little one-on-one."

It was a major part of their lives I'd always been left out of. I finished as much of my food as I wanted and wiped my fingers free of ketchup. "I want to learn to skate."

Both Neil and Rip wore the same surprised expression.

"What? Why?" Neil asked. "You tried and hated it."

I raised a shoulder. "I was a kid then. It's important to you, and I want to try again." Some of my old insecurities crept in. "Don't you think I can do it?"

"I think you can accomplish anything you want," Rip stated, and from the possessiveness burning in his eyes, he wasn't only talking about skating.

Later on, after we said good-bye to Neil and were in Rip's apartment, I brought it up once more.

"Do you think I can learn to skate at my age, or were you just humoring me?"

Rip kicked off his sneakers and peered at me with a furrowed brow. "You're serious about that? Why, all of a sudden?"

"I don't know. I just…I want something I can share with both you and Neil. Tonight, sitting with the two of you, I felt seen for the first time. I wasn't that annoying little tagalong getting in the way." Funny how merely saying it brought me back to those days when I'd watch Neil and Rip, shoulder to shoulder. No daylight between them. No room for anyone else.

Rip hauled me to his chest, and I grabbed on to his broad shoulders. "Are you kidding me? After everything, you still think that's how I feel about you?"

It was impossible to answer with Rip holding me so close. His heat, sweat, and woodsy cologne sent my stomach into free fall, and I dug my fingers into his skin. His mouth covered mine, tongue seeking entrance, and I sucked it with vigor. One big hand cupped my cheek while the other clamped on my ass. I groaned as Rip's erection slid alongside mine, and he rolled his hips, creating a delicious friction.

"Oh God, how do you do that?" I shivered.

He smiled against my cheek. "Do what?" He moved again, and I clutched his shoulders.

"That, you monster. You know exactly what you're doing."

Chuckling, he squeezed one cheek, then the other. "I can stop if you want."

"I might have to kill you if you do," I groaned and nipped his earlobe.

"You're halfway there already," he hissed, and popped open my slacks. His nimble fingers pulled the zipper and yanked my pants and briefs down. Still kissing frantically, I stepped out of them while Rip lost his sweats and underwear. He pulled me to the bedroom and ripped my shirt off.

"That was brand-new," I muttered as it fell to the floor.

"I'll buy you another one. As many as you want." Rip's head popped out from beneath his sweatshirt. "Matter of fact, you should have some clothes here for when you stay. Like tonight."

"*Mmm*, am I? Staying...ohhhh." I sighed as he wrapped his rough, big hand around my cock and began to work its length. His thumb swirled over the sensitive head, and I babbled, "Yeah, that's a good idea. Very, very good. Oh, damn." My head lolled on his shoulder as I felt his blunt, calloused finger enter me. Its rough caress had me shamelessly begging for more. "Please, don't stop."

"You like that? How about this?"

Now there were two, working deep in my ass, and with Rip playing my body like a musical instrument, Shaking, I came, my dick jerking against his sculpted abs.

"Damn, baby. Your face…" He kissed my gasping lips. "Like a fucking angel."

My long-ago crush was nothing compared to the reality of having Rip in my arms, taking me apart piece by piece. This complicated man was so much more than muscles and speed. People only saw that one side of him, but when the cameras turned off and the fans went home, he was like the rest of us–trying to make it in this muddled world.

"I-I need you," I managed, the words inadequate compared to what I held in my heart.

Under the bruises and scrapes from the game, his gorgeous face lit up, golden eyes sparking with desire. "I need you too. So damn much. Your passion and sweetness. Need to be inside you. Feel you take me."

I nodded, and he gently laid me on the bed. His fingers teased me, lips kissing my skin, leaving a scorched path wherever they touched. Still in a haze, I watched him roll on the condom, his penetrating gaze never leaving mine.

"Rip." My lips moved, but I couldn't be certain any sound came out.

Slowly, he entered me, and I welcomed the stretch as he filled me, inch by thick, glorious inch. A small moan broke free from my lips, and I arched up to meet him.

When he was buried to the hilt, he kissed me, slowly at first, with increasing hunger. I met him lick for lick. Touch for touch. He began to thrust, hard and fast. I tangled my fingers in his hair and met him with the same ferocious need. My nails raked down his back as he pummeled into me. Rip was everywhere—under my skin, burning through my veins, burrowed in my heart.

"Adrian. *Adrian*," he cried out, and I held on as he lifted my legs over his shoulders.

"I'm here," I answered, my hand working my rapidly hardening dick. "You've got me."

"Don't leave me," he begged. "Please don't leave me." Wetness fell from his face to mine, and seeing his tears, my heart shattered. I reached up, and his lips found mine. Locked together, he swelled and throbbed within me and came, his heavy body pinning me. I reveled in his complete surrender and held on to his sweaty body.

I love you, I mouthed against his skin. *I love you.*

"That was incredible," he murmured in my neck and kissed me.

"Yeah, it was."

"I meant what I said." With care, he pulled out and got rid of the condom, then returned to my side. "You should leave some of your stuff here. I like falling asleep with you." He pressed his lips to my cheek. "And waking up with you."

"Me too. But since I don't have anything tonight, I'm gonna have to go home at some point." The thought of moving from the bed was incomprehensible, but I couldn't go into the office with a ripped shirt and wrinkled slacks.

"That sucks." He sounded so petulant, I had to laugh, and he opened one eye and joined me. "I'll teach you," he said through his smiles.

"Teach me?"

"To skate." He sat up and flicked on the light. "After the season, we'll go up north where I rent ice time, and I'll teach you."

Wistful, I swung my legs off the side of the bed and stared at the shiny, dark wooden floor. A soft rug in varying shades of gray and blue lay under my feet. "On the weekend that'll be nice. But remember, I have a job. I know you're probably used to being with someone more like you–"

"Someone like me?" His brow furrowed. "Meaning what?"

"I told you, I've seen whom you've dated–models, actors, athletes. Never anyone with a nine-to-five job, like me. I can't be with you for months on end, doing fun stuff, or just go somewhere at the drop of a hat." I chewed my lip. "I'm afraid you'll get bored. I'm just a regular guy."

"Regular guy?" He put his arm around me. "Maybe so. But you're *my* guy. So that makes you special. Don't ever let anyone tell you you're not."

His words warmed me, but I still pressed on because I had to hear it from him. "And what I said? You're okay with a different kind of relationship? With a different kind of man?"

"As long as that man is you."

CHAPTER NINETEEN
Rip

The sound of our skates cutting through the smooth surface of the rink played like a familiar, comforting song. I sprinted toward the goal at the opposite end, the rest of the team on my heels. Our blades scraped the ice as we passed pucks back and forth. Coach kept the pace, shouting instructions.

"Tremaine, keep an eye on your left. You tend to concentrate on your right side. Chitson, don't hold the puck too long, otherwise they'll steal it right from under your ass. Varhov, Crowe, flank the centers."

It went on for two brutal hours, pushing harder and harder, yet it was exhilarating. I barely felt the burn of my protesting muscles when we finished. At the end of the regular season, there were fewer games, with more time between, but that didn't mean we rested. We practiced every morning, watched films, and studied the plays after. Much as I wanted to see Adrian, I was too worn out to do more than shower, eat, and sleep.

"You looked good out there, but I want it even better." Coach strode from one end of the room to the other as he spoke. "All of you need to release your shots quicker. And try and draw Nordstrom into the crease. He tends to be vulnerable. Good practice today. See you tomorrow, eight a.m."

Seb and I took our stuff from the locker. From the corner of my eye I watched Denis approach, and I tensed. I recognized that crafty look in his eyes. He'd grown his hair longer, holding it off his face with a headband, and stubble covered his jaw.

"You're looking good out there, *mon amour*. Must be that young lover of yours. He's keeping you on your toes, eh?" A blindingly white smile curved his lips.

"Stop calling me that." I shoved some things in my bag. "You have a fiancé. *He's* your love, not me. And what do you want, anyway?"

"Just to talk. We were friends...once. Before."

Seb snorted and picked up his duffel. "See you tomorrow, Rip. If I don't leave now, I might drown in all this bullshit being shoveled." Whistling, Seb walked away.

I zipped up my bag. "The key word is *before*. You lost my friendship when you cheated on me."

To my surprise, Denis didn't leave. He sat on the bench, his grin fading. "Rip. I'm serious. Can we talk?" Big eyes captured mine.

"I'm exhausted, and I really want to go home."

"We can talk there. C'mon. For old times' sake."

I'd forgotten how persistent Denis could be. And how charming when he wanted something. I could tell him to fuck off, and maybe I should, but thinking about it made me realize there was no need for me to hold on to my anger if we'd both moved on.

"Sure. Whatever. Are you ready?"

"Lead the way."

Inside the apartment we'd once shared, he set his things down and strolled around, nodding his head. "You've redecorated."

I kicked off my sneakers. "I wanted a fresh start, so yeah, everything's new—couch, chairs, rugs."

"Bed?" He arched a brow.

I turned away and took a bottle of water from the refrigerator. "Everything."

He flung himself onto the club chair and ran his hand over the smooth leather. "Very nice."

I chose the couch, across from him. "I doubt you came here to discuss my interior decorating."

That sharp gaze returned. "How have you been?"

My lips twitched. "You must be joking, Denis. What do you really want?"

"Like I said. We were friends. I miss you."

"I doubt Gordie would appreciate hearing you say that."

Denis huffed out a sigh. "Ahh, yes. Gordie. I love the man, but the hero worship gets to be too much."

This wasn't the Denis I knew. That man loved the attention and ego boost. "Is that so?" I asked, amused by his complaint.

"You know the type. All puppy-dog eyes and agreeing with everything I say. There's no tension, no back-and-forth." His eyes glinted. "Like...if I said I'd want a threesome with you, he'd be fine with it." The pink tip of his tongue swiped over his full bottom lip.

Speechless, I stared at him. "You've got to be kidding. A threesome?"

Was this the real reason Denis was here? To scope out my reaction?

"Come now. When we were together, we could hardly keep our hands off each other. I used to love our arguments." In the blink of an eye, Denis moved from the chair to the space next to me. "The make-up sex was passionate. Hot. I know you remember." His hand clamped on my arm. "Gordie is wonderful, but he gives in too easily, like I'm sure your lover does. He's sweet, *n'est ce pas*? But it's not enough for us. We like a little fight. Gordie would be the perfect in-between for the two of us. He could pleasure us while we pleasure each other."

The heated gaze that once melted me into a puddle of need no longer had any effect on me. I pulled away from Denis's grasp. "There is no two of us. I have no complaints or need for a third person in my bed. Adrian satisfies me completely."

Undeterred, he shifted closer. "*Mon amour*," he purred, his breath hot against my cheek. "Don't tell me that pretty boy satisfies you. I know what you need. I can call Gordie right now. No one has to know."

I pushed him off me. "Did you actually come here to seduce me and think you would succeed?" At Denis's silence, I laughed. "I should feel sorry for Gordie, but he knows you're a cheater. And I'm sure you'll find someone to satisfy your itch. It just won't be me." I rose to my feet. "Leave. I'm not in love with you anymore, and I don't want to be friends. We're teammates, and I'll defend you on the ice, but that's where it ends."

Handsome face blazing with anger, Denis pointed a finger at me. "You loved me. One day you'll get bored with your *petit ami*."

They say the opposite of love isn't hate but apathy. That must have been the reason I didn't give a damn what Denis said. At one point, I *had* loved him, but when love wasn't returned, it dried up, and like an autumn leaf, eventually crumbled into the dust of nothingness.

"And one day you'll wake up a lonely old man because you'll have driven away all the people who cared about you. I feel sorry for you, Denis, because to you, love is a game. But it's not about scoring the most points or coming out on top. Love is about finding that one person you don't need to compete with because they're your other half. They make you whole."

Denis grabbed his bag and stormed out, slamming the door behind him. Surprisingly shaken by our confrontation, I texted Adrian.

Can you come to my place after work?

He answered immediately.

Yeah. Is something wrong?

Revealing the conversation with Denis over text wasn't something I planned to do.

Tell you when I see you.

Obviously, that wasn't what Adrian wanted to hear, as my phone rang seconds later. "Hi."

"What's the matter?" Adrian asked, sounding concerned. "Did you get hurt at practice?"

"What? No. Nothing like that. It's not important."

"Are you sure?"

Still a bit rattled, I walked around the apartment, unable to sit still. "Yeah. It's nothing. I mean, Denis and I talked and...look, I'd rather wait until you get here."

"Denis?" His voice rose, then dropped to a whisper. "Oh. Yeah, sure. No problem. I understand. I'd better go."

"See you later." I set the phone on the kitchen island and decided to work off all this extra nervous energy at the gym. A hard session of pushing myself to the limit could only help. Plus, it would get me out of the apartment.

Two hours later and dripping with sweat, I returned and jumped in the shower. My phone was ringing when I walked out, towel-drying my hair. I smiled seeing it was Dev Summers.

"Dev. What's up?"

"Nada enchilada. I'm just calling to see if you wanna do the podcast before or after the playoffs. My thought is before so you can hype it up for the fans. But when you win, we can have you and some of the guys again, to celebrate."

"Shit, don't jinx it, man. But yeah, before would be cool."

"And Adrian is okay with it as well? You know there are gonna be questions."

"Yeah, sure. He's totally on board. When do you think you'll wanna do this?"

"Sooner than later since the playoffs start in two weeks. We meant to get to you earlier, but with the basketball playoffs already going on, and some high-profile football trades, we let you slip through the cracks. Sorry, dude."

"Not to worry," I reassured him. "I've been in and out of town for the past months anyway. Not much free time."

"Hold on and lemme look at the calendar." I heard him clicking. "I gotta get back to you. I need to confirm something before I give you a date."

"Sure. You know where to find me."

"Catch you later. We're rooting for you and the Blades."

The call ended, and I set the phone on the nightstand. Weary from the hard practice and my gym workout, my eyes closed. I awoke to the sound of my doorbell.

"Shit. Wait, hold on," I yelled out after it stopped. Wearing only briefs, I flung open the door to see Adrian halfway to the elevators. "Adrian, sorry. Come here."

He half turned to speak over his shoulder. "I don't want to interrupt anything."

I frowned, brows drawing together in puzzlement. "What're you talking about? I was sleeping."

His feet dragged, reluctance oozing from every step as he came closer.

"What's wrong?" I asked him, and he gazed around as we entered the living room.

"Nothing. Are you alone?"

"Yeah, of course. I punished myself at the gym after we spoke and was wiped out. Fell asleep after I showered. I just woke up."

Adrian stood unmoving, hands buried in his pants pockets. Tension radiated from him, and he wouldn't meet my eyes. "So, uh, what do you want to tell me about you and Denis?"

"Me and...oh, wait a second." Now I understood why he was behaving so strangely. "Me and Denis? Is that what you thought I meant after I told you he and I talked?"

"I mean...I guess." His eyes fixed to the floor, Adrian shrugged, and I held him, hating his stiff and unyielding body language.

"Let's sit, but put your backpack down first." I steered him toward the couch, and we sat side by side. I tipped his chin up. "Denis came to me after practice and asked if we could talk. I was curious, so I said yes, and we came here."

Defeat weighed heavily on Adrian's slumped shoulders. "It's fine. I understand."

"No, I don't think you do. Even I was surprised."

"What're you talking about?"

In hindsight, I could smile at the absurdity of it all. "He said he was bored with Gordie because he's too much of a yes man. Remember, I told you Denis is super competitive. That makes for a great player, but in relationships not so much because he always wanted to come in first. Gordie lets him, and Denis doesn't like it. He wants the push-pull."

"And you didn't."

"No. I can't lie and tell you our sex life was boring. But like I said before, competition with everything isn't healthy."

"So he wants you back, am I right?"

"Not exactly." I shifted and allowed a small grin, which Adrian didn't return. "Here's where it gets interesting. He wanted a threesome. Him, Gordie, and me. Classic Denis, wanting his cake and eating it too." I winked, and Adrian blushed.

"You're not serious," Adrian said, but at my nod, his cheeks turned pinker. "A threesome? That's...not what I was imagining all afternoon. How did you answer him?"

With Adrian already comparing himself to the previous men in my life, no way in hell would I reiterate Denis's subtle put-downs. What Adrian needed was validation that he was all the man I could possibly want.

"I told him to leave. I have you, and I am completely and utterly satisfied. My perfect lover."

"You told him that? And he believed you?" Doubt clouded his face, and I hated how he still hadn't learned to trust. In me, but more importantly, in himself and his capabilities.

"Why wouldn't he? I'm telling the truth." I brushed my lips to his. "Don't you believe me?"

"No...I mean, I know you're not a liar, but you also don't want to hurt my feelings. It's like I said last night—I'm not the type of guy you're used to being with."

"So you don't remember my answer? That I'm happy with you, and I want us to be together? This isn't a game that's finished once the fans go home. I'm playing for keeps. Winner takes all."

For some reason, Adrian was stuck on my past when I was trying to mold a future for us together.

"Isn't this fast? I thought building a relationship takes time, and yet—"

"It was all so easy," I finished for him. "Like it was waiting for us to come to our senses and realize it was always there. It seems quick, but if you look at the circumstances, it isn't." My hands curved over his biceps, holding him fast, aware his nerves had him dancing on the head of a pin. "What I'm trying to say—badly, I'm guessing, because words aren't my strong suit—is I know we started this thing between us as a way to help you in your career, but things changed."

"Changed how? You're doing everything you can to help me with my show. I know you are."

"Of course I am. And I always will because that's what you're supposed to do when you care about someone." I brought our faces close together, near enough that I could feel his breath on my lips. "Support your partner. But it's beyond all that now. I'm invested in you. Your wins are mine. I love seeing you gain that confidence and show everyone the strong, self-assured man you are. I love how you've embraced hockey because you want to learn about my life." I cupped his cheek, the words trembling on my tongue, ready to be freed. "I love you, Adrian. It took all these years to figure out what I needed, but I'm not letting go of you now."

"Rip." He shook his head. "You don't have to say that to make me feel better."

I drew back to meet his stunned, wide blue eyes. "Is that what you really think? That I'm laying my heart on the line so you won't be hurt?"

"I-I don't know," he stuttered. "I want to believe you. I used to dream of something like this, but dreams don't come true for guys like me with someone like you."

I took his hands in mine. "Maybe this time they do."

CHAPTER TWENTY

Adrian

It was hard to think clearly with Rip near enough for me to count the sprinkling of freckles across his nose and the scars crisscrossing his handsome face. His poor body had taken so much abuse throughout the years. While my heart wanted to burst with happiness, those old insecurities still threatened. This was me—Awkward Adrian. Quiet Adrian. Friendless Adrian. The kid who'd never had someone to sit with at lunch or to walk home with from school.

Megastar athletes didn't fall for the invisible man. The man no one wanted.

"You don't believe me?" Rip asked, more somber than I'd ever seen him. His lashes lowered for a moment, and when he met my eyes, I was shocked to see them shiny and brimming with tenderness. "Adrian. You're the most real thing I have in my life. At any time I could get hurt and my career would be finished. Would you walk away from me if that happened?"

"What? No," I answered automatically, horrified he'd allow that to cross his mind. "Of course not. I'm not with you because you're a hockey star."

"I know." Again his lips touched mine. "I know I can trust you with everything."

"You can," I said, barely recognizing my shaky voice. "And I feel the same. You've been part of my life forever, yet I never knew you. But these past few months have changed that. I've changed." Suddenly shy, I ducked my head to break his direct, unflinching gaze. "You made me feel seen. Heard. You let me in to see you're more than scoring points and breaking records."

He chuckled. "Goals, baby. We score goals in hockey." Face filled with emotion, Rip skimmed his fingertips down my face. "And tonight, my ultimate goal is to show you how much you've come to mean to me. There's a reason you're the first person I told about my father. You made me less empty. Less afraid to face an uncertain future. It's always been you. *You* are my ultimate goal."

At his kiss, I held on to his face, my lips clinging to his. So often the fantasy of a teenage crush didn't live up to the hype. But the reality of Rip as a lover far exceeded my childish yearnings. The few lovers I'd had in the past had made sex about pleasuring them and putting their needs first, and I'd been grateful simply to be wanted by someone to chase away the loneliness. I'd given them what they wanted without expecting anything in return.

Not with Rip.

"Open for me, Adrian. Let me taste you." His mouth settled on mine, warm and firm.

"Rip." I sighed as his tongue sought entrance, and dizzy with the need to become one, I held on to him as he nipped and licked, my body vibrating with desire. I sucked his tongue, licked and bit his lips, and he groaned in return.

"Off," he demanded, and without waiting for me to respond, flicked open the buttons of my shirt. "You're so beautiful." Rip buried his face in my neck and inhaled deeply. I held him close, running my hands over his broad shoulders, feeling the hard, sculpted planes of his muscles. "Smell so damn good."

God, I loved him. The way his hair curled at the base of his strong neck. The dimple that flashed when he smiled. The scar etched in his brow and all the ones on his body. How he made me feel special. Like I was the only one in the world who mattered. I wished I could take away all his pain.

"Fair is fair." I pulled at his Blades sweatshirt, and he yanked it off, displaying the ridges of his abs. My breath caught at his physical beauty. I rested my cheek against his chest, loving the scrape of hair, and hummed with pleasure.

"Let's go to the bedroom." Rip held out his hand. "There's not enough room here for what I want to do with you." He kissed me again. "Plus, I don't want to ruin the leather."

I laughed out loud, and together we ran through the living room. I jumped on his bed, so damn happy, afraid this was all a dream but willing to stay asleep forever if it meant this feeling would last. We shed the rest of our clothes, tossing them onto the floor.

Naked and resting on those powerful arms, Rip caged me underneath him, his thick cock still between us. I was rock hard too, halfway to orgasm merely from lying so close.

"Touch me," I begged, running a hand along the length of my shaft, shameless in my greedy hunger for him. I'd never been this sexual until Rip released a hidden side of me that simmered beneath the surface whenever he came near, waiting for him to set it free. "Please."

"Look at you," he murmured. "So anxious. So beautiful in my bed. Where you belong." A calloused hand encircled me, and as he pumped, I threw back my head, surrendering to pleasure. Wet lips suckled the head of my dick.

"Oh my God," I cried out and came so hard I saw stars.

Through half-open lids, I watched Rip lick his fingers, then lap up the remainder of the come running down my stomach. A wicked grin tipped up the corner of his lips, and he lowered his head between my thighs.

Anticipation crawled through my veins, and my breath caught as something soft and wet licked my hole. I widened my legs, and Rip settled in, his slick tongue penetrating me. I shivered and shook, my hands clawing at the sheets as he ate me out. Delirious with desire, I pitched my hips toward his face.

"More, harder, oh God, I need you. Please."

He stopped and rose. His lips gleamed. "I need you too, baby."

I licked my lips, my dick half-hard again as he rolled the condom on. He was huge, and I wanted him so bad, I almost swooned when he entered me. I was filled, yet Rip thrust deeper, pulling me taut, stretched to the limit. The burn of his slide left me crying out yet wanting more.

As if he sensed my craving, Rip drove in farther, opening me wider, pleasure intensifying with each movement. His pace increased, and he had me bent almost in half as he took me to the moon and back. Any control I had was lost. I was a single element. Desire. I thrashed on the bed as Rip continued to hammer into me, sweat dripping from his body and mixing with mine. Those bright golden-flecked eyes were pinned to my face, blazing with a passion I'd never seen before.

"Adrian," he called out, his raspy voice breaking. His hips punched into me. I wanted to wear his marks so I could carry him with me wherever I was.

"So good, don't stop," I urged. "Don't ever stop."

I grabbed his ass and dug my fingers into the tight flesh. Daring, I allowed my finger to slip into his crack, and Rip hissed and came, his cock jerking endlessly. He fell on top of me, and like other times, I welcomed his weight.

"Rip?" I reached for his hand, lacing our fingers together. "I love you too. So much."

He smiled against my skin. "Stay. Please?"

"Okay."

He remained heavy and half-hard inside me, and I played with his dark waves. "I checked the schedule, and you don't have a game for the next few days."

He yawned. "*Mmm*, yeah. At the end of the season, it slows down in preparation for the playoffs. There are only three more regular-season games." He stretched, and I couldn't help admiring his sleek torso.

"Then what?" I sat up in bed. "I didn't have a chance to tell you, but Rob wants to send me to follow the Blades for the playoffs."

Rip's brows shot up, and he beamed. "Yeah? I think I like Rob more and more every day." He kissed my shoulder, and I laughed.

"I have to tell you, Bryan is pissed. He was looking forward to going to the games."

"Tough shit. I'll make sure you get the scoop on our prep for the postseason and some other exclusives. And I'll give you the name of our hotel so you can book a room there, though we won't be able to stay the night together. Coach is pretty strict when it comes to playoffs."

"I'll have to see if the cost fits within the station's expense budget. But I'm excited to go. It'll be my first time.

Neil said he's coming as well, courtesy of the magazine, so I'll get to see him too."

"He gets complimentary tickets to all the playoff games." Rip's stomach growled. "I'm starving. What do you want for dinner?"

"I don't care. Italian?"

He nodded. "Yeah. I need the carbs. What do you want?" He grabbed his phone. "I'm getting Chicken Milanese with penne in vodka sauce and broccoli rabe."

"I'll have the same but with chicken parm. In the meantime, can I take a shower?" I gave my stomach a rueful glance. "I'm a little sticky."

"Yeah. I took some Blades merch for you before I left—track pants, T-shirts, and some sweats."

"Thanks. I-I brought a change of clothes. For the office tomorrow." I pretend-glared. "In case you ruined another one of my shirts."

Rip's eyes danced, and he pressed a soft kiss to my mouth. "Good." He smacked my ass. "Go take your shower. I'll leave the stuff on the bed for you."

I couldn't stop smiling under the water. I scrubbed myself and shampooed my hair. When I came out of the bathroom, I slipped on the sweatpants, and hearing Rip's voice, figured the food had come. Bare-chested, I walked into the living room, only to see Rip on the computer with Devlin Summers and Brody Martin on the screen.

"Is that Adrian?" Brody called out and waved. "Hi, there."

"Uh, hi." Guess there was no way to hide what we'd actually been doing.

Rip swiveled around on his chair. "They had some free time, so I told them it was okay to do the podcast now."

I waved a hand in front of me. "Can I put a shirt on, at least?"

Rip waggled his brows. "Personally, I prefer you like this, but if you insist..." He snickered, and my face heated even as I rolled my eyes.

"Very funny."

"Give us about twenty minutes to set things up," Dev said. "We'll be back."

"We'll be here." Rip rose from his chair. "The food should be here any minute. We can eat before or wait until after if you want."

"Now, as soon as it comes."

The bell rang.

"Aha. See? Perfect timing."

I hustled to the bedroom, grabbed the Blades T-shirt, and put it on. When I came out, Rip was setting the food on the table. A cozy domestic scene I'd never imagined being part of.

Rip glanced at me. "I was getting ready to eat yours as well as mine."

"That would've been a mistake on your part." I grabbed a hunk of bread and chewed. "*Mmm.* Good stuff."

"The best. Let's do this so we can be ready for Dev and Brody."

Rip powered through his food, and I found it fascinating to watch him eat. Chewing the last of his chicken, he pointed to my plate. "You gonna finish that?"

I toyed with my pasta. "Have at it."

"*Mmm,*" he hummed as a *beep* sounded from the computer. "Showtime," he mumbled through his chewing. He swallowed and wiped his face.

With a bit of trepidation, I sat by his side, watching as they set up. Rip handed me headphones. I put them on and waited. Rip nudged me.

"You look like you're going to be sick. It's just like having a conversation."

Tell that to my brain.

My heart pounding, I sat, mentally preparing. Dev and Brody finished looking at their notes, and they nodded and met our eyes.

"Ready?" Dev asked. "We'll begin with intros, segue into talking about the regular season and the upcoming play-offs, and finish up with the main event." He cackled. "The two of you. Your relationship—how you first met, recon-nected, and everything in between."

"Okay?" Rip murmured, for my ears. Out of sight of the computer, he took my hand and squeezed it. Warmth filled me, igniting something that curiously felt like courage.

"Yes." I straightened my shoulders. "Yes, I am."

After the introduction, Brody started the interview.

"Somethin' I always wondered about. How do you guys take such a beating and two days later gotta be out there doin' it all again? And on skates." He shook his head. "Man, I gotta give you hockey players your props. I know I couldn't do it. What about you, Dev?"

"No fucking way. You guys are total badasses out there. I can barely get on the ice without falling on my face." He shifted, and I braced myself. "So, Adrian. Do you skate?"

"I'm like you. Face-first on the ice."

Dev's brows winged high. "Oh, wow. I figured you two would have that in common."

I gulped. "Nope. I plan on learning, though."

Brody's turn. "You and Rip knew each other growing up?"

"Yes. He and my brother were—are—best friends. Rip came to live with us when he was about eight or nine."

"Eight," he whispered. This time I squeezed his hand, and he hung on to me.

"He left for college when I was turning nine, so we didn't really have much interaction, except when I was being the proverbial tagalong little brother. When Louie Rozner—the Channel 8 sports reporter—got hurt, I was asked to step in and interview the Blades players." I smiled at Rip. "We reconnected then."

"Did you always want to be a sports reporter?" Dev

checked his notes. "I see you were at several news stations but doing lifestyle reporting."

Shit.

I took a deep breath. "My dream has always been to be a news reporter. And eventually an anchor. But you don't begin your climb at the top of the mountain. Working with a sports reporting team of professionals the caliber of Louie and Bryan is something people in my position rarely achieve. I'm still learning, and I'm so grateful for Channel 8 and my news director, Rob DeVine, for giving me this amazing opportunity."

"And your new show? How's that coming along?" Rip gave me an encouraging nod.

"Good. My first interview was a little scary, but once we talked, it just flowed, and before I knew it, the time was up."

Dev chuckled. "I never had that problem, did I?" He snickered, and Brody rolled his eyes.

"More like we have trouble getting you to stop talking."

"Maybe you'll come on the show," I offered.

"Just give us a holler. So how serious is it between you two?" Brody asked me. "It's gotta be easier for you knowing each other for so long, even if you are younger, Adrian."

I looked to Rip, who raised his brows at me but kept quiet. "Uh, well...we're having fun. Enjoying the time we have together. Right now, Rip is busy gearing up for the playoffs, and I'm concentrating on my career."

"It's hard to make time for each other, isn't it?" Dev nodded in sympathy. "My advice is to never let it slide. All the years Brody and I were separated, we spoke every night just to connect, and we'd meet up whenever we could."

"You gotta make the time," Brody agreed. "Dev always knew there was no one else but him for me, but I still always made sure to tell him how much I loved him. And I still do, every day. Most importantly, don't let the job take over your life. I know how busy you are right now, Rip, plus Adrian also has these great opportunities, but make time for each other. Prioritize the two of you. The game is here for only a little bit. Your relationship is for a lifetime."

"I know." Rip's husky rasp reached down to my toes. "We're going to work it out."

An uncharacteristically thoughtful and somber Dev folded his hands together. "I hope so. Because in the end, nothing is more important than love."

Again, a subtle pressure of Rip's fingers to mine. I met his burning gaze.

"I agree."

CHAPTER TWENTY-ONE
Rip

We'd done it.

Won the first round of the division and were at home for the rubber game of the conference championship. All the games had been hard fought, and our bodies were tired and beaten but not broken. First series against the Atlanta Arctics we took four straight, but the next one was tougher—the Eastern Conference Final—and we were now tied at three wins a piece. I had the highest number of penalties called on me in any postseason, which I attributed to scoring a hat trick in the first game and assisting on four other goals in the next three games. The Nordics were out for blood—mine, personally, it seemed—and they'd achieved it. I'd earned a fresh set of stitches on my chin, bruised ribs, and a wobbly front tooth that would require a visit to my oral surgeon, but that would have to wait until after the season was over.

Adrian had come to all the games, and each time he'd interviewed the players, I'd seen his confidence growing.

It was the day of the rubber game, and I was eating my lunch, trying to keep calm. All previous games with the Nordics played on a loop in my head, but at the moment I was more focused on Adrian's wide eyes and pale face as he talked on the phone to Rob.

Shit. That didn't look good. I set my sandwich on the plate, a sinking feeling in my stomach. For weeks now, ever since his show aired, Adrian had been waiting to hear when he'd be able to prepare for his next show. Rob, of course, kept him on a string, telling him they were trying to work "things" out. But he remained cagey as to what those things might be, which meant Adrian took it personally and was a nervous wreck every day going into work.

Adrian ended the call and joined me at the island. "We have a meeting tomorrow morning with the station manager. Won't say what about."

I knew enough to keep a positive attitude. "That's good. They want to tell you in person."

"Or more likely, Rob wants to see my face when he gives me the bad news because he's a sadistic SOB who enjoys delivering pain." Adrian stared off into the distance.

"No way. Tonight we're going to win the division, and tomorrow you'll go into Rob's office and hear what he has to say." I rose to my feet and stood behind him so I could slip my arms around his neck and kiss his cheek. "You'll get the show, and the Blades will win the title and go to the final." I tugged at his earlobe. "And you and I will celebrate all night long."

"Of-of course you'll win." A shiver ran through Adrian, and I smiled.

"I love the support you give me. And I love you." He settled into my chest.

"I love you too."

That was the affirmation I began every day with.

I drank the rest of my water and shoved the last bite of my turkey sandwich into my mouth. "I gotta go. See you tonight." Without waiting for an answer, I hustled out of the apartment, shoving my keys and phone into my pocket. The car I'd arranged waited to take me to Blades Arena. I could've walked off some of the nervous energy accumulating before such an important game, but I knew it would be best to hold off on that until I got on the ice for practice.

"There he is. *El Capitan*," Chitty yelled when I entered the locker room. "Are you ready?" He stood up and beat his chest. "We're gonna win this thing. Smash it."

"Try and be a little more enthusiastic, Chitty. Your negative attitude is bringing me down." I punched him on the shoulder as I passed him on my way to my locker. "Keep it together, Rookie. Focus all that energy on the game."

Seb slammed his locker door shut. "Rookie, if you think it's been intense so far, you ain't seen nothin' yet. Be prepared and don't act like we've got this."

"Okay, listen up." Coach came in and stood in the middle of the room. "This is it. Season's on the line, and I have to say, this has been one of the hardest-fought series we've played and that I've ever seen. The Nordics want this because it would be their first division title in over twenty years. We want this because we've been here and know the next step is the finals. We want the Cup."

Everyone's gaze swiveled to Seb and me. The elders on the team.

I folded my arms. "Coach is right. We can't afford any slipups, misses, or almost-had-its. Don't wait for an opportunity. Make it happen. We know where they're weak and where they're strong. Play to their weaknesses. Force errors. We can do it. We've already won the division. We need to do it one more time for the ultimate prize. The Cup."

Everyone cheered and Seb pumped his arm. "Let's go do this."

We practiced, then rested. By the time the evening rolled around, we were on a hair trigger, ready to explode onto the ice. I gathered the guys for one last huddle.

"This is practice. Don't go all out. Take shots on goal, do some breakaways, but nothing that'll use too much energy. Save it for the game."

"Got it, Cap." Peter raised his stick. "We've got this!"

"Damn right. We will not be denied," we all chanted and sped off in different directions.

My concentration remained solely on the ice—hitting slapshots, sprints, and shots on goal. I didn't sneak a peek to see if Adrian or Neil had arrived, yet I sensed they were there. I couldn't help but see Gordie in his usual spot, right behind the goal. Poor bastard. I wondered if he had any idea what he'd gotten himself into.

After the announcements, I skated out to center ice and faced off against Nolan Larsson, the Nordics' young, hotshot captain. He had an attitude as wide as the Hudson River and just as ugly. Larsson's lips drew back in a pretend grin, which was more of a grimace. The final game of the regular season he lost several teeth in a fight, and under his mouthguard, I knew he looked like a Halloween pumpkin.

"Ready, old man?"

I smirked. "Ready to teach you how to wipe your ass, punk."

"Stay away from my ass, freak." He glared.

"Enough already," the ref snarled and held the puck between us.

I snapped to attention and kept my eye not on the puck, but on the ice so I could move the moment it hit the ice. Our blades battled and I won, taking the puck across the red line. Two Nordics wingers came up behind me, smashing into me on both sides, aiming to steal, but I was ready.

"Rip, to me," I heard Seb scream, and I shot the puck his way. Immediately, he spun it out to Chitty, who drove past the blue line to Peter, who passed back to Chitty. The Nordics' goalie, Siminov, came out in the crease, and Chitty prepared to take a shot, but on his left flank a Nordics' defenseman sped up to block him.

"Peter, to your right," I shouted. "Chitty, to Peter."

Peter zipped through a tangle of bodies and blades to grab the puck and take the shot. Siminov kicked it away, but Chitty, bless his rookie heart, stayed right there and grabbed it, smashing it with his blade. It bounced off Siminov's shoulder pad and sailed right into the net. The light came on, and we'd drawn first blood.

We celebrated for all of two seconds before play resumed.

It was one of our toughest games, and the Nordics, for all that I razzed them about being young and inexperienced, were like a pack of starving wolves. They weren't going to roll over.

During the shift change, I had a minute to sit and take a breath. I watched as Denis saved three shots on goal and got pissed that our defense was letting it happen. Seb was next to me on the bench.

"We gotta be tighter on the passes, man," he said.

I chewed on my mouthguard. "Yeah. Next time we're out there, we'll do a split run."

"You got it."

Our rest time was up, and we jumped in. I nodded to Seb, and we took off. Within four seconds, he was slammed into the boards, and I let out a vicious curse, but Chitty was right there to retrieve the puck. He sliced it to me, and I dug my skates in, passing center ice. I had one thing in mind, and that was to get the puck in the net, no matter what. A hard smash to my shoulder only made me bite down harder, and I shot the puck to Seb, who flicked it to Lemoine, his counterpart. Lemoine sent it up ice to Chitty, who didn't have a clear shot.

"Chitty, to me, now," I yelled, and he hesitated.

That inexperience cost us, as Rembowski, the Nordics' hulking defenseman, zoomed in and took possession. He broke away and powered across the rink, where he faced Denis. His shot somehow slid past Denis's pads, and the score was tied. The buzzer sounded, and it was time for the first intermission.

We trooped into the locker room, where I stomped over to Chitty. "I told you to send it to me."

"I thought I could make the shot if I moved."

I had no time for egos. "Fucking hell, Chitty. I gave you the play, but you wanted to get the glory of making the shot, didn't you? That's not how it works. The best person to make the shot gets it. Understand? We're fighting for our lives here."

He hung his head. "Yeah, Cap. I get it. Sorry."

I cuffed him. "Look at me." He met my eyes, misery clouding his normally cheerful face. "You're a good player, but if you want to be a champion, you need to start thinking of the team. Sorry isn't gonna be enough if we lose because of your ego." I gazed around the room, where my teammates sat in silence. "That goes for all of us. I know we can do this. We're gonna raise the pennant at the end of this game. Eastern Division champs, then Stanley Cup champions. Am I right?"

"Fuck, yes," everyone screamed, and the atmosphere, which had been mostly subdued, morphed into a passionate outburst of how we planned to kick the Nordics' asses in the second period.

Coach Chopard came into the center of the room, and we quieted down. "I think Rip said it best. There's no time for egos. We have the experience and the talent. Make it work in our favor." He outlined several plays he wanted us to make and pointed out weaknesses in our strategy.

Reenergized, we grabbed our freshly taped and waxed sticks, ready to get out there.

"One more thing," Coach said. "Lindstrom. You're starting this period. Rip, take the bench."

Protest sprang to my lips. "But, Coach—"

"No egos here, Rip. Remember?" He strode out, leaving me stunned. Seb nudged me.

"It doesn't mean anything. He's saving you for the end game, when it's the most important."

I refused to show how bad the slight affected me and nodded. "Yeah. Let's go."

We took to the ice as if we were a brand-new team and scored two goals in twelve minutes. I got some playing time, but not as much as I wanted, and didn't get to face off until later on. But we were ahead, and that was what mattered. I had to eat my own words of taking one for the team.

Third period, we were holding our lead of 3-2. Coach signaled to me.

"Rip, go in. Cycle the fucking puck. Make sure you get the team net-front present if they're in our zone. I don't want anything getting near Denis."

"You got it, Coach." Relieved, I took to the ice for the face-off. The rest had done me good, and I grabbed the puck, reinvigorated. A Nordics defenseman slammed me into the boards, and I felt a pain in my side where he jammed his stick.

"You like to suck cock? You're gonna be sucking mine when you lose."

I threw an elbow backward, connecting with his midsection, happy to hear a grunt of pain. He punched me low, an illegal kidney shot that sent me sprawling to the ice. Whistles blew, but it was too late. The benches emptied, and it was a brawl. Several minutes passed before the ice was cleared, and the fans were screaming and booing. The team doctor came to check me out.

"Rip, you okay?"

I nodded, still a little winded. "Yeah, I'm fine. Bastard."

"He's been suspended, and he won't be on the ice for the rest of the game. You okay to play?"

"Fuck, yeah. Let's bury these assholes."

When I rose and skated to the sidelines, the fans roared and cheered. I lifted my stick in appreciation and caught sight of Adrian's scared face. I gave a thumbs-up and took a seat. Without Coach even saying a word, I knew I was off the ice for now.

"Cap, you okay?" Chitty, who'd been one of the first to dive into the mess, had a cut over his lip.

I spit out my bloody mouthpiece. "Yeah, I'll be fine. Don't let them goad you. Concentrate on keeping the puck away from our side of the ice. Now, get out there."

He gave me a quick nod and skated off, while I reassured the rest of the team I was okay. Coach, always with his eye on the game, nevertheless addressed me.

"That was a low blow. What caused it? Did you have words?"

I met his eyes. "Yeah. He told me since I liked to suck dick, I'd be sucking his after the game." My smile was thin. "Just another day in the life of a gay pro athlete."

To my surprise, he put a hand on my shoulder. "I'm sorry. He has no right to say that. No one does." Then he walked away to consult with the other coaching staff. His actions left me somewhat confused, as I'd always gotten the impression that Coach wasn't fond of having a gay player. His words dispelled that feeling and raised my spirits.

More energized, I watched Lindstrom take the face-off, and we were off. He passed to Seb, who cycled to Chitty. I was happy to see he'd taken our talk to heart, as he sent the puck to Lindstrom. A Nordics defenseman forechecked Lindy, sending him into the wall, where they battled for control.

"Peter," I screamed, my throat raw from the effort. "To your left."

Though I knew he couldn't hear me, Peter had that puck instinct, which made him one of the best in the league. He got to the puck and shot down the ice directly at the Nordics' goal, only to have the puck stolen in what I hated to admit was a beautiful move by their defenseman. In a breakaway, he sped toward Denis, who waited close to the net, and my heart pounded hard and fast. This was where Denis excelled. The defenseman took a shot, but Denis stuck his glove and sprawled across the net, and it went nowhere.

The arena went wild. Lindstrom skated to the bench. "Rip. Go."

I zoomed out of there like a bat out of hell. There were three minutes remaining, and my adrenaline was through the roof. I blocked out everything except that puck drop. We were going to get to the finals. I refused to think of anything else.

Larsson won the face-off, but I went after him like a tiger to an antelope. The Nordics had pulled their goalie to get an extra offensive player on the ice, but I refused to allow them to gain any advantage. I pinned Larsson, but the kid was a wily fox and shoved me off, taking the puck and trying to pass.

"The fuck you will," I spat and took it off his blade. Open ice beckoned me, and I had a breakaway to an empty goal.

The crowd was hysterical with joy, and I sent the puck into the net. Not the most exciting goal of my career, but I'd sure as hell take it.

With less than a minute remaining, there was no way the Nordics could catch us. We'd won, and I was mobbed by the team as the fans cheered. I swore I could feel the arena rocking and rolling beneath my skates.

"We did it. We did it. We're going to the finals." Even Coach was smiling as we shook hands with the opposing team. Almost all were good sports and congratulated us on a hard-fought win, but when it came time for Larsson to shake my hand, he spit on the ice at my feet.

"I don't shake hands with cocksuckers."

Stunned by his words and action, I merely nodded. "No problem." I couldn't hold back a smirk. "But this cocksucker is going to the Stanley Cup Finals. Have fun watching my ass on television."

Finished with the pleasantries, I spun around and skated to where Adrian and Neil were seated. They each wore my jersey, and their faces were bright with joy. I raised my stick to them and shouted, "We did it!"

I didn't think he could hear me over the din, but Adrian raised his fist and mouthed to me, *I love you.*

And thrilled as I was to win the conference and as much as I wanted to raise that Cup, knowing I had Adrian in my corner and by my side meant win or lose, I could handle whatever came my way.

CHAPTER TWENTY-TWO
Adrian

I asked Rob for the day off since win or lose, I wanted to be with Rip as a boyfriend and not a reporter. Watching the joy on Rip's face as they celebrated their win, I didn't understand why the fans were on the ice, but Neil explained that they often joined the players when the team won the division championship.

"Come on," Neil pointed up the steps. "We'll meet him outside the locker room after he does the press conference. Trust me, we don't want to be near him until he takes a shower."

"You got that right. Talk about smelling rank." Laughing, I walked with him, the elated fans jostling us as they hustled past us.

Neil checked his watch. "I told Lisa I'd be late as it was the final game. If they won, I'd go out for a drink to celebrate, and if they lost, I'd go out for a drink to help drown his pain." He leaned against the wall. "How's it going with you two?"

"Fine." I allowed a quick smile, my mind still on the earlier conversation with Rob. "But I have a meeting with Rob and the news director tomorrow about the show." Staring off into space, I voiced the fear I'd kept to myself. "I think they're not gonna give me the show after all."

Startled, Neil peered into my face. "Why the hell would you think that?"

"I don't know. He sounded so serious, and there's no reason for the two of them to want a meeting. If he wanted to tell me the show is a no-go, he could just put me out of my misery."

Neil's lips twitched. "Rob isn't like that. And I think you might be surprised."

"Why? Do you know something?"

Neil shook his head, sending my hopes crashing. "No, but I know him. Wait and see."

"And you haven't heard anything?"

His brows knitted. "No? Why would I?"

I chewed my lip. "I don't know. Just that you got me the job–"

"Again with this? I got you the interview. *You* got yourself the job. And kept it. And from the show I saw, you did great. But I also saw you two on *The Huddle*. The way you two behaved with each other...it's gone beyond pretending to be boyfriends, hasn't it?"

As much as I wanted to tell Neil the truth, Rip and I had already discussed not telling him anything until the season was over. And it sure as hell wouldn't be in a public forum, with drunk, screaming fans surrounding us.

"Nothing's changed between us."

How had I become such a good liar? Because from that night on, everything had changed—the world had turned upside down. Rip said he loved me, and nothing would ever be the same.

"I'm gonna let that slide because you have this meeting tomorrow. Let's do some role-playing." Neil folded his arms. "I'll be Rob." He pulled his thumbs through imaginary suspenders and pursed his lips. "So, Adrian, before we get into why I called you here, tell me how you think you're doing."

I snickered because the imitation was spot on. "I, uh—"

Neil put up a hand. "First mistake is hesitating. Be prepared with an answer to that question."

"Such as?" My insecurities spun a spiderweb of fear around me.

Neil frowned. "Come on. You know what to say. Stop letting him intimidate you. Think."

I closed my eyes for a moment, then straightened my shoulders and met Neil's gaze. "I'm doing great. Everyone I've met who's seen the show loved it and asked me when the next one will be aired. I asked good questions, not cookie-cutter ones. And I've prepared for the next show."

Neil broke out in a smile. "Now that's the perfect answer. Confident without being cocky. Plus, it shows you've already planned for the future." He squeezed my shoulder. "You speak exactly like that, and you'll be fine. Rob wants winners working for him. And you and that show will be winners."

"Thanks." Something still bugged me. "Have you heard anything about Louie? I tried calling him, but he's always in therapy or the person helping him answers and says he can't come to the phone."

"No." A puzzled expression settled on his face. "Do you want me to make some inquiries?"

About to eagerly accept, I stopped. Time for me to grow up. Handle my own shit. "Thanks, but I'll wait until tomorrow and try and find out myself."

"You'll let me know, of course."

I heard the excited voices of the fans calling out their favorite players.

"Seb, Seb. Sign my program, please?"

"Look, it's Rip. Rip, you were great. Can I get a pic?"

"It's Chitty and Peter."

I nodded to Neil. "Yeah, definitely. Good news or bad."

We hung back, letting the people get their time with their stars. Watching Rip, I couldn't help but notice him favoring his knee. An almost imperceptible falter, but knowing intimately every inch of Rip's body, that slight hesitation was apparent and troubling.

Neil nudged me. "God, I hope he wins the Cup this year. He's hurting—I can see by how slowly he's walking. I'm not sure how much longer he can do this without really injuring himself. The guy's given everything to the game, and I'm afraid it'll catch up with him." His face was grim. "Age is a ruthless thief of joy in hockey."

Rip laughed at something someone said to him as he signed their cap, but my heart ached for him. Perhaps he sensed my stare, because he turned around and gave me a wink.

"Okay, everyone. Be sure to get your tickets, because the final against the Polar Bears is gonna be epic. Love you all. Catch you later." Rip waved and joined us. "Thanks for waiting. Great night, huh?"

He hugged Neil first, then me, leaving his arm slung casually over my shoulder. A warm glow settled in my chest as people streamed past us, a few rolling their eyes, but more shouting words of encouragement to Rip. I even caught a few nods of approval directed my way. One couple wearing matching Blades Pride T-shirts walked by but stopped and retraced their steps to us. Both were in their mid-to-late fifties, in good shape. The taller of the two had ebony skin offsetting a beautiful white beard, while the other was freck-led with a head full of russet waves. Their hands were entwined, but I saw the gleam of wedding bands.

"We're sorry. We don't mean to interrupt."

I tried to step away, but Rip held me firmly. "You're not. At all."

The bearded man shot me a quick look before addressing Rip. "We've been fans of yours from the beginning, but since you came out and became an advocate for LGBTQ sports players, we've followed your career. I hope you know what an inspiration you've been."

"Thank you. That means a lot to me. I've tried, along with other players, to normalize queer players in sports. It's why the GAINS organization is so important, not only for players, but for fans. When players from all sports get together, we can push boundaries. When I was a kid, I never thought I could be an out-and-proud NHL player, but here I am. And our ranks are growing every day. This helps people believe they can be whatever they want to be."

"It helped our son. He grew up watching hockey, and he's a huge fan of yours. He came to us from foster care six years ago when he was twelve, and now he's gotten a hockey scholarship to college."

Rip pulled out his phone. "Give me your email. I'll make sure the three of you get tickets to our opening game."

"What?" They spoke in unison, staring at us in shock. "That's...so incredibly generous. We weren't asking—"

"Of course not. But I'm offering."

"He means it. Go on," I urged. "You'll have an incredible time."

"Th-thank you so much." They each gave Rip their email and left after shaking his hand and taking several pictures.

"That was very nice of you," Neil said.

"I'm a nice guy, don't you know?" He again put his arm around my shoulders, and we walked out of the arena. "There's a big celebration at Slapshots. Tonight's the night to let loose. You coming?" Rip asked Neil when we made it outside to the street.

"I thought I might, but it's running late and I gotta get home. After the finals, you'll come to the house, and we'll hang out." He hugged Rip. "Take care of yourself."

I could hear the concern in his voice, one I shared. Rip either ignored it or didn't notice.

"Sounds like a plan." Rip squeezed me. "Ready? All the guys will be there, and I want you to meet Seb's wife, Jolie. He told me she got a babysitter to watch the girls tonight."

"Uh, yeah, sure." Even after these past few months together, it still took me a moment to reconcile my anonymous old life of solitude with this new social, public life. I should've realized he'd be celebrating their win.

"You okay?" Concerned eyes met mine. "Is something the matter?"

Tonight was Rip's night to celebrate. There was plenty of time for me to prepare for the meeting tomorrow with Rob. I beamed a bright smile. "Not at all. Time for me to buy you a drink."

Neil whispered in my ear, "Tell me how it goes. Talk to you tomorrow."

He got into the car he'd called for, and we watched the headlights melt into the hoard of cars leaving the underground parking lot from Blades Arena. Rip took my hand, and I laced our fingers together as we walked to the bar.

"You were so good tonight." I leaned to put my lips to his ear. "And so hot. All I thought of was, that's my guy on the ice."

His eyes glittered, catching the streetlights above. "Initially I couldn't find you, but I sensed you were there, somewhere in the crowd. It's like a force pulling me toward you. I know when you're near me, and it gives me strength that I have someone always in my corner, cheering me on."

"I'll always be there for you."

He kissed me right there in the middle of Flatbush Avenue, with the lights of Blades Arena shining blue and gold down on us. Cars honked as they drove by, and Rip laughed against my mouth.

"Seems we're giving Downtown Brooklyn a show."

I held him around his neck. "Bring it on."

"Shit. Where's my tie?" I stumbled into the bedroom and bumped my knee on the bedframe. We hadn't made it home until past midnight, I'd had quite a few drinks, and then we'd stayed up making love. My last recollection of time was pale light breaking through the blinds.

"Wha..." Rip rolled over, mumbling, but I had no time to admire him in all his gorgeous nakedness. I was running late for my meeting with Rob.

"Who the fuck calls for a nine a.m. meeting on a Monday, the day after a crucial game?" I grumbled but didn't expect an answer. It was my own stupidity to get caught up in celebrating the Blades' win and forget to keep a clear head.

Rip yawned and pushed the hair out of his eyes. "A sadist. Don't worry. Take one of mine from the closet. You're gonna kill it. Call me after. I might be at practice, but I'll check my messages."

I nodded and ran into the shower, barely wetting myself but enough to get the smell of the bar and Rip off me. I dressed in my best suit, a freshly washed and ironed shirt, thanks to dry cleaning preplanning, and Rip's tie. I brushed my hair and gave my reflection a pep talk in the hall mirror.

"You got this. *You can do it.*"

I arrived at Rob's office a minute before nine, stomach empty because I didn't want to come to the meeting with sesame or poppy seeds caught in my teeth from my usual everything bagel. Rosalind smiled as I approached her desk.

"He's waiting for you. Go right on in."

I took a deep breath and knocked on the door.

"Come in."

When I entered, I expected to see Rob and the station manager, but Rob was alone.

"Good morning," I said.

Rob pointed to the chair in front of his desk. "Sit, Adrian."

Heart thundering, I took the chair and waited.

"Ed couldn't make it. Great game last night. How's Rip doing this morning?"

There was no leering or innuendo, which I appreciated.

"He's good. Sore, but eager to start practicing for the finals."

"I'll bet he is. I don't know how those guys do it."

My heart sank, as I wasn't getting a single positive vibe from Rob, but I had to ask. "What's going on with Louie? I've tried calling him, but I haven't been able to get through to anyone."

The first sign of true emotion clouded Rob's face. "Ahh, man, it sucks. Louie's leg isn't healing as well as they'd hoped. He's going into a rehab facility down in Florida, where his sister lives. He lives alone up here and can't take care of himself."

The news hit me like an arrow to the heart. "Oh, no. Damn. I can't believe it. I thought he was doing so well."

"We had hopes he'd be on his way to a full recovery by now, or at least be able to do the sports from home, but he's in too much pain."

"That's horrible. He's so active, it must kill him to have to sit and do nothing."

"Yeah. So that brings me to our meeting. We asked Bryan to take Louie's spot full-time, and he agreed. But he doesn't need an intern. He prefers to do the work on his own."

My heart slammed, then did a deep dive to the pit of my stomach. "I understand." We'd never really vibed, and I sensed that for all his buddy-buddy words, he resented my in with Rip and the Blades. I blew out a breath. "What about the show? Are you going to tell me if I'm going to get a chance to continue?"

He steepled his hands under his chin. "Ed still has concerns about your qualifications, so for the second show, we're thinking to have Bryan do the interviews. He's got the name recognition."

"B-but it was my idea. It's *my* show," I sputtered, outraged that someone else would get the credit. "That's not fair to me."

He shrugged. "No one said it had to be fair."

Angered by his brush-off, I grew heated. "I think that's wrong. *You're* wrong. I came up with the format. I pitched the guests. You can't just steal my idea and think that's okay. And Bryan gets to benefit from everything I set up and put into place? No way." I rose to my feet. "You know you're screwing me, don't you? I've worked my ass off doing whatever anyone asked of me, even pretending to date Rip to get the show."

"So you're not together? You're faking it?" Rob folded his arms. "Didn't look like that to me from the pictures I've seen of you together."

My cheeks burned. "Whatever. That's not important. My personal life—"

"Is the reason you got the chance."

His casual dismissal of my work pissed me off even more. "Yeah? So what? Everyone has an in with someone. Big fucking deal. I did great on the show and you know it. I've gotten great sound bites from the other players. You can't take the show from me. I've proved I can do it." I leaned across the desk. "If you take the show from me, I'm going to go over your head and talk to Ed."

Rob glared at me. My breath came hard and heavy, but I held his gaze. All of a sudden, he began to laugh. "Bravo. You aren't the same scared kid who came here a few months ago. You stood up for yourself, stood up to me. That takes balls."

Still angry, I didn't break. "So what?"

"That's why we're giving you the show." He folded his arms and gave me a big, cheesy grin. "Just wanted to see how you'd react if I poked the bear. And it was better than I expected."

"You what? You think it's funny to make me feel like shit? Is that what you think great management style is—torturing people mentally?" Trembling, I paced the office. "I can tell you it's not. Thanks for letting me know. Is there anything else?"

"No. I'm expecting full coverage of the finals. Bryan will be here in the studio, waiting for your feed."

I gave a sharp nod. "And the show?"

"We'll be starting the promos this week, so make sure you have your final lineups on my desk for the next one by the afternoon so I can get the names to production."

God, I wanted to punch him right in that smirking face, but I wasn't stupid. An interview show, even if it was solely sports-related, could lead to bigger things. I was only twenty-eight and could bide my time.

"That's fine. Thank you."

"You're welcome."

I left his office and found my way to my cubicle. My phone buzzed, and I saw it was Rip.

"Hi."

"So? How'd it go?"

I decided not to bother telling him about Rob's idiocy and concentrated on the positive. "I got it. They're gonna start promos right away."

"Yes, baby. I knew you could do it. We'll celebrate tonight. I love you."

"I love you too. It's good, isn't it? My own show. I can't believe it."

"I can. And it's great news. You're gonna nail it." His voice dropped to that sexy rumble that never failed to turn me on. "And I'm gonna nail you tonight when you get home."

"I'm counting on it," I murmured.

"You can count on me no matter what. Us together is all we need. Now go do your job, and I'm going to practice." He hesitated. "I'm proud of you, Adrian."

After we ended the call, I took some time to think about what Rob had said. In the heat of the moment I'd been strong enough to make my case, yet I felt the same—I still wasn't sure if I could handle the weight of a show all by myself.

My desk phone rang.

"Hello, Adrian Hunt."

"Kiddo, how's it goin'?" Louie's cheerful voice brought a smile to my face.

"Louie. Jesus, I'm so glad to hear your voice. I just saw Rob, and he told me you're down in Florida?"

"Yeah. Man, it sucks. Everyone here is old and looks like me, but the docs say I gotta come here and rehab this bionic ankle and knee they made for me." His sigh hurt my heart. "I ain't comin' home, kiddo. It's gonna be a long road. I gotta retire."

"I'm so sorry, Louie."

"Me too, kiddo. But Bryan'll do a good job. And hey, I hear they're gonna go forward with your show. I thought you did a great job—you're a natural. Must be your love life." He cackled, and I grew warm, glad we weren't on FaceTime.

"You're a real comedian, Louie."

"You know I'm joking. Truth is, you have a natural ability to draw information out of people. It's definitely a gift, and you've got it. I could see it, and so could Rob."

"Come on, Louie. You don't have to jerk my chain. I know—"

"You think I'm lyin'? No fuckin' way. You know Rob's not one to give out praise, and neither am I. We're both straight shooters, and we call it like it is."

Why was I getting emotional? My family had always encouraged me to follow my dreams, and of course Rip had given me all the praise and help I could possibly want, but it wasn't enough. Maybe because it was the first time someone in my field had ever given me that pat on the back I'd yearned for.

"Thanks. I think that's what I needed to hear. I-I really miss you, Louie. It's not the same around here without you."

"Yeah? Well, that's the thing, kid. Life goes on, whether you want it to or not. It's how you choose to live that life that makes the difference. I had my turn, and now it's time for me to move on and make room for the new cowboys. Like you."

Hearing Louie call me a cowboy had me laughing despite the gaping loss his departure would leave for both the station and me.

"Thanks, Louie. I'll be calling you. You can't get rid of me that easily."

"Anytime, kiddo. You can take the old dog out of the newsroom...yadda, yadda. Talk to you soon."

The moment I ended the call with Louie, the phone on my desk rang again.

"Hello, Sports Desk. Adrian Hunt speaking."

"I'm Mel Banfield, Pedro Espinoza's publicity agent. We'd like to see about getting him a spot on your new show. The New York Empires just signed him last week as their new outfielder."

I hadn't kept up with baseball news—my concentration had been solely on hockey—but I could fake it with the best of them.

"Sure. Send me your media kit, stats, and a highlight reel, and I'll get back to you with a date. You have my email?" I recited it to her.

"Excellent. Thank you. I'll have that for you today."

"I'll look for it."

I sat in my chair, savoring the moment, and glanced up to see Rob at my door.

"Good work, Hunt. Ed's free and wants to talk now."

Finally, I felt like I belonged.

CHAPTER TWENTY-THREE
Rip

Practice was light—we went through the playbook and watched films of the Polar Bears from the past five seasons. They were tough, and I anticipated a seven-game series that would be as physical as I'd ever played.

When we broke, Coach beckoned to me. "Rip. Come with me."

Curious, I shut my locker door. "What's up, Coach?"

"Not here. In my office."

Seb raised his brows. "What's that about?"

"Not a clue."

"Never a good sign when you get called to the coach's office," Denis called out.

"Shut up, Denis. Do what you do best—blocking shots on goal, not running your mouth."

I knocked on Coach's door and opened it.

"Sit, Rip."

Nervous, I folded my arms. "No thanks. I'll stand. What's wrong, Coach?"

He sighed. "You've been playing some of the best games of your career."

Not what I expected to hear, but the glow of his praise settled the dancing butterflies in my stomach. "Thank you. It's been rough, but I'm ready to bring the Cup to Blades Arena."

"Well, we're armed and ready for a hard fight. It'll take real team effort."

I allowed myself a grin. "That it will. But we've been waiting, and this time we'll do it. No egos, just pure hockey guts."

"No ego is correct." Coach's returning smile was thin. "Which is why I'm starting Lindstrom in Game One."

The door opened, admitting our defensive coach, Alexi Aranov, along with the team physician, Dr. Mike Hutchinson.

A pain hit me center mass, as if I'd been kicked in the nuts. "What? Starting Lindstrom? Why?"

"Rip, we watched the tapes during and after the game and at practice. You're clearly favoring your knee." Hutch, as we called him, was sympathetic but firm. "I'd like to take a look at it."

Goddamn it. "I mean, yeah, I fell on it hard and a few pucks slammed into it, but I'll be one hundred percent by game day next week."

"Rip." Coach pointed. "Lift your pants. Now."

I did as told and presented my bare leg. Hutch bent in front of me and prodded the skin above, below, and on top of the patella.

"It's swollen. There's no apparent damage, but it's obvious to me the knee is not in its best shape."

"And with a week of rest, heat, and therapy, it'll be fine by game time," I insisted.

As I spoke, Coach shook his head. "We can't take that chance, Rip. It's not the beginning of the season. It's the Stanley Cup. If you improve and Hutch gives the okay, you'll play."

No use arguing. Coach wasn't about to budge. "Sure. Yeah. Lindstrom will do a great job."

To my surprise, Coach left his seat behind his desk to sit beside me. "I know how disappointed you are. And I wouldn't do this if I felt you were one hundred percent. Believe me, the moment Hutch gives us the go-ahead, you'll play."

I couldn't break down. Not here. Not now. "What if that doesn't happen?"

His hand rested on my shoulder. I gazed at him, mute and trembling with a myriad of emotions. "I promise. You'll get ice time. I know how much this means to you. Therapy every day, but only light practice. And you'll suit up for the games."

All I could do was nod at him and Hutch, get up, and walk out of the office with my head high. I left the arena and called a car for home. I could have sworn I didn't take a breath until I shut the door behind me and collapsed on the couch. That was when I started to shake. I wanted Adrian, but he was at work and I couldn't bother him with my problems. Not when he'd had the best news of his career. I didn't want to be the one to dull his shine.

I picked up my phone and called Neil. "Great news about Adrian."

"Yeah, he texted me. I hope this'll boost his confidence. From what I heard, the station is very pleased with the show. And with Louie having to retire—"

"Whoa, he is? I haven't heard that."

"Adrian didn't know," Neil explained. "He's not going to get the news slot, but they do like how he handled the interview. But this isn't why you called. I hear it in your voice. What's going on?"

Neil always was a sharp bastard. I sighed. "They're pulling me out of the starting lineup for at least the first game, most likely the next as well."

"Your knee? Is it bothering you that much?"

My heart sank. "You noticed?" *Dammit.*

"Rip. Come on. It's me." A gentle Neil was a Neil I never wanted to hear.

"So you agree with them that I should be benched."

"Listen. No one knows how bad you want this more than me. It's all we talked about growing up, only you're the one who made it to the top. And you don't get to your level without giving everything you've got, which you do every game you play. But the goal is the Cup. And if your coach thinks the road to getting there entails resting your knee, then that's how it's got to be."

"Realistically, I know you're right. But dammit. Sitting out the opening game? Maybe the whole series?" I pounded the pillow with my fist. "It's killing me."

"I doubt that's gonna happen. What did Hutch say?"

Over the years, Neil had visited me enough to become familiar with the whole Blades team.

"He said it's swollen, and I should rest and take hydrotherapy, acupuncture...the works."

"It sucks because you're the fiercest competitor I know, but promise me you'll listen to him. You don't want to wreck your health in pursuit of the Cup. What happens if you don't win it this year and you wreck the knee to the point where you end up permanently injured and have to retire? You'll never be able to play again."

At his words, a chill ran through me. Never play another game? The thought was inconceivable.

"Yeah, I know. Just...sitting while everyone else is skating...I don't know if I can do it."

"You can because you're the heart of the team, and if they sense your anger, their concentration will be off."

I rested my head on the pillows lining the couch, gazing upward. "It just sucks."

"I know. Take the therapy and rest."

"Thanks. I'll let you get back to work."

I didn't know how long I remained sitting in a fog of despair before I picked up the phone.

"Hey, Hutch? It's me. When do you want me to come in?"

"Ahh, man. What the actual fuck?" Seb shut the door to his locker. Coach had made his announcement that Lindstrom would be starting the series while I rested and took care of my knee. The weight of everyone staring felt like a thousand pounds on my shoulders.

"Coach isn't wrong. I hate to admit it, but my knee did take a shot in that last game, when it was already sore. And I don't want to slow down the team. I'd never forgive myself if I cost the team the Cup because of my ego and unwillingness to step aside for the betterment of the Blades organization. I went home, wallowed in some self-pity, and talked to Neil. I kicked my ass in gear, came in and did hydrotherapy, acupuncture, and stretches."

"You're gonna be one hundred percent, and we're gonna win this Cup, *with* you on the ice." Seb gripped his stick, his expression fierce.

"Thanks. I'll do everything in my power to make that happen."

Denis strode over, and I braced for a sarcastic comment or a smirk. Instead, he sat beside me, serious. "I'm sorry, Rip. I know we haven't been good to each other—"

"We haven't?" My lips twitched.

An unexpected and surprising blush rose to his cheeks. "Okay, you got me. I haven't been good to you. In fact, I've been a petty shit. But I'd never wish this on you. I know how bad you want to win." He stuck out a hand. "Shall we call a truce?"

Call me a sucker, but being at odds with Denis was exhausting. Aside from it creating tension on the team, at one point I did love him. I could tell he meant what he said. Maybe he was growing up. And though he'd cheated on me, I'd moved on. I had Adrian.

I grasped his hand. "That would be a good idea." Our eyes met, and the anger and hurt no longer hung around me like a dense fog. Nothing remained but a gentle pang of what had once been but now was gone forever.

"I truly am sorry, Rip. For everything. I wish you and Adrian the best. The two of you are better than we ever were."

"Thanks. And for the record, I hope you and Gordie are happy together."

He broke eye contact. "Well, let's say I'm zero for two in relationships. He and I...*finis*."

"I—Denis, I'm so sorry."

"It wasn't meant to be." He shrugged and rose to his feet. "Make sure your boyfriend takes good care of you. Better than I did. And I expect to see you on the ice as soon as you're able."

He walked off, and Seb waited until he disappeared to speak. "What the hell was that about?"

"Maybe Denis has finally woken up."

"And realized what he lost?" Seb waited. "He has lost you, hasn't he? You and Adrian are solid?"

At the mention of Adrian, I grinned. "Yeah. We are. As a rock."

It was well after six when I opened the door to my apartment and saw Adrian behind the island. God, I loved seeing him. Loved coming home and finding him there, waiting for me. At his welcoming smile, all the bad in my day vanished. I hefted the bottle of chilled champagne I'd picked up after I left the arena.

"Congratulations to my hot and sexy boyfriend. The newest TV star of Channel 8."

Adrian blushed. "Stop."

"I'm serious. How'd the rest of the day go?" I leaned in for a kiss. "*Mmm.* I've never kissed a real television news star."

Adrian gave me a playful shove before reaching for two flutes. "And you still haven't."

I popped the bottle and poured us two glasses. "Don't downplay your accomplishment." I lifted the crystal to make a toast. "To you and your show. I know it will be a massive success."

We clinked and sipped. Adrian set his glass on the counter. "How was practice today? Must be so exciting to be heading to the finals."

My stomach tied in a tighter knot. "Yeah...well, no. I-I didn't practice today. I can't." Anxiety made it impossible for me to sit still, and I walked past the island to the living room and stood by the expanse of windows overlooking the river. "Matter of fact, I spent my afternoon sitting in a hydro bath, then having a massage and acupuncture, after which I watched my team practice." Adrian touched my shoulder, and when I turned, his puzzled gaze met mine. "Yeah. You heard me. I've been benched." My voice caught, and horrified, I turned away, but Adrian put his arms around my waist.

"Tell me everything." He led me to the sofa and we sat.

I repeated my conversation with Coach and Hutch from the morning, and I could see Adrian's heart breaking for me in his eyes. I struggled to control my emotions.

"It'll be okay. I'll rest and get treatment—it already feels better after only one day. I'm sure I'll be on the ice for the series."

"Rip. You don't have to pretend with me. Come on." He patted his lap. "Lie down."

"I'm fine. Really. I've made peace with it."

His gorgeous face remained stern but tender. "I doubt it. Stop trying to pretend you're tough. I know what being in the final—what winning the Cup—means to you."

I held on to him, fighting the tears. "No you don't, but that's okay." Self-conscious, I sniffled. "Something funny. Denis apologized for his behavior and wished us the best. And told me he and Gordie broke up." I tried to laugh. "Maybe there's hope for him yet."

Adrian kissed me. "There's always hope."

The Blades needed all the hope we could get because it was the seventh and rubber game of the Stanley Cup finals and we were tied, 3-3. The Polar Bears had taken advantage of Lindstrom's inexperience both as a center and team leader to capitalize on our mistakes, plus we'd failed to exploit on any of the multiple scoring opportunities. It wasn't all hopeless because the Bears had suffered a major loss when their All-Star goalie tore his meniscus diving for a power-play shot on goal. Their backup goalie, Marcus Bernard, was only a second-year player, and hopefully, his newbie status boded well for us.

I'd come in for short shifts at the end of the past two games to test my knee, and it had held up after each turn on the ice. I'd even assisted on a goal. That morning, Hutch had proclaimed me ready to play, and I was vibrating with barely restrained energy. The entire team gathered around me.

"You're starting tonight?" Chitty asked, hopeful. "You're playing?"

My cheeks hurt from smiling so hard. "Yes. My knee feels great, and Hutch says I'm a hundred percent. So we're gonna do it tonight. Bring that cup to New York where it belongs."

"Yes, Cap!" everyone shouted.

"You know they're gonna come after me with everything they got. Dirty tricks and all. But we don't need tricks. When we get the puck, drive to the net to the far post, set up whoever's following the puck carrier, and look for a chance to score. Press the defense. Make them turn over the puck. Look to intercept when they've got control. And remember." I faced each of the guys. "No one is to be a hero or looking to score the most goals. You see someone open in front of the net, or with a clear shot on goal, you pass the puck to them. Got it?"

"It's good to have the captain on the ice with us, where he belongs, *n'est ce pas*?" Denis said, meeting my eyes. "We will win tonight because we are the best. I feel the destiny in my bones."

Denis wanted this win as much as I did—he'd come from the Icers, having missed their glory years, and part of our initial bonding was from our mutual, ferocious desire to win.

"Protect the net. Don't let Denis get drawn out into the crease. Are we ready?" I stood and grabbed my stick.

Everyone trailed after me, and we walked through the tunnel to the rink. The roar of the fans to watch us practice was as loud as if we'd scored the game-winning goal. God, it felt good to be on the ice instead of watching from the sidelines, and as I got the feel of it under my skates, I saw Adrian, Neil, and Lisa sitting with Jolie and hers and Seb's two girls, along with an older woman I believed was Jolie's mother. Seb, Chitty, Peter, and I sped down ice toward the net, cycling the puck as we traveled.

The arena was ready to rock and roll when the starting lineup announcements were made, and I couldn't help but raise my stick to the thunderous cheers as my name was called. I skated to the red line for the face-off with their center, Piers Hansonn.

"How's the bum knee, Tremaine?"

"As solid as your thick skull, Hansonn, but thanks for asking."

My nerves were on fire and tingling. The energy of the arena flowed through me as I waited for the three-inch circle that controlled my entire life to drop. I heard my guys calling out to me and each other. The puck hit the ice, and we were off. My knee held strong as Hansonn and I battled for the puck. He grabbed it away from me and passed to his right winger, but it was intercepted by Seb, who flicked it to Chitty, already on the move. The screams from fans made it impossible to hear anything my team-mates were saying, but we'd practiced for this all year, and we were in sync.

I whizzed past Chitty, and he passed the puck to me. Surrounded by Bears players, I didn't have a clear shot on goal. I fought to keep control but lost it to the groans of fans. Peter picked it off and sent it to Chitty, who smashed it at the goal. Bernard slapped it away, right onto the blade of Seb, who flicked it between Bernard's legs. The light went on, and we'd drawn first blood.

We held that tenuous one goal lead well into the third period. Coach had rested me periodically throughout, which I didn't mind, but now there were only two minutes left. We took a time-out.

"How's the knee, Rip?"

"Great. No problems."

"All right, then. You know what to do. Protect the goal at all costs. Don't let them near Denis. And you"–he pointed to Denis–"don't allow them to draw you out in the crease. You fucking superglue your body to the net."

"*Absolument.*"

I'd never taken drugs, but I imagined this out-of-body sensation must've been what it was like to feel high. My heart hammered, goose bumps popped up on my skin, and my breath came short. We stood in a tight circle on the ice and I spoke to the team.

"I don't care what happens. Don't get called for a penalty. They're gonna come after us to try and force us to make stupid mistakes. Keep your head. Be smart."

As predicted, the Bears attacked us like beasts after raw meat. They tried to draw us into our end, but we anticipated that, and when the puck hit a bump in the ice on a pass, I grabbed it and sped away.

"Fuck you, Tremaine," Dubois, their defenseman, spat and slammed me into the boards.

"No thanks," I snarled and fought for possession. Covering my body with his, he punched the base of my spine, and I grunted but pushed through the pain to jam my elbow into his stomach. He fell off me.

Hansonn slid his stick in, and to my horror, sped off on a breakaway. Just him and the puck. Straight at Denis.

"Get him," I screamed. "Seb, Chitty, Peter, go."

I tore after them, but I was too far behind. My teammates were gaining. I knew time was running out, but my entire focus was on Hansonn facing off against Denis.

The crowd was on its feet, and I vaguely heard them counting down. Hansonn pulled his stick back to take the shot, and I sent a silent prayer.

Please, please, miss.

Helpless, I watched the puck sail toward the net, certain it was going in. A big black glove reached up and out, and at the last second, pushed the puck off to the side, halting its forward motion.

The buzzer sounded, and the arena exploded.

We won. We fucking *won*.

I threw my stick up in the air and screamed with unbridled happiness. "We did it. We fucking did it." I skated to Denis. He ripped off his face mask, tears of joy streaming from his eyes. There was no animosity—only absolute joy.

"Rip."

"Denis. We made it."

We jumped each other, and the rest of the team surrounded us and we hugged en masse. Seb and I embraced as the team broke its huddle.

"I can't believe it. Finally. *Finally*."

Coach joined in our celebration, and we each hugged him and shook his hand, then the hands of everyone on the Bears team. The Commissioner and his assistants set up the small podium. I could see Adrian and Neil filming the ceremony. Denis was rightfully named the most valuable player of the series, and I didn't feel a single twinge of jealousy. He'd played the best games of his career. The Commissioner finished his speeches and handed the Cup to me.

I kissed it, the metal cold against my overheated skin, and I could barely see through the tears. Fifteen years of hoping and waiting, all came to this moment in time. A moment I knew I'd never forget. I kissed the Cup again and held it up to thunderous applause and cheers.

"Thank you to the Blades organization and Coach Chopard and all the coaches for teaching us how to be a team. To the best teammates in the world. We did it." I held the Cup closer. "I owe this to my mother, Abby Tremaine. She's no longer with us, but she sacrificed everything so

I could play hockey. And she taught me to never give up my dreams." I took a deep breath. "Thank you to my best friend, Neil, for being my brother in every sense of the word, and to my boyfriend, Adrian…thank you for being you. To Mom and Dad Hunt, for giving me the chance. And most of all, to the fans who've stuck with us through good and bad. This is for you."

I held up the Cup and skated around the perimeter of the rink, showing it off to the cheering crowd. I savored this experience, wishing I could hold on to it forever.

I returned to my teammates and handed it off to Denis, who in his usual showboating behavior, did spins, then approached an older man in a wheelchair and held it high. The man blew him kisses, and I recognized him as Denis's mentor, the famous Canadian youth hockey coach, Gil Girard, whom I'd met once at the beginning of our relationship.

Each teammate had their chance with the trophy, and the noise inside the area was growing louder. I looked over to where I knew Adrian and Neil were sitting when screams and shouts diverted my attention.

In horror, I watched as the top-level railings on the right side of the arena, a new section that had been installed the year before, collapsed, and all the people disappeared in a shower of crumbling concrete and metal. The rubble fell on top of the crowd below. Plaster dust and screams filled the air, and I lost sight of Adrian, Neil and Lisa, and Seb's family.

"Holy shit. Oh, my God."

CHAPTER TWENTY-FOUR
Adrian

"Neil?"

Choking from the dust, I spied him getting to his feet. Relief filled his eyes.

"Adrian, are you all right?"

"Yeah, I'm fine. You?"

"Yeah, but you're bleeding."

Feeling a wet trickle on my cheek, I touched my face, and my fingers came away with blood on the tips. "Just a slight cut. Where are Lisa, Jolie, and the kids?" The seats by us were empty.

"I don't know. After the ceremony, Lisa and Jolie went inside with the girls and Jolie's mom."

"This is a disaster. How many people might be hurt? It's terrible."

"Adrian, go find out. I'll dial 9-1-1, but you should see if you can talk to some people and find out what happened. Get their stories."

I stared at him. "Neil, that's morbid. This is a disaster."

Serious, he nodded. "Yeah. Exactly. And you're on the scene, and you can tell the audience what's happening live. There are people watching who have relatives here. You're their connection, their lifeline. Record using your phone." I hesitated, and Neil grew impatient with me. "If you want to be a news reporter, you have to put yourself in situations that might not always be pleasant. Go. I'll look for the others."

I pulled out my phone and saw texts from Rob.

I know you're at the game. Go get the story.

Taking the stairs two at a time, I saw several people with blood running down their faces, in obvious pain. Instead of getting the story, I stopped to help move some broken concrete, and I could see people standing around, uninjured, filming us. Why wouldn't they help instead of recording... on their phones? They could do both if they wanted. I found a woman crying and moved a heavy piece of railing off her legs, then smoothed the tangled hair off her face.

"Don't worry. We've called 9-1-1, so help should be here soon."

"Coming through," I heard the shouts.

"Over here," I called out and waved to the paramedics. I stood back as they put the woman on a stretcher to carry her out. I followed them.

"You'll be okay now."

"Thank you for staying with me." She reached out a hand, and I took it. "I appreciate it. I don't know where my sister is. She came with me but went to the bathroom. I haven't seen her since it happened."

I squeezed her fingers gently. "I'm a reporter with Channel 8. Do you want me to get it on the news so she'll know you're okay and you're in route to the hospital?" I turned on my video.

"Yes, please. Katelynn, it's Megan. I'm okay."

I turned to the paramedics. "What hospital?"

"Mercy."

I gave her one last reassuring smile before they hurried away, and then I was patched through to Rob.

"Please put this video I'm sending you on the live feed so that this woman's sister will know where she is."

"Good job, Adrian. You're already on national television as helping that woman. Keep doing what you're doing."

I frowned, again annoyed that someone would stand around to film a tragedy and not do what they could to help.

"I'm going to see if anyone needs assistance. Talk to you later." I returned to the area and helped move the debris and winced at the people's injuries. Other more fortunate people were simply sitting and waiting for directions. I approached one woman in a Blades jersey, sitting next to a younger woman who was crying.

"Hello. I'm Adrian Hunt with Channel 8. What are your names, and would you like to say something to your families at home who might be watching?"

The woman with the Blades jersey spoke first. "I'm Amanda Owens from Rego Park. I'm okay. Just a few cuts." The woman next to her continued to cry. "This is my sister, Chloe. She's just scared. Mom, Dad, we're both fine."

The man next to her winced as he pushed up. "My name is Jason Sears. This is my wife, Madison. We're from East Seventy-eighth Street in the city. We're okay." The dark-haired woman by his side gave me a shaky nod.

"Yeah, I feel lucky. One older man standing next to me got hit in the head. They took him away already. I hope he's all right."

"Can you tell me what happened?"

Jason spoke first. "We were all standing by the railing to watch the ceremony, jumping with happiness, celebrating the Blades' win, when I heard, like, a groaning sound. Then *bam*, the railing gave way and we fell."

Firefighters appeared along with EMS paramedics. "Is anyone here hurt and needing assistance?"

I pointed to Jason. "His leg's injured." I backed away and let the first responders take my place. "I'll let the experts do their job. Thank you, and I hope everything works out well."

I took to the stairs again and pushed my way through the crowd. I found several people on the floor crying. With trepidation, I approached two men, one older, one younger, and from their facial features and red hair, obviously related.

"Hi, I'm Adrian Hunt from Channel 8. Are you okay? Do you need me to call the paramedics to help you?"

The young man wiped his eyes. "It's okay. They checked us out and said we're not hurt."

"Can you tell me your names and where you're from?"

"I'm Ryan McGee, and this is my father, Timothy McGee. We're from Brooklyn. It was my twenty-first birthday yesterday, and these tickets were my present."

The older man looked rather pale, and I peered closely at him. "Are you sure you're feeling all right?"

His lips lifted slightly. "Yeah. Just a little freaked out."

"I'm sure. What do you remember?"

Ryan rubbed his face, his blue eyes wide with what I assumed was shock. "Me and my dad were cheering the Blades. I had my first beer to toast the win when I heard this awful creaking noise. Then it looked like a movie, with pieces of concrete tumbling down along with these metal railing pieces. We ducked and ran toward the exit, but some other people weren't so lucky."

I followed his quick glance to see people being carried out on stretchers. I shuddered. "Yes, you were very lucky. Thank you for telling us your story."

I left them, and seeing an official-looking firefighter directing others, turned on my video camera again. "Chief, I'm Adrian Hunt with Channel 8. Can you tell us what's happening—what you know so far?"

He pushed the hat off his face. "We have around fifty people en route to local hospitals with varying degrees of trauma, but none life-threatening. From our preliminary investigation, looks like this area's railings became loosened from the weight of the people leaning on it, and it collapsed. The seats are fortified underneath, so that remains intact."

"So only the front railing was affected where there was excess weight? You don't think it was anything deliberate?"

"No, but we'll do a thorough investigation, as will the Blades. It could've been a lot worse. And as for something deliberate, it's always a possibility, but I don't think so."

"When does the investigation start?"

"It already has. See?" He pointed over my shoulder.

I turned to see several men in Department of Buildings jackets walking through the rubble with people wearing NYPD jackets. Through the static, I heard firefighters' voices.

"Squad 43 reporting in. We're clear at the arena. All injured removed and rubble secured."

"10-4."

"Squad 43 returning to base."

"Thank you, Chief. I'll let you get back to work."

The loudspeaker blared an announcement. "Attention. Attention, please. All injured parties have been taken to Mercy Hospital. There is no damage to the structure of the arena. It is limited to that one section. We're happy to report that thanks to the quick and heroic efforts of our first responders, none of the injuries are life-threatening. The Blades have set up an emergency number for people to call, and we've given it to all the local news stations." The announcer stated the number, and I entered it into my phone.

I videoed a panoramic view of the broken section of the arena and kept my camera on as I picked my way through the mess to get to rink level. Once I found an area with good signal, I called Bryan, and he picked up immediately.

"What's going on? Are you hurt?"

"No, I'm fine."

"Good. We've got a live feed. What did you manage to get?"

"I interviewed some of the injured and the fire captain on the scene. I have it all on video from my phone camera."

"That's great. Send it, and we'll put it on the news in a few. Good thinking to capture it all."

"Yeah, thanks." Now that I'd finished with the impromptu interviews, I wanted to see Rip. I felt so horrible that he'd waited his whole life for this moment, and it was being overshadowed by a tragedy.

The ice was empty, and when I searched the crowd, I picked out Rip, Denis, Seb, and other members of both teams helping people. I wove my way through people until I reached them.

"Did you see Neil?"

Rip held on to a woman's elbow as they maneuvered past me. "Yeah. He's inside with Lisa, Jolie, the kids, and Jolie's mom. Where were you?"

"I went upstairs to talk to people and the fire department. Neil thought it would be a good idea to get a news story. I'm really sorry I wasn't here to congratulate you."

Rip hugged me. "That's okay. You did the right thing. People were hurt. This is just a game. Their lives are more important."

"Rob told me I was on the national news. I needed to help some people more than getting a story."

"Baby, you helping them *is* a story. I'm proud of you."

A warm glow enveloped me. "It was the right thing to do. Give me a minute. I'm gonna send my videos in to Rob."

I collected all the footage I'd taken and sent it to Rob along with an explanatory email. He called me immediately.

"Obviously, we're running with this story first. Bryan's gonna put you on live. Pick up when he calls. We know where you are—the sports department cameraman is there."

"But—"

"But nothing. This is real news, not a game."

I looked up and watched as a Channel 8 cameraman walked toward us.

"What's going on?" Rip came up behind me, and I explained what Rob had said. "He's right. You want to be a reporter, Adrian. This is as real a news story as it gets. Just pretend you're telling it to me."

I recalled Louie's story of how he was supposed to be interviewing soccer stars the morning the towers were hit. *Time for me to get my story.*

Gerrard, who'd worked with me on *Playing the Field*, waved. "Ready, Adrian?" He tossed me a headset and a microphone. It felt heavy but natural.

"News on the fly." I put it on and adjusted the earpiece. "Ready."

He got behind his camera and held up a finger, and then the light came on and I waited for Bryan's cue.

"We've got Adrian Hunt on the scene at Blades Arena, with a live report. Adrian, what can you tell us?"

"Thanks, Bryan. After a triumphant and thrilling Stanley Cup win by the Blades, disaster struck as the railing of the upper deck collapsed, sending metal and chunks of concrete tumbling to the level beneath it. Several people were injured, but I was personally assured by the Chief Battalion Officer that no one was in critical condition. First responders were on the scene immediately to transport people to Mercy Hospital." My earpiece hummed before Bryan spoke.

"Can you tell us about the atmosphere in the arena now, Adrian? How is everyone doing?"

I thought for a moment. "People are tense and worried about friends and loved ones, but there's also that New York spirit of coming together in an emergency. Everyone's helping each other."

"Of course. We saw video of you assisting first responders, as well as many Blades and Bears players assisting with the rescue efforts."

"We all want to help. It's times like these that make people realize that winning is about more than playing a game. To win at life, we need to come together and help each other."

"Very wise words."

I held out my hand, and Rip took it, coming into the camera view. "I have Rip Tremaine, the Blades captain, here with me. I figured we should snag him to say a few words about winning the Stanley Cup—his first." I held the microphone to him. "How does it feel to finally bring the Stanley Cup to New York?"

Rip's grin lit up his face, and his absolute joy made my heart turn over. "It's like nothing I can express in words. All my life I've dreamed of this moment, and now that it's here, I'm just so incredibly grateful." His face turned somber. "The Blades organization is coordinating with the FDNY and NYPD to make sure the injured are taken care of. Our main concern right now is to get everyone the help they need."

"Thank you and congratulations to you and the entire Blades team. To our viewers, let me repeat, the injured are being transported to Mercy Hospital. If you need to check on a family member or friend, the Blades have set up an emergency number." I recited it.

"Thanks, Adrian, we also have that number up on the screen. Great job tonight. We saw how you helped the injured people in the stands when no one was certain of the stability of the area, putting your own life at risk. Channel 8 is very proud of you."

I gave a wave. "Just doing what's right. This is Adrian Hunt from Channel 8 Sports."

Gerrard gave me the thumbs-up, and I handed him the headset and microphone. "Great job, Adrian. I'll get to the station." He paused. "Congratulations, Rip. Fantastic season."

Rip shook his hand. "Thanks, man."

The Jumbotron flashed the colors of the Blades—blue and gold—and then the announcer came on: "*Congratulations to the Stanley Cup champions, the Brooklyn Blades.*"

A cheer rose from the people who'd remained in the stands, and they began to clap and chant, "*Blades, Blades, Blades.*"

Rip held me close, and I kissed him.

"I'm so proud and happy for you, Rip. It was such an incredible game. My heart was in my throat at the end."

Joy spread across his face. "Is it wrong for me to feel so happy even though such a terrible thing happened?"

"Not at all. You heard the announcement. No one is going to die. You're entitled to celebrate."

Seb reappeared with Jolie at his side, holding both his little girls. They clung to his neck, and his joy matched Rip's. "There he is. How's it going, Adrian?"

"I'm good. Congratulations. It was an amazing game."

Denis approached and didn't stop to talk to Rip or Seb, coming directly to me. "Adrian. I'm very glad you're here so I can speak to you. I acted so foolishly when we met previously. *Je suis désolé.*" He held out a hand. "Please forgive me."

It was a day filled with surprises, and when I met Rip's eyes, they were soft, and for the first time, filled with peace. "Of course. As far as I'm concerned, I'm a winner as well." I put my arm around Rip's waist. "I've got Rip."

Denis's face fell, although he tried to smile. "Yes, you are. Rip is a great guy."

"The best," I answered and leaned into Rip's chest. Smelly and dirty as he was, I wanted to sink into him and never let go. This night might be the culmination of Rip's dream, but it was for me as well.

Shoulders hunched and head bent, Denis walked away.

"Funny enough, I feel sorry for him," I mused, and Rip kissed my neck.

"That's because you're a very nice guy."

"Nice only goes so far because if he ever tried to come between us, Bad Boy Adrian might have to get activated." As heartfelt as Denis' apology was, I didn't trust him. He'd shown himself to be the type of person who'd say and do anything to get what he wanted.

A spark lit the golden flecks in Rip's eyes. "Bad Boy Adrian, *hmm*? I like the sound of that."

I took his hand. "Let's go home, and I'll show you."

We barely made it to the bedroom. I pulled off his clothes, then mine. I held Rip close and kissed him, leaving him gasping for air.

"What's gotten into you?"

I licked the head of his dick. "I've never made love to a Stanley Cup champion." I swiped my tongue over it again, then nuzzled into his thigh. "I'm so proud of you."

He played with my hair. "This is the best night of my life. I have you and the Cup. Nothing could ever top this."

I arched a brow and grinned. "Is that a challenge?" I grabbed the lube and poured it on his thick shaft. "Tonight there's going to be nothing between you and me."

We locked gazes as I held on to his shoulders, and inch by delicious bare inch, sank onto his cock until he filled me so completely, I couldn't catch my breath. Naked skin to naked skin, I clasped him tight within me, wishing this moment could go on forever. Together, we were the forces of life. Fire and water. Air and earth. I couldn't let him go.

"Rip. God, Rip," I moaned, his fingers digging into my hips. I moved on top of him, pleasure chasing the pain, and gasped after he rolled me underneath him and lifted my legs to my chest. The hard thrust of his cock left me aching with a desire that transcended any emotion prior to this moment. I grasped my shaft, and the mere touch to my sensitive skin sent me flying. Rip held me as I shook, then swelled inside me and came with a harsh cry, filling me with heat.

"I love you," he whispered in my ear, and I rubbed my cheek to his.

"I love you too."

He slipped out of me, but neither of us had the strength or will to move, so we lay together, tangled in an embrace. My eyes fluttered shut.

The next morning as I walked into the office, every person I met stopped to congratulate me both on my helping with the rescue efforts and my on-the-spot reporting. I finally had a moment to myself in my office, when the phone rang.

"Adrian Hunt. Sports Desk."

"I think after last night, that might change, kiddo."

Happiness settled in my chest. "Louie. How are you?"

"Not as good as you, I'm thinkin'. Great work. Really great."

"Thanks a lot. It sure wasn't how I expected to spend my night. But I'm just glad there weren't more people seriously injured."

"Listen. On 9/11, I never thought I'd be interviewing survivors of the World Trade Center Towers, but someone else had a plan for me. We find ourselves in a position we never dreamed possible, but it's how we handle what's thrown at us that proves our mettle. You proved yourself last night."

My throat grew tight. "Thanks, but I did what anyone else would've."

"I didn't see no one else climbing over the broken concrete to help people. Only you."

My other line buzzed, and Rob's number flashed on the screen. "Louie, I gotta go. Rob's calling. I have a meeting with him."

"I bet you do. Call me later."

"I will," I promised and hit the button. "Rob?"

"I'm ready for you."

"I'll be right there."

I already figured he was going to thank me for stepping up and doing the live feed from the game. When I entered his office, he was standing in front of his desk with a big smile.

"There he is. Channel 8's hero reporter."

He shook my hand, but I cocked my head. "Reporter?"

"Adrian, last night you showed incredible poise and the ability to think on your feet. Your instinct to dive right into a chaotic situation, handling it seamlessly, proved you possess the skills required of a news reporter. So effective today, we'd like for you to move to the news division. Working as an intern in the sports division would be a waste for both you and us."

My heart pounded. "Oh, wow, th-that's amazing. Thank you. I'd love to."

"Great. We're assigning you to the political division. You'll get a press pass and whatever else you need. You'll be working with Sterling Forest on the evening news. He was very pleased to hear it."

Goose bumps prickled over my skin. "Sterling Forest?" I repeated. He was the anchor and new face of Channel 8 News. I had very little to do with him—he'd come from Los Angeles and kept to himself, coming into the studio only to do the news, leaving immediately after. On the rare occasions we'd cross paths, he'd nod and give me a quick hello.

"Yes. We've briefed him, and he thinks you'll be a good addition to the team. I told him and the rest of the political staff to expect you around eleven." He sat behind his desk, effectively dismissing me. I turned to go, then remembered something. "What about my show? I did like the idea of *Playing the Field* and hate to give it up when it had barely begun."

"You can still do it. Maybe now you can bring in other people besides athletes."

"Really?" Damn, I didn't want to sound like an eager kid, but this was a great opportunity.

"Welcome to the big leagues. Now, get to work."

"I will. Thanks, Rob."

He picked up his ringing phone, and I returned to my office, anxious to tell Rip everything that had happened.

I took out my phone, prepared to call him, when a text popped up.

I'm at the hospital. My father was at the game last night and was one of the people injured. He's in a coma.

CHAPTER TWENTY-FIVE

Rip

Adrian left early, around seven thirty, and I showered and changed and got on the phone with my agent, Ezra Green. He was bubbling, and I could picture him bouncing in his chair like a blond Energizer bunny.

"Dude, you were awesome. Congratulations. Roe and I were screaming at the set at the last second."

I could laugh about it now. "Me too. If Denis hadn't made that save, it could've been a whole other story."

"Well, it's not, and you're a Stanley Cup champion. I've got you booked on Channel 8's morning show at ten, Dev and Brody want you on *The Huddle* at one, and ESPN Hockey at three, and..." He rattled off several more names.

"Whoa, Jesus. When do I get a chance to take a piss?" I joked. "Seriously, it sounds good. Just tell me where I need to go and when, and I'll be there."

"I'll send you the list. I'm really happy for you, Rip. You worked so hard for this. I know what it means to you."

"Thanks. I still can't believe it myself." My phone beeped, and I frowned, seeing a call from Mercy Hospital. "I gotta go. I've got a call I need to take."

"No worries. Talk soon, and I'll send you the schedule."

"Great." I ended that call and picked up the new one. "Rip Tremaine."

"Mr. Tremaine. This is Dr. Alvin Kim at Mercy Hospital."

"Did something happen to Adrian or Neil?" My stomach bottomed out at the thought of one of them hurt. Oh shit, was it the kids?

"I'm sorry, that's not whom I'm calling about. There's a John Carver here who says he's your father."

My father? What the hell? Obviously he'd come to see the game. Conflicting emotions buffeted me. I didn't want to care, but I couldn't help feeling sorry for the man, lying hurt and alone in a strange city without a familiar face.

"What's his condition?"

"He received a blow to the head during last night's collapse at Blades Arena. When he arrived he was conscious, but there's swelling in the cranium, so right now he's in a coma."

My stomach bottomed out. "I...see. I-I'll be right there. What room is he in?"

"Room 428."

"Thank you."

I ended the call, and realizing I had commitments I could no longer make, I texted Ezra about my change of plans, citing a family emergency.

I'll call you later and let you know what's what.

He responded immediately.

Don't worry about it. Hope everything's okay.

I took off, and once I was in the car, texted Adrian, but figured he'd be in a meeting with Rob and wouldn't be able to answer me. The hospital was only ten minutes away, and the car had barely slowed to a stop before I was out and rushing toward the entrance. I gave my name to the receptionist, who thankfully wasn't a hockey fan, as I was given a visitor badge and waved through without any acknowledgment.

In the elevator up to the fourth floor, I wondered why I'd come running for a man who'd turned his back on my mother. Maybe because at one point she had loved him enough to leave her family for him, and she'd kept me even after he left. I followed the numbers to his room, where I found him lying in bed, white as the sheets and on a breathing machine that beeped every second. Stunned, I sank into the chair by his bedside.

A man in a white lab coat entered. "Mr. Tremaine? I'm Dr. Kim."

"Good morning. What can you tell me about his condition?"

"We won't know more until the swelling comes down. His scans were normal, but we have to wait and see."

"I understand."

"Are you his only family member? Does he have a wife? I know he came in alone."

I didn't want to get into a discussion of my personal life, so I gave the most innocuous answer possible. "I think it's only me."

"Do you know if your father has a DNR?"

I blinked. "You mean whether he wants to be resuscitated if something happens? No, I don't know."

Dr. Kim nodded. "Right now he's on a ventilator, but we'll see if he wakes up."

"If?" My mouth dried. "You mean...he could stay like this?" I swallowed. "Permanently?" It was inconceivable to imagine a person lying like this for who knew how long.

"Like I said, we don't know. It's too early to tell." He checked my father's chart. "I'll be by later to check on him."

He left, and I sank to the chair, still in shock that all this happened. Here I was, the day after winning the Stanley Cup, sitting by my father's hospital bed. He hadn't let me know he was coming to see the game.

You blocked his number. How would he have told you?

He must've bought a ticket and flown to New York without asking me to get him a seat. Something I could've easily done without a second thought.

But would you have?

A question I wrestled with throughout the morning, as nurses came by to check on him and he was wheeled in and out for tests. At one point, I was approached by an efficient-looking man with a clipboard.

"Are you Mr. Carver's relative? I'm Edward Rose, the hospital's patient-family coordinator."

"Yes. I'm...his son." The words felt awkward on my tongue.

"I see. Do you know what medical insurance he has?"

This wasn't a conversation I wished to prolong. "No idea."

The man held out the clipboard. "Are you willing to sign a DNR?"

My heart skipped a beat. "Are you saying he's never going to wake up?"

Rose shook his head. "No, I'm just here to get Mr. Carver's paper work in order for the administration. Only the doctors can determine that."

I thought for a moment. "It hasn't even been twenty-four hours. Let me think for a while, please."

"Of course. I'll take care of the rest of this. Thank you."

He left, and I finally had the chance to call Adrian.

"Hey."

"What happened? Are you still at the hospital?"

God, it felt so good to hear his voice. "Yeah. He's still unconscious. The doctor said something about swelling in his brain from the hit he took on the head. They're waiting to see if it comes down."

"I'm so sorry. You didn't know he was coming to the game, I'm sure."

"No. He was the last thing on my mind."

"It's not your fault."

Then I remembered Adrian's text and his early morning meeting. "What happened this morning with Rob? You said it was something amazing."

"I almost feel bad talking about myself."

"Don't you dare," I scolded. "Tell me," I insisted.

"They're giving me a news reporter position—real news, not bullshit or sports." He chuckled. "Sorry, dammit. Not that sports is bullshit, but you know what I mean."

"No offense taken. I know how much this means to you, and I'm so happy you're getting the job of your dreams."

"Thanks. I'm nervous but excited at the same time. Today I'm off to City Hall for a press briefing, but I'll come to you right from work. Give me the info."

I could hear the hesitancy in his voice and tried to build up his confidence. "You're gonna kill it. I have total faith in you." I gave him the room number. "I can't wait to see you. It's hard sitting here all day just waiting and watching a machine breathe for him. Even though we're basically strangers, I can't help feeling for him."

"Of course you do. It's why I love you so much. You have such a big, forgiving heart."

Did I? I wasn't so sure.

"I'm not a saint," I pointed out. "I didn't say I forgave him for what he did to my mother."

"I understand. But you and Denis have worked it out now. If you could forgive him for cheating on you, maybe you can find a way to forgive your father for walking away, not knowing your mother was pregnant."

"I'll see you later." It was too much for me to think about, an overload of information I couldn't process. I wished I could go back to the previous night, when I'd skated with the Cup. A moment of pure happiness.

The next several hours I sat with him. The doctors told me there was no change in his condition. I left for a while to have lunch and talk to my lawyer, Ethan Phillips. I wanted to ask him what my legal responsibilities were regarding my father.

"None, as far as I know," Ethan stated. "He's not your dependent, and you aren't his guardian."

"That's what I thought."

"I didn't know your father was in your life. You never mentioned him."

I chewed my lip. "He wasn't when I was growing up. Matter of fact, I didn't know who he was. When I made it to the NHL, he popped up, and I had him take a paternity test. You know my best friend, Neil. His parents are both attorneys and insisted on it. That was before I hired you."

"I see. What's your relationship with him like?"

"Basically nonexistent." I huffed out a laugh. "He's been calling me on and off for years, but I refused to listen to him. On a recent road trip, he came to where I was staying and tried to explain everything about why he walked out on my mom, but I didn't want to hear his excuses. I still don't, but seeing him lying in bed on a ventilator...I don't know. Maybe I'm just a sucker."

"I've had plenty of clients who support their entire family, from grandparents to cousins, and others who refuse to give anyone a dime. You should do what you feel is right."

"I wish I knew what that was." I explained the situation, from my childhood to my mother's death and what my father had revealed to Adrian. "So you can see, I'm still angry and upset, but like Adrian said to me earlier, if I can forgive Denis for cheating on me and breaking my heart, maybe I can make room for one more."

"One thing I've learned is that forgiving someone often benefits the person who's giving it more than the one it's being given to. You don't have to have a close relationship with him—or one at all, if you don't want. But the fact that you're having all these doubts might mean you want to be able to say those words to him. The ball's in your court."

"Wrong sport," I joked but sighed. "Maybe you're right. You should've been a psychologist instead of a sports lawyer."

"I've got a Jewish mother who'd agree with you. She wanted her son to be a doctor but settled for a lawyer. Now listen. If you want to set up a medical trust for your father to pay his bills, you don't have to be personally involved. It can all be done through me."

"I'll have to see if he has any health insurance, but...yeah, I think so, because he'll likely need help afterward. If he wakes up."

"I'm sorry, Rip. Whatever your relationship is, it's got to be tough seeing him like that."

"Yeah." I managed to squeeze the word out past the dryness of my throat. "Talk to you soon."

"I'll get started on the paper work."

I left the cafeteria and returned to my father's room, where I saw several people standing around his bed. Fearing the worst, I moved closer.

"What's going on?"

"Mr. Tremaine, I'm glad you're here." I recognized the neurologist, and there was another doctor I hadn't met before. "Your father has woken up and is making purposeful movements. A very good sign. We're going to remove the intubation."

"Isn't it too soon?"

"No. We'd rather have him breathing on his own."

I watched and winced as they pulled this ugly long tube out of his mouth and he began to cough and choke. After inhaling and exhaling several times, it appeared my father could hold his own. He met my eyes.

"Rip," he rasped.

"It's okay. How do you feel?"

"Like crap," he whispered.

"Mr. Carver, do you remember what happened?" Dr. Kim asked. "Do you know where you are?"

With a wry smile, he plucked at the bedsheets. "This looks like a hospital. And yeah. Of course I remember. My son just won the Stanley Cup, and we were in the stands cheering. All of a sudden, the railing gave away and we fell below. Something hit me on the head, and it went dark."

The doctors took his blood pressure, checked his eyes, and requested he perform simple commands, all of which he was able to accomplish.

"We'll be back to take you for another MRI, Mr. Carver. In the meantime, rest."

The group of white coats left, and then it was only the two of us. He tried to sit up but fell onto the pillow, his face pale and sweaty. "Damn, that hurts. And the room is kind of spinny."

"You had a head injury. It'll probably be a while before you can return to normal."

Fear rose in his eyes. "No, I gotta get home. I'm supposed to work tomorrow."

"I doubt that's happening. You can call them and tell them what happened. By the way, do you have health insurance? They'll need your info."

He shook his head. "No. No insurance. I've been lucky and been pretty healthy. Just got some blood pressure meds my doc gives me generic so it's not too expensive."

Lines marred his forehead. "I can't afford to be in the hospital. I don't have money to pay for it."

I was afraid he would say that. "Well, you can't go home. And don't worry about the money. I'll take care of it."

"No, no way. I'm not letting you pay for me."

I could see he was getting worked up, which couldn't be good for him. The monitors he was hooked up to started beeping faster. "We don't have to talk about it now. The most important thing is for you to recover."

A smiling man entered the room. "Time to go for a ride, Mr. Carver. I'm here to take you for your MRI."

"I don't need that. It's expensive," he protested. "I'm feeling better."

"The doctors said you need it," I argued. "Let them do the test."

He didn't answer me, and the transport people moved the bed. They pushed him out as Adrian walked in. Relief flooded me.

"Rip." He rushed into my arms, and I held on to him, feeling as if he were my only shelter in this storm-tossed world.

"Thanks for coming." I buried my face in his neck, needing this skin-to-skin contact. "Tell me all about your new position." Anything to get my mind off this disaster. We sat in the chairs by my father's bed. "How was it going to City Hall?"

Adrian's face shone with happiness. "I talked to Sterling Forest for the first time. He's so damn intimidating, but I held my own and went to the press briefing and even managed to ask some tough questions." His eyes sparkled. "And I gave my report on the six p.m. news and didn't freeze up or make any mistakes."

"Dammit, I wish I could've seen it. And of course you didn't." I hugged him tight and kissed him. "I'm so damn proud of you, baby. You're on your way to making your dreams come true."

"It'll repeat at ten p.m." He rested his cheek on mine. "I've already got my dream. Here with you. Twenty or thirty years from now, I'll be replaced by someone younger. I don't want to be the person who made their job their life."

"I don't want that either. You and I together are all the life I need. I've won it all in hockey, and if I never play again, it'll be okay. Loving you is the greatest win of all."

We sat in the hospital room, Adrian's head on my shoulder. My father returned and Adrian sat up straight. I squeezed his hand.

"How are you feeling?" I asked. "You remember Adrian?"

"Yeah, sure. And I feel like I've been hit in the head with a pipe." He attempted a smile. "They said they'd come in after the doctor had a chance to review the results. You don't haveta stay. I'll be fine."

"I wanted to talk to you." I stood at his bedside. "I was surprised to see you at the game."

He shrugged. "Even after the way we left it the last time, I wanted to be there. You don't haveta acknowledge I'm your father. I know you're my son, and I wanted to be there for the most important moment of your life."

My eyes burned. "I wish my mother could've been there. She sacrificed her life to give me everything."

A tear streaked down his cheek. "I'm sorry I was a coward. I never should've left without her. If I woulda known she was pregnant, I would've taken her with me."

I couldn't answer because I had no idea what my mother would've done. Maybe she would have left with him. I'd never know. But nearly thirty years had passed. She was gone. I could choose to remain angry, or I could move forward.

"I think...we can talk more when you leave the hospital."

Hopeful eyes met mine. "I know I was wrong the way I first came to you. You probably thought I wanted money, and in the beginning, yeah, I was stupid. But I don't want to take anything from you."

"It's not taking when it's freely given." My father and I might not ever get to be best buddies, but maybe we—or I—could put aside the hurt and anger and begin to forge a relationship together. "I think the time has come in my life that I'm ready to learn about who you are."

Adrian's hand crept into mine and squeezed, and I returned the pressure.

His lips trembled. "I'd like that. But I don't wanna be a burden."

"Family isn't a burden."

The doctor entered the room. "Mr. Carver, good news. There doesn't seem to be any permanent damage. Your brain activity is normal. Tomorrow we'll see how you do out of bed, and if all goes well, you should be able to go home in a few days. You'll have to take it easy, though. You've had a concussion and will need to rest."

"That's great news," he said with a smile. "I'm feeling better already."

"Me too," I responded. "Me too."

Dr. Kim turned to me. "I also wanted to say congratulations on the win last night, Mr. Tremaine. We had the game on in the doctors' lounge, and it was thrilling right to the last second. I've been a Blades fan my whole life."

"That's awesome. Thanks so much." I could see he wanted to ask for a picture but was hesitant. "I'm happy to take a picture if you want."

"Oh, wow. If you wouldn't mind."

Adrian took the doctor's phone, Dr. Kim and I posed for a few shots, and then I signed his lab jacket. My phone buzzed, and seeing it was Ezra, I excused myself.

"What's up?"

"How's your father?"

"He's going to be fine."

"Great. I've got you rebooked on tomorrow's morning shows. There's going to be a parade on Saturday down Flatbush Avenue and over the Brooklyn Bridge, ending at City Hall."

"Can't wait," I drawled. "Did that sound as sarcastic as I feel?"

Ezra laughed. "The price of fame, my man. I saw Adrian on the six p.m. news. He did a great job."

"Yeah, I'll catch it at ten after we get home."

"I'll send you the schedule and talk to you tomorrow."

"Take it easy." I ended the call and Adrian adjusted my father's pillows. "We should get going. I have to be up early for a morning-show interview."

"Thank you for everything. I appreciate it."

I held out my hand. "I'll see you after I'm done tomorrow. Have a good night...Dad."

I didn't think the word could make me so emotional, but seeing the tears spring to his eyes, I knew he was as affected as I was.

"Good night, Rip. You too, Adrian."

We left, and Adrian called a cab.

Later at home, as we were sitting on the couch watching the lead-up to the news, Adrian suddenly faced me wide-eyed. "Oh, shit. I never told Neil about my new job."

"I never told him about my father either. Let's FaceTime him."

He picked up after one ring. "I assume you're going to tell me what you've been doing all day that you didn't answer my calls or texts? And neither did my brother?"

"I think when you hear what I have to say, you'll understand." I gave him the condensed version, knowing I'd have much more to say when we met in person.

"Shit, Rip. I'm glad he'll be all right. And truthfully, I'm happy to hear you're willing to talk to him. I can't imagine how heavily that must've weighed on you."

"You're right, of course. I'll just have to see where it leads. I couldn't let him lie there alone and hurt."

"No. So let me ask you. How long are you going to keep up this lie that you and my brother aren't together? He's there with you now, isn't he?"

Adrian popped in over my shoulder. "Yeah, I am. And yes, we're really together even though it didn't start out that way. The more time we spent together, the closer we became. I love him, Neil, and I hope you'll be happy about it. As happy as I am."

Before Neil could answer, I jumped in. "And don't give Adrian shit. I was too deep in the season to take my focus off the game so I could explain everything to you." Hearing the tension in my voice, I softened my tone. "Neil. You know you're my brother in every sense of the word. I didn't want to lie to you. We were gonna tell you after last night's win, and then all this other shit happened. But you have to believe me when I tell you, I love him. It wasn't planned. It just happened. This isn't a rebound relationship either. He's the one. The only one."

I held my breath, waiting for Neil to respond. And when he smiled, the last weight holding me down vanished, leaving me lighter than air.

"I couldn't be happier for both of you. All my life I've considered you my brother. Welcome to the family."

EPILOGUE
Adrian

One year later…

"Guard the net," I screamed. "Guard the net."

"Look at Mr. Hockey Fan now." Neil snickered.

"I'm a Blades man through and through." I sniffed.

"I'll just bet you are, little brother." Neil elbowed me, and I ignored the innuendo to concentrate on the final minutes of the game, but my face burned.

"Idiot."

To the roar of the Blades' fans, Rip came out of nowhere and stole the puck from the Drifts' winger about to take a shot on goal.

"Rip's gonna score," John said, unruffled, his gaze firmly on Rip speeding down the ice toward the Drifts' net. If he did, it would be a hat trick for him, and the Blades would win their second Stanley Cup in a row. Blades Arena was on fire.

"To the left," Neil yelled, jumping out of his seat, his cheering as loud as mine.

The Drifts' goalie, Pieter Lindell, spread himself in front of the net, but at the last moment, Rip spun off to the side and smacked the puck, sliding it behind Lindell's bulk and into the net. The light went on, and the arena erupted. The Blades' lead had increased by two with less than five minutes left.

"He did it. He did it." I threw my arms around John, the gold band on my finger catching the overhead lights. We'd gotten engaged over Christmas, and I'd been promoted to Channel 8's full-time political reporter, after uncovering a huge scandal in the city's Finance Department, which had led to the resignation of its top commissioners. Sterling Forest had the anchor job locked down and strangely enough, I was okay with that. I still had the sports show, *Playing the Field*, which the station believed was best as a monthly program, so between that and my news reporting, it was a perfect balance.

I had the job I'd dreamed of, the man of my dreams, and I'd never been happier.

John remained standing, never taking his eyes off Rip as he hugged it out with his teammates, then skated to the side for a final shift change. The Drifts pulled Lindell to put an extra skater on the ice, but the Blades would not be denied. The sticks flew fast and furious as the Drifts attempted to control the puck, but Peter Varhov stole it from their center and skated away with Chitty and Seb guarding him. The Drifts refused to go quietly. Two defensemen flanked Varhov on either side, and he had no clear shot at the empty net. I winced when they smashed him into the boards and their defenseman stole the puck, but he only made it to center ice before the buzzer sounded and the game was over.

"Yes, yes! Two years in a row!" I threw my arms up in the air, and we jumped for joy while the arena lights flashed and "We Are the Champions" blasted over the loudspeakers. The entire Blades team piled out on the ice, and after shaking hands with the Drifts, they skated to center ice for the Cup ceremony.

"Damn glad to be sitting here this year." John laughed. "Rip told me the engineers did a walk-through and checked the entire arena last night to make sure everything was secure."

"You're where you belong," I said, squeezing his arm. "With family."

I watched as the NHL commissioner made his speech, and Rip was named most valuable player and handed the trophy. He stepped in front of the microphone and it took him a moment to collect himself. I knew him so intimately, I could see how he struggled for self-control.

"Thank you to the league and the Blades organization for making my dreams come true. To my teammates, who are more like a family. To my fiancé, Adrian, for always being by my side, cheering me on, and for loving me, no matter what. To Mom and Dad Hunt, Neil and Lisa—I love you all so much. And to my father. I'm glad you're in my life and here to share this night with me." He wiped his face with the back of his hand. "And everything in the future to come."

He hopped off the podium, and to thunderous applause, skated the circumference of the rink, holding up the Cup to the cheering fans. He handed it off to Seb, then skated to the section where we sat, and though we were separated by the plexiglass, he placed his hand on it and I reached out to line my fingers up with his.

"I love you. See you outside. I'm gonna get cleaned up."

"Okay."

"Dad?"

Even after a year, my heart still squeezed tight seeing Rip with his father and hearing him call John *dad*. They'd had some hard conversations, but each day brought them closer. John had moved to New York when recurring headaches and dizziness from the head injury made it impossible for him to work. Rip had bought him a small house with a garden, and he had a service dog who helped him with balance support when the unsteadiness hit.

"Yeah?"

"We're having a celebration at Slapshots afterward. Can you come?"

A smile lit up John's face. "I'd like that."

"I've got some press to do, so I'll meet you outside the locker room."

Rip rejoined his team celebrating on the ice, and we stood for a while as he, Denis, and the rest of the team were interviewed by sports networks and local stations.

The three of us waited until the arena emptied out. We made our way to the locker-room area and it took about half an hour for Rip to appear. He'd showered and was dressed in street clothes. He put his arm around my shoulders.

"Ready?"

"Yeah."

"I gotta get home," Neil said, and Lisa kissed Rip on the cheek.

"Mom and Dad are babysitting so we need to relieve them, otherwise we'd stay for the celebration." She hugged him, then me.

Neil shocked me by wiping his eyes. My brother rarely got emotional.

"I am so goddamned proud of you, Rip. You're the best of the best. Two Cups in a row. I think it's the Adrian effect." He winked at me.

My cheeks burned. "Shut up," I mumbled.

Rip tightened his hold on me. "I think you're right. Everything's better with Adrian."

They hugged, and Neil pulled me close.

"This year has been incredible. I've loved watching you grow and come into your own. Never let anyone change you. You're the best."

"You are too. Thanks for always believing in me."

"And remember, you and Rip are coming to the house this weekend. Mom and Dad are dying to see you both, and the kids want to see their uncles."

"We'll be there." We hugged again, and I watched him get into the car he'd called.

Hand in hand, Rip and I walked to Slapshots, with John holding on to Rip's other arm. Once inside, a cheer rose from the crowd. Win or lose, Rip and the rest of the team had rented the bar out for the evening for family and friends, and the corks were popping as we got a table. Rip made sure his father was settled before he raised a hand to quiet people down.

"To the Blades and our fans, and to keeping the Cup where it belongs. Brooklyn, baby!" He gulped the champagne straight from the bottle.

"You know that's right," Seb shouted, standing on a chair. "To our captain." He drank from his own bottle, and he and Rip hugged. I loved their friendship, and Seb and his wife had become my good friends as well.

His face flushed with happiness, Rip pulled me close for a kiss. His mouth tasted warm and sweet, and I clung to him.

"To my guy, the one who never lost faith in me. This is where our story began, and it's only gonna get better. I love you, baby. Here's to us."

As I drank my bubbles, I caught sight of Denis, a wistful expression on his face. He'd gone out with numerous men over the past year, and I wondered if he even knew what love was. Rip had forgiven him for his bad behavior, but I didn't trust him. It still upset me that he'd wanted a threesome with Rip knowing the two of us were dating. Was his loneliness an act? With Denis, no one could ever be certain.

Rip nuzzled me close. "What're you so deep in thought about?"

I smiled against his cheek, the plight of Denis Bouvier's love life forgotten. "You. What else?"

"*Mmm*. Good answer." He played with my hair. "I've been thinking. Let's do it."

Confused, I met his dancing eyes. "Do what?"

"Get married. This weekend at Neil and Lisa's. What're we waiting for? We'll bring everyone together who can make it, and we have the whole off-season to celebrate the honeymoon."

I blinked. "Are you sure? It's so spur-of-the-moment. Shouldn't you check with Neil first?"

He held me closer, his laughter rumbling through me. "Neil is oblivious. I've already mentioned it to Lisa, and she's chomping at the bit to get it done. Especially with your parents visiting. It's the perfect time."

I grinned, settling into his arms. "You've thought of everything, haven't you?"

"I did. Because you are my everything. I've never been happier than I have been with you."

Overwhelmed, I drank in the sight of everyone celebrating the Blades' win. Even Denis had come out of his funk and was toasting away. Like Rip said, a team that was more like a family.

"I love you so much, Rip, and I'm so happy, I don't know what to do with myself."

"You can marry me, that's what." He brushed our lips together. "Before you, I was alone and lonely. I thought I'd lost my joy. Then you appeared and became the one constant in my life I could count on and turn to. The one I could confess my secrets to without any judgment."

"Do you know how long I've loved you?" I gazed into the face I used to dream about, wishing he were mine, knowing it was an impossible fantasy. "All I wanted was you to be my boyfriend."

"And now I'm going to be your husband."

I kissed him. "Guess we'd better get ready to handle all the good stuff coming our way."

Rip held me tight. "Bring it on, baby. Time for us to take that shot at forever and score the ultimate goal. You and me. Together forever."

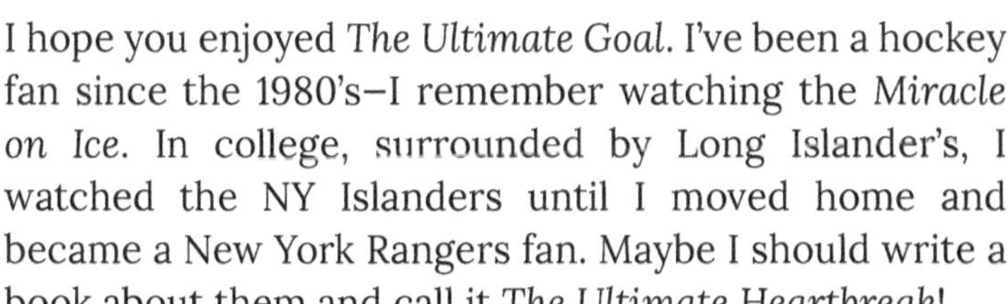

I hope you enjoyed *The Ultimate Goal*. I've been a hockey fan since the 1980's—I remember watching the *Miracle on Ice*. In college, surrounded by Long Islander's, I watched the NY Islanders until I moved home and became a New York Rangers fan. Maybe I should write a book about them and call it *The Ultimate Heartbreak*!

I hope you'll consider leaving a review for *The Ultimate Goal*. Reviews are so important and appreciated. Thank you for your support!

Don't miss out! I have a sweet little Adrian and Rip bonus scene for you that you can access here:

https://dl.bookfunnel.com/7sblthp8g0

Are you curious about our bad boy goalie, Denis? I hope so, because his redemption story is next in *The Ultimate Save*. I confess to having a soft spot for him, and I think you will too, once you know his backstory. Besides, I love when the bad boy falls hard. I fell for Denis and his love interest, heart and soul. You haven't yet met the man who wins his heart, but opposites attract doesn't even begin to describe these two! The fun and snark are strong with them. Make sure you subscribe to my newsletter to get the latest updates on all my releases, plus exclusive cover and art reveals and so much more!

FELICE STEVENS writes romance because what is better than people falling in love? Her favorite part of a romance novel is that first kiss...sigh. She loves creating stories of hopes and dreams and happily ever afters. Her stories are character-driven, rich with the sights, sounds, and flavors of New York City, and filled with men who are often deeply flawed but always real.

Felice writes gay romance because she believes that everyone deserves a happily ever after. Having traveled all over the world, she can safely say that the universal language that unites people is love.

Felice has written in a variety of sub-genres, including contemporary and paranormal, and she has a mystery series as well. You can find all her books listed on her website.

Felice is a two-time Lambda Literary Award nominee and a Lambda Award winner in Gay Romance for her book *The Ghost and Charlie Muir*.

BOOKBUB

https://www.bookbub.com/profile/felice-stevens

NEWSLETTER

https://tinyurl.com/y85e69ab

READER GROUP

https://www.facebook.com/groups/FelicesBreakfastClub/

FACEBOOK AUTHOR PAGE

https://www.facebook.com/felicestevensauthor/

INSTAGRAM

https://www.instagram.com/felicestevens

GOODREADS

https://www.goodreads.com/author/show/8432880.Felice_Stevens

WEBSITE

felicestevens.com

PAYHIP STORE

https://payhip.com/FeliceStevensAuthor

TIKTOK

https://www.tiktok.com/@felicestevens